TALES OF DERWENTDALE

&

The Extraordinary

Mr Fawcett

TALES OF DERWENTDALE

First published in 1902
This edition published by Land of Oak & Iron, 2019

ISBN: 978-0-244-49126-0

Wood-cut illustrations: Thomas Bewick
Cover design : Geoff Marshall
Layout and type-setting: Geoff Marshall

Printed in Great Britain by Martins the Printers
Sea View Works, Spittal
Berwick-upon-Tweed
Northumberland
TD15 1RS

Land of Oak & Iron
Heritage Centre
Spa Well Road
Winlaton Mill
NE21 6RU

www.landofoakandiron.org.uk

FOREWORD

The riches of the Land of Oak & Iron lie not only in fertile soil, mineral wealth, invention, industry and a history that goes back to the Romans. Its greatest wealth lies in its people, and people love stories. In setting down these myths, legends and anecdotes from history at the beginning of the twentieth century, James William Fawcett drew on centuries of traditional tales, many of them passed down by word of mouth.

But it turns out he's a story in himself, and in his own corner of north-west Durham, the man is a legend.

I must confess I hadn't heard of him until David Marrs, a local historian from Dipton, suggested to the Land of Oak & Iron volunteers that the perfect counterpoint to *Men of Iron*, the industrial history we'd just republished, would be a new edition of *Tales of Derwentdale*. He mentioned, almost in passing, that the man who wrote them had been an interesting chap.

That turned out to be an understatement.

I thought I'd find out a bit about him and write a short introduction. I was completely unprepared for what we would find and what a quest we had embarked upon.

Google took me immediately to Ray Thompson of Castleside, who in 2009 had directed his considerable energies into telling the world about J. W. Fawcett in a quest to bring 'Satley's Forgotten Son' the recognition he so richly deserves.

When Ray was a little lad in the 1930s, he sometimes used to go along with his uncle, Harry Dent, to visit a kindly old man who lived in a house stuffed with books. After a hugely adventurous and productive life, James William Fawcett was eking out a frugal existence in the village of his birth. When he passed away in 1942, at the height of the Second World War, he was buried in an unmarked grave.

Throughout his career as an electrician and union convener at Consett Steelworks, Ray Thompson never forgot 'Major' Fawcett. In his old age, he thought often of Satley's most famous son, who lay in an unmarked grave in the village of his birth. His conviction grew that the legacy of the renowned scholar, naturalist, antiquarian, linguist and author should be preserved and celebrated. At the age of seventy-seven, Ray decided to tell the story of this 'son of Satley of whom great cities would have been justly proud' and raise funds to erect a gravestone.

He brought to his mission all his powers of determination, industry and persuasion and the resulting memorial is a testament to the lives of not one but two marvelous local characters.

Ray, now almost ninety, was invaluable to our research as we took up the torch. From that house filled with books and lit by candles, via the treasures of Durham County Records Office, to the wonders of the internet, we bring you the astonishing story of the extraordinary James William Fawcett.

Val Scully

CONTENTS

PART ONE
TALES OF DERWENTDALE

PART TWO

THE EXTRAORDINARY MR FAWCETT

The Life and Works of James William Fawcett

ILLUSTRATIONS

Woodcuts by Thomas Bewick appear on pages:

PREFACE to the First Edition

Written in 1902 by J. W. Fawcett

The Derwent Valley, one of the most picturesque in scenic beauty in the North of England, and which has been the theme of many a poetic effusion, is also rich in historical lore and traditional tales, in fact, history, legend, superstition, and tradition vie with each other throughout the length and breadth of the valley. Some of the old legends and traditions, which had only an oral permanency, have long since passed down the traditionary channel into the sea of oblivion, and become lost. Others with the march of common sense and a more enlightened age are rapidly passing out of remembrance, and will in the course of time become forgotten.

To give these a more enduring worth and to make them known to a new generation, who have become residents in the locality to which they are associated, has been the chief aim of the collector and compiler of these Tales of Derwentdale. In their collection he has delved into old volumes long since out of print, and has also been greatly beholden to the memories of old residents, in whose families some of the traditions had passed down from one generation to another.

They were first published in a serial form in the pages of the Consett Guardian in 1901, and an unanimous request for their republication in volume form has resulted in their present issue to subscribers, whose kindly appreciation is valued by the compiler, and his sincere wish is that the work may always prove interesting to its many readers, and that his feeble endeavours to preserve local stories of the past may at all times provide entertaining matter for readers, not only in "lovely Derwentside," where they are of especial value, but to those subscribers and readers in other parts of the "homeland," as well as to those natives, or at one time residents, who "in lands across the sea" have made homes for themselves, and into whose hands the work may fall.

J. W. FAWCETT.
Satley, Darlington.
June 14th, 1902.

PART ONE

TALES OF DERWENTDALE

THE DEVIL AT EDMUNDBYERS

The fifteenth, sixteenth, and seventeenth centuries were eras when a belief in the supernatural was almost universal and numerous are the tales which exist of marvellous apparitions, wonderful miracles, and remarkable occurrences in various parts of England. The County of Durham, in common with the rest of the English shires, has its share of these tales and traditional accounts, and more than one belong to the Derwent Valley.

In the year 1641 there lived in the village of Edmundbyers, a yeoman named Stephen Hooper, who besides cultivating his own farm at that place, had also another one in his own hands at Hunstanworth. In November he was taken ill and not able to look after his farm, so one day he sent his wife, Margaret Hooper, to see how things were going on at Hunstanworth. She went, stayed a day, saw much that did not please her; and determined, that should her husband get well again, they should be reformed. On her return she found her husband much better, and told him what she had seen, and what should be done to put the place aright. A day or two later, however, Mrs. Hooper began to show signs of being deranged in her mind, or, as it was called in those days, of being bewitched, or haunted with an evil spirit. She talked at random, told all kinds of idle tales concerning the farm at Hunstanworth, and also about an old groat, or fourpenny piece, which her little son had found a few days previously.

Her husband tried to pacify her, and got her to say a portion of the Lord's prayer after him, but this she would not finish, and demanded to see the old coin and her wedding ring, which she evidently did not wear on her finger. Her husband took no notice of her request, but prayed to God to send her a more quiet spirit. The more he prayed, and begged her to do the same, the more she seemed to be troubled with an evil spirit. Suddenly she began to stare at him with a vacant and unnatural look which so frightened him, that he called in her sister and others. She then commenced to rave and foam at the mouth, and it was with difficulty that they could keep her in bed. Then in a somewhat strange manner both the bed and the room in which she was, commenced to move and shake, frightening her attendants, and half an hour later, when all was quiet she spoke and said that she had been in the town "to beat away a bear which had followed her into the yard, when she came from Hunstanworth." Her husband and friends persuaded her not to talk of such things telling her that her brain was light for want of rest; and got her to repeat the Lord's prayer after him.

This happened on Wednesday, and she remained quiet until the Saturday, when she again commenced to rave at times. She, however, quietened down again until Sunday night, when she suddenly roused her husband, by calling out that she saw a strange thing, like a snail, carrying fires. Her cries also roused her brothers and sisters, who were in the house, and on their bringing a lighted candle into her room, she got excited and called out, "Did you not see the Devil?" They tried to pacify her, but she got worse, and said, "If you see nothing now, you shall see something by and by." By the time she had finished, the whole party heard a great rumbling noise outside the house, like as if a number of carts were passing, and some of the party cried out, "Lord help us!"

After the rumbling was over her husband and those with him saw a strange beast, about half-a-yard in height, and half-a-yard in length, much like a bear, but without head or tail, coming to the bed, and Mr. Hooper immediately got up from his seat, and struck at it with a stool, and the stroke sounded as if he had hit a feather bed. The stroke did not harm the beast, which went up to the bed, struck the woman on her feet three times, and then pulled her out of bed and rolled her on the floor, to the great amazement of those present who were too astonished to prevent anything. Then the beast, who is generally supposed to have been the devil, rolled the woman up like a hoop, feet and head together, and rolled it downstairs into the hall of the house, where it kept her for a quarter of an hour; the husband and friends being too much afraid to follow, on account of a most horrible smell and fiery flames which proceeded from the place where the beast and the woman were. After a while they heard the woman cry out, "Now, he is gone!" and the husband immediately answered, "Then, in the name of God, come up to me" The woman at once obeyed. When she reached the room, her friends put her to bed, and four of them kept down the bedclothes and prayed for her. But all of a sudden she got out of bed, and thrust her feet and legs out of the window, which opened of its own accord, and those in the room heard something knock at her feet, and flames of fire issued therefrom, from which proceeded a most " horrible stinke." Those in the room then invoked the aid of the Almighty to save the woman.

After prayer for some time, the candle in the room, which had hitherto burned so dimly that they could scarcely see one another, began to burn brightly, and on looking round they saw a creature like a little girl with a bright shining countenance. Then all the party fell flat on the ground and thanked the Lord who had so wonderfully answered their petitions, and the child vanished away. Then the woman was put into bed, and when she came to her proper senses, she asked forgiveness, at God's hands, and of all that she had offended, acknowledging that she was so sorely tormented by the evil spirit on account of her sins.

Such is the "most feareful and strange newes" of a marvellous apparition at "Edenbyres, neere the river Darwent" in "the Bishopprick of Durham," as told in an old pamphlet published in London in 1641, and which is witnessed as being true by no less than six persons, residents of the place, named, Steeven Hooper, John Hooper, John Iley, Alexander Eagleston, Anthony Westgarth, and Alis Eaglestone. We are also told that the above-named Margaret Hooper had continued in good health, after the occurrence of this curious event, and that she had been visited by many godly and learned men from various parts of the country, anxious to ascertain particulars of the case.

THE MUGGLESWICK GIANT

"Once again behold the smiling miles
That spread their wealth of beauty on the view;
And we must wade their sunny maze of smiles
If we would learn the tale of Ward's romantic shoe."

Barrass.-"*The Derwent Valley.*"

In Muggleswick churchyard are said to have been interred during the seventeenth century, the remains of Edward Ward, who is understood to have been a person of gigantic stature, and who on this account has sometimes been called the Muggleswick giant. This man was also like Nimrod, a mighty hunter in his day and tradition says that his limbs were so enormous that his favourite female hound littered in one of his shoes. This may be true or it may not, but there can be little doubt that the man was very much above the common size.

Unfortunately we know nothing more of him. The exact year of his death is not known, and even were it so, the parish registers, which might have given some information of him, have long since been destroyed, and there were no newspapers in those days to chronicle the chief events of his career or give the date of his death.

Some writers seem to think that Ward was probably one of the seditious associators, who, in Muggleswick park in 1662, banded themselves together, to overthrow the new state of things in Church and State, after the Restoration of Charles II, and from the enormity of his exploits obtained the name of a giant. This conjecture, however, has no verification, and can only be recognised as a suppositive tradition.

THE MOSS-TROOPERS
AND
BORDER THIEVES.

"Hail! hail, where wild Moss-troopers roamed of yore!
We rove, enraptured, our engaging way,
To delve the mines of legendary lore,
Or sniff the scent of primrose patches gay;

For in these woods, and in that wilder day,
When lawless minds essayed no beaten track,
But loved adventure as they loved the prey
They hugged, transported, on their journey back,
Have planned their purpose fell full many a savage pack!

Ay! here they ran, the tameless and the wild,
The doughty and indomitable raid
Who looked on frowning danger till she smiled,
Or in their hearts a frenzied gladness made;

Or till their blind contempt of fear betrayed
And hurled them headlong into waiting gins;
Else Muggleswick, the hapless priest that said
The Litany o'er thy sorrows and thy sins,
 Had not been huddled through this maze of leaves and whins!"

Barrass.-*"The Derwent Valley."*

Muggleswick, it would appear, was, in olden times, notable as the scene of some of those predatory excursions, commonly called moss-trooping. Its isolated position and the scattered condition of the farmsteads probably made it favourable for such-like adventures. Like many of the neighbouring districts, it had its share of the border raids. One, more than ordinary, of these happened in January, 1528, when a band of Border thieves, led by one William Charlton, or, as he was better and more generally known, Willie o' Shotlyngton, a place near Bellingham in Northumberland - a famous moss-trooper in his day - entered the county of Durham, and, after robbing a number of persons in the neighbourhood of Wolsingham, returned by way of Muggleswick, from whence they daringly captured the parson, one Robert Forrest, and carried him off with them as a prisoner. The inhabitants, however, rose in arms and pursued the moss-troopers, who fled for their lives towards the Tyne. When they reached that river they found it in flood, and were unable to get across. They then made their way to Haydon Bridge where, however, they found the bridge "barred, chayned, and lokked fast." Here their pursuers came upon them, and a skirmish ensued, in which some met their death, some were made prisoner, and others escaped. Charlton and James Noble, his chief coadjutor, were killed and two others named Roger Armstrong and Archibald Dodde, were captured, and afterwards executed. All their bodies were eventually hung in chains as a warning to others - Charlton at Hexham, Noble at Haydon Bridge, Armstrong near Newcastle, and Dodde at Alnwick. Of what became of the poor priest the historian gives us no intelligence. Evidently he escaped in the fight and returned to Muggleswick, where he continued to minister to the spiritual wants of his scattered parishioners for some years.

It was probably the frequency of these border raids which caused some of the inhabitants of Muggleswick to follow the example of the invaders, and to commit those depredations on their neighbours, which the Scots and others committed on them all, for we know that in later times the neighbourhood became a noted harbourage for moss-troopers, few of whom scruppled to commit "pillage and plunder" on their Weardale neighbours on the one hand, and their Tynedale neighbours on the other, as well as, when occasion served, on the Scottish raiders themselves. Two of these famous (or infamous) moss-troopers and reivers - Rowland Harrison and Thomas Raw - have left behind them a more than ordinary fame.

Fig. 1 Moss-Trooper by Frederick Tayler 1802-1889

ROWLEY HARRISON:
THE MOSS-TROOPER.

"Where elate,
The doughty Rowley's blustering dame espied,
Her lord come home with Hodge's live estate,
And proudly, loudly 'Well done Rowley!' cried;
'When dost thou gang again?'
Most avaricious bride."

Barrass - "*The Derwent Valley.*"

Rowland, or, as he was better known, Rowley Harrison was a famous moss-trooper in his day and many singular adventures are related of him. He lived at the close of the seventeenth century, and the beginning of the eighteenth century, and during the latter part of his career resided at a farm called the Shield near Muggleswick.

Harrison's hazardous occupation furnished his household with a good store of beef, the cattle which he captured on his free-booting excursions and brought home from time to time being slaughtered for family use, cut up, salted, and packed into what was locally known as the "flesh boat," or beef cask. His wife, who according to tradition had the blood of the Graemes, a famous Cumberland family of moss-troopers, in her veins, was considered almost as bad as, if not worse, than her husband, for though she did not go "foraging" herself she looked out that the family food box was never empty. Like a good many other housewives, not very deeply versed in domestic economy, she always took care to keep the choicest pieces of flesh meat uppermost in the tub; and on one occasion when her good man's exploratory raids into Weardale and Teesdale had not been as successful as they often had been, and no fresh supply of stolen beef had been got till the tub was nearly empty, she roused him with the exclamation, "Ride Rowley, the hough's i' the pot." This remark is traditionally said to have been her favourite mode of ordering her plundering husband to go on a raid.

On one occasion when the Fates bad been more propitious to him than usual, Harrison was returning home at break of day with eight cows and a bull, the result of his moonlight night's work, his wife, whose eye was never satisfied with seeing, greeted him with - "Well deyun, Rowley," and immediately added - "When dost thou gan ageyn."

Like everyone who followed the precarious profession of a moss-trooper, Harrison lived constantly from hand to mouth. It was successively feast and famine; one day, full and plenty and jovial festivity, the next an empty pantry and an empty stomach. If we are to judge from oral tradition and from the absence of his name in the criminal annals of those days, he does not seem to have ever come within the clutches of the law of the land, such as it then was. He however came under the ban of the church, which fulminated its then much dreaded edict against him by excommunicating him and refusing him Christian sepulture. He died September 24th, 1712, and according to tradition was buried outside the walls of Muggleswick Churchyard. His gravestone, however, now lies in the floor at the west end of Muggleswick Church, and is inscribed

HERE LIETH

ROWLAND HARRISON

OF MUGELSWICK

WHO DEPARTED

THIS LIFE

SEPR. XXIV

ANNO DOMINE 1712.

Another tradition states that when Muggleswick Church was rebuilt about 1728 the moss-trooper's last resting place was considered to be the best site, and it was in this way that his memorial stone came to be in the centre of the new, and present, building. This, however, is incorrect. The church, which was rebuilt in 1728, was erected on the site of the previous one, and in all probability the gravestone was removed, perhaps about then, to its present position by some kindly hand who wished to put it in a safer place, and keep it safe from destruction. The parish registers, which might have thrown some information on the career of the moss-trooper for the year 1712, and for many years later, were wilfully destroyed by the wife of one of the sub-curates of Muggleswick during the system of pluralities, who was in the habit of tearing out the leaves to put her teacakes and spice wigs on, on baking days.

Fig. 2   Blanchland

14

THE BLANCHLAND BELLS

"Their lives in Alba Landa's holy dome,
Flow'd sweetly, as in summer days, the stream
Meanders by the ruins of their home,
Till those inured in plundering raids to roam -
I tell the story that tradition tells -
Blent on these heights, malignant joy and foam,
And savage laughter with the chime of bells,
That led them to their spoils athwart the realms of fells.

From wanderings wild and filled with foul and feud,
And dripping shrines aglow with human gore,
To startle this supernal solitude.
With damning deed they came!
And o'er and o'er
The hills that, purple-blossom'd, base the shore,
They roamed and nursed their ignominious will,
Till cursing loud the luck that held the oar,
And lone and lost among the moorlands still,
The Convent bells rang out on wild Dead Friar's Hill!

They came! the nameless, bloody men, they came
Whose long-nursed vengeance stilled the voice of prayer;
Whose eyes red-gleaming with a frenzied flame,
Glared, gloating round on treasures rich and rare;
Whose hands assigned to silence and despair,
The plundered temple and the sainted dead
They came, and lo! the monks are lying there,
As heedless now of man's inhuman tread
As of these flowers that fling their fragrance o'er their bed."

Barrass - *"The Derwent Valley."*

15

In connection with the history of Blanchland Abbey there is a curious tradition, that on one occasion a party of marauding Scots, in one of their raiding expeditions across the borders, found themselves in the neighbourhood of the head of the Derwent, and hearing that there was an abbey at Blanchland on that river, resolved to pillage and plunder the monastery. On their way thither, however, they lost the track over the fells, in a thick mist, and were unable to find the place on account of its secluded situation. They wandered about for some time, in which they had either overlooked it, or passed it by at some distance, for having crossed the Derwent, either on the east or west side of the Abbey, they had reached a spot to the south of Blanchland, on the Durham side of the river, now called Dead Friar's Hill, when their attention was arrested by the distant sound of bells.

Whether this peal was a paean of joy rung by the monks for their supposed deliverance, or a call to vespers we are not told. If, and it is possible, that the monks had become aware of the presence of the marauders, and had been apprehensive of their intentions, and had watched them pass their house without noticing it, and had let them get as far south as they did, and then thinking that they could not celebrate their deliverance in a more fitting manner than by ringing the abbey bells, they made a mistake, for guided by the sound, the Scots made their way to the abbey, where they broke through the gate, and after slaughtering some of the imprudent brethren, set fire to the buildings, and retired with a vast amount of plunder. This raid is said to have taken place in the early part of the fourteenth century.

There is another tradition referring to the Blanchland Bells, which is said to have originated at a later date.

The great struggle of the Reformation in England from 1529 onwards broke, link by link, the chain which had so long bound England to Rome, and first one Parliament and then another passed acts which gradually widened the breach that commenced between the two powers. The divorce of Queen Catherine in 1533, increased the tension betwixt the King, Henry VIII, and the Pope, and the question arose, "Who was to be the head of the church in England-the King or the Pope ?" The Parliament of 1534 decided the point by declaring Henry "supreme head on earth, next under Christ, of the English church." The King's spiritual supremacy was enforced, and those who denied it were executed, or cast into prison. Then the papal thunders of excommunication were hurled at Henry, and the English monarch proceeded to reduce the strength of the pontiff by the dissolution of the religious houses. He gave orders that all the religious houses, or abbeys, monasteries, priories, etc., should be dissolved or suppressed. Thomas Cromwell, " the hammer of the monks," as he was called, was appointed Visitor General. for the purpose of making the requisite inquiries. This was done in 1535-6, and in the latter year an Act of Parliament, based on Cromwell's report suppressed 376 houses whose income did not exceed £290 a year. This caused great dissatisfaction amongst a portion of the population, and was the cause of an insurrection called the Pilgrimage of Grace, in the northern counties. After a while it was suppressed and its leaders executed. As the, monks were suspected of having been the prime movers in this rebellion, Henry ordered a visitation of the larger monasteries to be made, and in 1539 and 1640 they were suppressed to the number of over 500.

The second tradition relating to the Blanchland Bells refers to the period of the dissolution of the larger monasteries in 1539-1540, and is to the effect that the Commissioners appointed by King Henry VIII to make the general visitation of the large religious houses, missed their way to Blanchland, and were only directed to the place, after they had passed it unawares by the sound of the abbey bells.

This circumstance is referred to by John Carr, L.L.D., a native of the Derwent Valley, having been born at Watergate, near Castleside, in 1732, in his "Ode to the Derwent," as follows:-

"Hot Henry in choler decrees,
His fingers to snap at the Pope,
Alba Landa, embosom'd in trees
Had well-nigh eluded his hope.

Alba Landa's inquisitors made
Small progress in finding the place,
Till a bell the dread secret betray'd
Like a Lollard bereft of all grace.

Hall mynish'd their mete and their wyne,
As the guise of black chronicle saith,
But could the good father's repine,
While he stoutly defended the faith."

THE BLANCHLAND MURDER

On Thursday, January 1st, 1880, a farmer named Robert Snowball, 26 years of age, residing at Belmount, in the parish of Hunstanworth and the county of Durham, and about two miles from Blanchland, was barbarously murdered at that place. He was a single man and lived on the farm with his father - Robert Snowball - and a housekeeper named Jane Barron, and, besides the. occupation of a farmer, he occupied himself with joiner work, and had a room fitted up above a byre as a carpenter's shop with bench and tools.

On the afternoon of the day in question he left the house remarking that he was going to visit a neighbour, but he failed to return that night. On the following morning a quantity of blood was discovered in the byre, dropping from the ceiling, and on an examination being made the dead body of the unfortunate man was found in the room above, with a large wound in the back of his head, the jaw fractured, and a bruise on the breast. The wounds had been made with a large hammer similar to those used for breaking stones in road-making, and it was supposed that the murderer had approached from behind and struck the fatal blow whilst Mr. Snowball was looking in a closet, beside which his body was found.

Dr. Montgomery, of Blanchland, was sought, and after having seen the body and made some examination he telegraphed to the Superintendent of the Police at Stanhope, who immediately took the matter up.

On Monday, January 5th. an inquest was opened before Coroner Graham in the house of Police Constable Ferguson, at Ramshaw about a mile-and-a-half from Belmount, the scene of the murder, at which, after hearing certain evidence, he gave orders for the burial of the body, and adjourned the inquest until the 21st.

The interment of the murdered man took place in Blanchland Churchyard on Tuesday, January 6th, at which there was a very large attendance of persons from many miles round the district. That same evening Jane Barron, the housekeeper, was arrested by Superintendent Thubron, and placed in the police cell at Ramshaw. Early the following morning she was taken to Stanhope, and brought before Mr. Valentine Rippon, J.P., charged with killing and, murdering Robert Snowball, at Belmount, on January 1st, by striking him on the head with a hammer; and remanded.

The inquiry into the circumstances attending the murder of Robert Snowball, on New Year's Day, was re-opened on Wednesday, January 21st, before Coroner Graham, and resumed on the two following days. After the hearing of a vast amount of evidence, twelve of the thirteen jurymen returned a verdict of "Wilful murder against some person or persons unknown" - the foreman of the jury, the Rev P. C. Jones, Vicar of Hunstanworth, not signing the verdict.

On Tuesday, January 27th, Jane Barron was charged at Stanhope Police Court for the wilful murder of Robert Snowball, and committed for trial at the Durham Assizes, where, on Saturday, April 17th, she was indicted before Mr. Justice Stephen, and acquitted. The Belmount or, as it is more generally called, the Blanchland murder is yet an unsolved mystery, and is one of the, most mysterious in the history of this section of crime.

Over the grave of Robert Snowball, in Blanchland Churchyard, is a granite cross inscribed:-

ERECTED
IN AFFECTIONATE
REMEMBRANCE OF
ROBERT SNOWBALL,
OF BELMOUNT,
AGED 26 YEARS.
HE WAS CRUELLY MURDERED
AT THAT PLACE ON THE
1ST JANUARY, 1880.

THE MUGGLESWICK MURDER.

On Sunday, May 7th, 1843, a barbarous murder was committed at a farm called Lamb Shield, sometimes, but erroneously, designed Lang Shield, on Muggleswick Common, about two-and-a-half miles north-west of Waskerley. The sufferer was the tenant of the farm, one William Lawson, and the culprit was his brother, Thomas.

William Lawson, the farmer in question, was a bachelor, and a man of some means, and resided on the farm with a housekeeper, one Elizabeth Patterson, a native of Rookhope. On Saturday, May 6th, his housekeeper went to Rookhope for the week-end, leaving her master alone. Early on the Sunday morning his brother, Thomas Lawson, a married man with a family, who resided on the farm called Cote House some three-quarters-of-a-mile distant from Lamb Shield, paid him a visit, and from what afterwards transpired, for there were no witnesses of the crime, they had some conversation relating to money matters, in which they quarrelled. In the struggle which ensued, and which took place in the cowbyre, they both fell to the ground, William being on the underside, and whilst in this position Thomas took a stone and struck his brother three or four times on the head with it, fracturing his skull, but not killing him outright. He then left him and went on to the adjoining fell, or common, to see his sheep.

William then seems to have attempted to go for assistance, and weakened by the loss of blood, had to crawl on his hands and knees. That same night a couple of Lawson's neighbours, John Bainbridge, farmer, of Pedom's Oak, and William Ritson, farmer, of Calf Close, went to Lamb Shield to spend the evening with William Lawson, but on their arrival at the house they found the place deserted, the kettle on the bar, the fire out, and Lawson nowhere to be seen. On proceeding to the cowbyre, they found the milk-cans standing empty. That same evening Thomas Lawson's children went to their uncle's house, but failed to see him, as did also Thomas Lawson himself, with a similar result. When they saw that William was missing they never seem to have troubled about looking for him.

Early on Monday morning John Bainbridge, the farmer who resided at Pedom's Oak, having an idea that something must be wrong, went again to Lamb Shield to see if William Lawson had returned home, and he found him on the fell, near to a slate quarry, about three hundred yards from his house, resting on his hands and knees, still alive, but unconscious, having laid out in the cold and wet for about twenty-seven hours without a jacket on. Bainbridge then went to Shotley Bridge and gave information to the police, and an Irishman who was draining at Edmundbyers was taken into custody on suspicion.

The policeman (Leybourne Wilson) afterwards went and questioned Thomas Lawson, about his missing brother, and he stated that he had been that morning at Waskerley looking for him and making enquiries about him. The policeman, however, doubted his word and as the morning had been very wet, he examined Lawson's clothes and boots, and found them quite dry. He then made a search of the place and found a shirt stained with blood. He thereupon arrested him and took him to the Shotley Bridge lock-up - a temporary room in the Bridge End public-house.

Two days later, on May 10th, William Lawson, who had never recovered his senses or speech, died from his injuries. When his death was communicated to his brother in the lock-up Thomas enquired if he had spoken before he died, and on the constable replying in the affirmative, Lawson said, "It's all up with me now," and confessed the crime, stating that he did not kill him with a stick, which the policeman at that moment was holding, but with a stone. Soon after William Lawson's death an inquest was held at Edmundbyers, at which Thomas Lawson, the culprit, made the, following statement:-

"I live at Cotehouse in the township of Muggleswick. I am a farmer and keep about four score of sheep and lambs. I am the brother of William Lawson, the person that is dead.

I went up to his house on Sunday morning, between six and seven o'clock. I had some talk with him in the house. He said he was going on the fell after he had milked. He then went into the cowbyre, and began telling me about a letter he had got, and said it was for me. It was an attorney's letter, about some money I owe to Harry Ritson; he told me it was 11/- in it. I wanted some money off Willy (his brother) - some mother had left me - and £2 5s he owed me for sheep that were sold of his and mine together. I asked him for the money, or to go and speak to Forster Raine to give me time to pay what I owed him . He refused to do so. This vexed me, and as he was beginning to milk, I took him by the neck and we had a struggle. He struck me with his foot, and hit me on the inside of the left thigh. It did not hurt me, but it raised me, and we went down together. There was a stone behind the byre door, and I hit him with it on the head three or four times. I thought I had done so much for him, and he nothing for me - that was what made me take hold of him.

When I went out of the byre he got up, and leaned upon a stick between the stalls behind the door. I then went on to the fell among the sheep, and fell in with Tommy Anderson, and a man looking for a galloway - I don't know who he was. I thought he would not be so bad so I did not tell anybody. My children went to his house, and I went afterwards, but he was not there. I saw Thomas Ritson and Willy Bainbridge. I have never told anybody anything before today.

Things being in such a bad state, and him doing nothing for me, made me take hold of him.   One bad thing begot another. After he kicked me I got worse, and that made me do it. I would have helped him into the house when my passion cooled, but I had not power or strength. I never told my wife; I only told her we had some words. When I say "things," I meant stock was so bad, and he would not give me anything. I have a family of two children, and five altogether of family, and my brother had no family, and being distressed for money made me apply to him."

Thomas Lawson was tried at the Mid-summer Assizes, at Durham, in 1843, found guilty of manslaughter, and sentenced to transportation for life. He died at the hulks about a couple of years later.

THE MUGGLESWICK PARK CONSPIRACY.

During the brief reign of Presbytery and Independency under the Commonwealth and Protectorate, from 1649 to 1660, the bulk of the inhabitants of Muggleswick and the neighbourhood, seem to have abjured Episcopacy and Prelacy; and the Rev. Richard Bradley, Master of Arts and a High Churchman, who had been appointed to the Perpetual Curacy of Muggleswick, and the spiritual oversight of the parishioners, on the 20th of November, 1641, was expelled, or ousted from his living five years later. The Civil Wars which broke out in 1642 ended in the abolition of monarchy and the establishment of a Commonwealth in 1649. During this period every effort was made to desecrate the Established Church, and considerable damage was done to the ecclesiastical buildings, their monuments, and their parish registers, and all the established clergymen were driven from their livings.

In 1646 Episcopacy was abolished and the use of the Book of Common Prayer, whether in public or private, was prohibited; fines being inflicted for the first offence, and a year's imprisonment for the third. In the county of Durham the Bishop (Thomas Morton) was driven from his seat, and his estates and property seized and ordered to be sold. All the Clergy in this diocese, as elsewhere, were thrust out of of their livings, and Puritan preachers, or intruders as they are generally called were put in their places. These intruders were not clergymen, but sectaries, thrust into the livings by the Parliament, or by Oliver Cromwell, after the Church and Crown had been overthrown by the rebel.

The name of the intruder into the living of Muggleswick was Thomas Roger, who, however, did not occupy the perpetual curacy very long from the restoration of monarchy in the person of Charles II., in 1660 when everything that had been done in the Church and State during the interregnum was annulled, and when by the Act of Uniformity, all the Clergy were obliged to subscribe to the Thirty-nine Articles, and use the same form of worship and the same Book of Common Prayer, Mr Roger was, with about two thousand other Nonconformist ministers, deposed in their turn.   Roger did not stay until the final ejection of Nonconformist ministers on Black Bartholomew's Day on the 24th of August, 1662.

This violent change was naturally distasteful to the Puritanical portion of the inhabitants of Muggleswick and the neighbourhood, who complained loudly, but in vain, that an unsuitable person was to be imposed upon them to guide and rule them in spiritual matters. They thereupon drew up a petition containing their grievances, which they gave to Mr. George Lilburne, one of the members for the county, to present to the House of Commons. It was signed by sixty-two persons, including women and children, whom the Rev. Richard Bradley had indicted for absenting themselves from Holy Communion.

A copy of this petition, which was printed, is amongst a series of pamphlets presented to the British Museum by King George III. (Folio. Sh. 1. No. 121) and is quoted by Robert Surtees in his *History of Durham*. It is as follows:

> *"A most lamentable information of Part of the Grievances of Muggleswikk Lordship, in the Bishopric of Durham, sent up by Master George Lilburne, Major, of Sunderland, to be communicated to the House of Commons.*
>
> *"To all Christian people to whom these presents shall come, know that we are a people in that our parish of Muggleswicke, who have been destitute of a preaching Minister; yea, ever since any of us that are now breathing were borne, to our soul's great griefe and dreadful hazard*

of destruction; neither is it our case alone, but also ten, yea or twelve parishes all adjoining are in like manner void of the means of salvation, whose case and condition is deeply to be deplored: And as for us in Muggleswicke, we have had neither good nor bad since Martinmas (November 11th) Anno Dom., 1640, but such as the Scottish Presbiterie furnished us withal (bemoaning our miserable estate) for hee who then supplied the place, departed this life the day of the date above mentioned; and we immediately after his death rode to one Master James, minister of Riton, being one of the prebends of Durham, entreating him with all earnestness, with an humble petition, because he then was in authorite, and no more of that sect left in the countre, but all fled because of the Scots, that this our poore parish of Muggleswicke might once at length have the fruition of a faithful minister, but hee answered that they (viz.) the prebends, had already appointed us a man, namely, one John Duery, whom we knew; then with all our soules we besought him that we might be exempted of that Duery, because we knew him to be no preacher, and his life and conversation scandalous, and had two places at that present; as we told him; and also that he publicly confessed in a pulpit before an open assembly, that he could not preach, and yet that aspiring prebend (whose lifeless conscience, we leave to your censure) replyed that they had once authorized him, and wee neither could nor should depose him; and he also told us in plaine tearmes, that if he could reade the prayer booke and an homily, it was nothing to us what kind of man he was; so when things would be no better, it behooved us to come home with these cold comforts having heavy hearts that our soules should a longer season be inthralled to such a simple, yea (we dare say) sinful minister, who is ignorant of the very principles of religion; yet our all sufficient God (seeing that we were but

29

breeding and beginning in Christianitie) would let no more be laid upon us (than we were able to beare), and so seeing us unwilling to accept of him he gave over. Thus the place being voide for the space of a whole yeare, we ourselves betwixt grief and necessitie, went abroad to seeke, and it pleased our God to send such an one as our soules longed after, and no sooner found we one to whom our minds affected, but immediately those prebends (who whether they were friends or foes to Christ judge yee), that will not sticke to hazard their heads so they may hinder the truth, doe impose one Braidley upon us, a bird brought out of the nest of their bosomes who (we may say without sinne) is one of the most deboist amongst the sonnes of men, for hee will neither preach himself, nor yet permit others; but upon the Sabbath day he, took the locke from the Church doore, and fastened on one of his owne, so that the parishioners were forced for to stand in the church yard to discharge divine duties with their minister in cold, frost, and snow, to the, infinite dishonour of the Almightie, the great griefe of their minds, and the dreadful indangering of themselves in that stormy time of the yeare; other times before, he came into the church, whilst our minister was in his exhortation, and stood up beside him, reading with a loud voyce in a book to overtop the sound of his words; afterwards pulled him by the coate when hee was in the pulpit; but when neither of these would cause him to desist from duty, he goes and rings the bell all aloud; neither is this all, but out of malice cals a communion and enters upon the sacred action without any preparation sermon before the day."

Under the circumstances described in the terms of the petition, it was no wonder that the parishioners felt deeply aggrieved, and Surtees observes that "it was perhaps owing to the calmer temper of the people and the milder genius of the country rather than to the leniency of the Government, that the same scenes were not acted there which soon after occurred in Scotland, when the Covenanters were hunted into the wilderness, and found consolation in anathematising those persecutors amidst woods and water and waterfalls." The proceedings on the part of the clergyman at Muggleswick unquestionably in a great measure fomented the Anabaptist and Presbyterian plot hatched at that place. The local gentry and others of Muggleswick parish who had been imbued with this Puritanical spirit during the Commonwealth, were, after the Restoration, viewed with suspicion by the Royalists. In such a state of things every movement was liable to be misconstrued as treasonable; whilst on the other hand their proceedings of the Government were naturally thought tyrannical by those who had contended for the "good old cause."

Muggleswick Park at this period became the scene of several supposed seditious meetings, which an ill-judged display of force might very easily have converted into dangerous armed assemblies provided there had been some leader to inflame their godly zeal and to lead them forth to fight the battle of the Lord of Hosts. The "psalm singing rascals," as such individuals were called in those days, on the banks of the Derwent, however, were few in number and devoid of influence; and the gentry in the neighbourhood were almost to a man against them. The actual state of matters may be inferred from the following affidavit (from the Harleian M.S.S. in the British Museum) sworn to by John Ellerington, of Blanchland, in the county Northumberland before Samuel Davison, Cuthbert Carr, Thomas Fetherstone, and Richard Neile, justices of the peace, on the 22nd March, 1662, at Durham.

> *This informant saith:-*
> *"That he hath known divers seditious meetings in Muggleswick park, within the last six month, sometimes in the house of one John Ward, who is one of their chief preachers, sometimes at the house of John Readshaw, Robt. Blenkinsopp and Rowland Harrison, who were met together. The said John Ward, John Readshaw, Robert Blenkinsopp, and Rowland Harrison, together with Capt. George Gower, Robert Readshaw, son of the said John, Robert Taylor,*

Mark Taylor, both of Eddis Bridge, John March of the same, John Joplin of the Foxholes, John March of Ridley Mill, Cuthbert Newton of Flendsey, Richard Taylor of Cronkley, Henry Angus, Cuthbert Maughan of Birchenfields, George Readshaw of Edmondbyers, John Oliver of the same, Lewis Frost of South Sheales, Cuthbert Coatsworth and Michael Coatsworth of the same, Richard Ord and John Ord of Birchenhaugh, James Carr of Ardley, Nicholas Dalmer of Crawcrook, Rowland and Nicholas Harrison, sons of Rowland Harrison above said, John Hopper of Carpsheales, Thomas Readshaw of Peddamack, Michael Ward of Shotley Field, Cuthbert Ward of Black Hedley, Ralph Iley of Edmundbyers, Richard Johnson of Sunderland, and ---- Foster of the same; where they did mutually take an oath of secrecy not to discover their design, which was to rise in rebellion against the present government, and to destroy the present Parliament, which had made a law against liberty of conscience, and to murder all bishops, deans, and chapters, and all ministers of the Church, and to break all organs in pieces, and to destroy the common prayer books and to pull down all churches; and farther, to kill the gentry that should either oppose them, or not join with them in their design. That they intended first to fall upon Durham, to seize any magazine that might be there, or money in any treasurer's hands, and to plunder the town. They did boast of many thousands of Anabaptists and Independents that were to join with them in the nation, with whom they had daily correspondence by letters and messengers, upon which employment the said informant had been divers times sent to divers persons ; and he heard them lately say that some Papists were lately come in to their party, and they did not doubt of their real intention to join with them in their design; That they have already in their hands some provision of arms, and do expect great proportion both of arms and ammunition from Lewis Frost above said, who hath undertaken to provide for them. And he further saith, that for divers months by past it was resolved amongst to rise on the 25th of this instant March, but they did lately agree to defer the execution of their design for a month longer, till they see what the Parliament would do concerning indulgence to tender consciences and toleration of the party, and withal by putting off their rising they would be much stronger by many that would come to their party daily. And this informant saith that he knows to depose what he hath said because he was one of their party, and was re-baptised by the above John Ward, and was with them at most of their meetings, and did take the above said oath of secrecy, but being pricked in his conscience at the horror of such a, bloody design, he could have no rest nor quietness in his mind, till he had discovered the same."

In the second information Ellerington accused several gentlemen of considerable rank as participators in this crime of high treason. Amongst them were Sir Henry Witherington of Northumberland (who had been High Sheriff and also an M.P. for the country), Edward Fenwick of Stanton, Esq.; Timothy Whittingham of Holmside, Esq.; and Captain George Lilburne, of Sunderland. Witherington and Fenwick were probably Roman Catholics. Whittingham was a Presbyterian, and Lilburne whose name aforetime had been a terror was ominous, was an independent.

Whittingham and Lilburne were apprehended on the information of Ellerington, detained in custody three months, and then liberated for want of the slightest evidence to criminate them. Against Witherington and Fenwick there seems to have been less suspicion, probably their hereditory adherence to the old faith rendered it unlikely that they would ever make common cause with the Roundheads in an endeavour to upset Charles II's government and replace it by something to their mind far worse. In the Bishopric of

Durham the seditious Derwentdale plot excited no little commotion, and to oppose the conspirators, Dr. Cosin, the Bishop, called out the trained bands of the Palatine, under Sir Thomas Davison, and the principal gentry and their retainers, embodied themselves in the different wards of the county, under Sir Nicholas Cole of Brancepeth Castle; Colonel Cuthbert Carr of Dunston; Colonel Byerley; and Henry Lambton, Esq.

After all the alarm proved to have been a "much ado about nothing," without solid foundation, resting simply on the evidence of the one rascally informer and infamous scoundrel - John Ellerington, of Blanchland, who, in order to gain himself favour, and finding his audience had itching ears, accused every Anabaptist, Independent, and Presbyterian, or whoever leaned to the presbytery, of participation in the alleged plot, and manufactured cock and bull stories to startle them and subserve their own vile purpose.

It is true, however, that in various parts of the Kingdom all the Dissenters showed symptoms of uneasiness under the Bartholomew Act of 1662 which demanded episcopal recognition, the use of the amended Book of Common Prayer and the adjuration of the league and covenant, and the Cavaliers could never forgive "The psalm singing rascals who drubbed them so well." Loyal addresses poured in, and armed associations formed in all quarters, and such a face of general resistence was displayed, that all the discontented residents shrunk from showing any unpleasantness.

The following is a copy of the text of one of these loyal addresses dated 14th January, 1663:-

> *"For-as-much as this county palatine of Durham together with others, the northern parts of the Kingdom, have been lately disturbed by many seditious plots and devices of disaffected persons, who in their frequent and secret designs in their unlawful designs, may much endanger the peace of his majesty, and of his loyal subjects we therefore as faithfully promise and undertake to be ready with our horses*

and arms, and with all the free assistance we can procure,
to repare unto such place etc., and to oppose the designs
either of Quakers or Anabaptists or other disaffected and
disloyal persons, and to dissipate the dangerous assemblies
and seditious conventials, etc., in the several and respective
quarters of our habitations."

During 1663 several inquiries were held concerning the plot and various evidences taken. In a letter written by Mr. Edward Arden to Mr. Stapylton, dated Auckland Castle, 27th March, 1663; we have the following:- "My Lord (the Bishop, Dr. Cosin) is now and was yesterday examining several Anabaptists, who have a witness come in against some of them that upon oath swears that they at their meetings entered into a solemn oath upon the Bible to destroy the Parliament, the Bishop, the Clergy, and the Gentry too if :they opposed them. We have now horse and foot, with no great number, heare in towne, and at Durham in readiness, &c."

In the month of December several witnesses were examined before Henry Widdrington, James Ogle, and Ralph Jennison. It is impossible however to give the whole of their evidence, but the following extracts will show what sort was adduced:-

George Proud, of Ebchester-bridge-end, Webster, on
December 1st, 1663, stated that "Being in company with
one John Suirtes, of Highfield, about five or six weeks since
at a place called the Hollins, he heard the said Suirtes say
that there was two troops of horse that were in arms there;"
and Proud also stated that two persons with broad swords
came over the ford at Ebchester.

The same day Thomas Richardson deposed "that he told Thomas Marshal that John Wilkingson told him that Joseph Hopper was and had been abroad with his horse and armes, and that there were some men upon horseback with swords, seen ryding by over at Ebchester and Shotley Bridge, and John Wilkinson said that he feared Joseph Hopper was with them."

Joseph Hopper was then examined, and he stated that he had been "abroad five weeks in Ireland, to see some friends he had there" and that when he went "he would not acquaint his wife therewith, for he knew she would be unwilling to let him go."

After the most minute inquiries, conducted by parties by no means disposed to extenuate the case, it turned out that the terrific array of mounted Anabaptists whom the informer alleged to have been mustering by night on Muggleswick Common, and the two troops of horse seen near the Hollins, and the, same men who forded the Derwent with glittering broad swords was reduced to one man - Joseph Hopper - who had taken a jaunt to Ireland, and had reasons for not acquainting his wife, showing, indeed great want of gallantry, but nothing to intimidate the Cavaliers, and had come back again on horseback. As Ellerington had accused every person in the neighbourhood who favoured the presbytery and was opposed to prelacy, of participation in the alleged plot had there been a tittle of evidence against any of them they could not have escaped the severest punishment, such was the inflamed spirit of the time, and if such had been the case, of the fifteen hundred men then sent on an average to the Virginian colony in North America, Muggleswick would probably have provided a considerable instalment that year to labour as slaves in the tobacco plantations.

KING ARTHUR'S ENCHANTED CAVE.

"The scenes which, all enchanting,
threw their spell O'er old King Arthur,
who in dreamy state,
Abides for ever caverned in this dell;
Or till the subtle hand that fixed his fate
Dispels the dear delusion!"

Barrass. - *"The Derwent Valley"*.

"King Arthur's round table is near,
Though none has declared how it came;
He lifts up his head once a year,
The sceptre long lost to reclaim.
Enchantment its hold must forego,
Could any strange arm draw the sword,
The trumpet could any man blow,
That lie at the feet of their lord."

Carr. - *"The Derwent,"* an Ode.

In the north-east side of Muggleswick, and on the north side of the Derwent is a tongue of elevated woodland, called the Sneep, round which the river, in other parts of its course generally impetuous, patiently and beautifully describes the form of a horse shoe. In the neighbourhood of this romantic headland - one of the prettiest pieces of landscape scenery in the Derwent Valley - tradition says is a certain deep cavern, inaccessible to common mortals, in which King Arthur - that mysterious British ruler whose career has furnished more excellent good matter for romantic writers than any other ancient British hero - is said, together with his Queen, and several of his gallant Knights, and their steeds, to be lying in a trance, every one of the last equipped and ready at the King's command to march and assist him to regain his kingdom, when the time appointed shall arrive and the enchantment be broken.

Arthur was born A.D. 501 succeeded to the throne of his father in 516, and ruled until his death in 542. During his reign he is said to have gained several victories over the Saxons, and to have defeated them so severely that they were obliged to seek refuge for a while on the sea; to have defeated the Picts and Scots; and to have caused his name to be known to the uttermost parts of Ireland, Norway, Muscovy, and Gaul by his great victories. At last he was mortally wounded in a battle in Cornwall against his rebel nephew Modred, and was buried by the monks of Glastonbury in the isle of Avalon.

Tradition, however, states that his remains were spirited away to a spot which the hero himself had chosen during his lifetime. This feat was performed by his half-sister, who carried him off to Fairyland, there to be healed of his wounds. When this was accomplished the monarch was placed asleep, with the flower of his chivalry round him, in a subterranean hall, there to remain for a certain period of time. The traditional cave at the Sneep is, however, only one of the many in the North of England assigned as the scene of this slumber of ages. Its entrance is concealed by a wealth of foliage, and in the centre of the hall a flame of fire arises from the ground. Around the fire are placed two couches formed of many various kinds of herbs and wild flowers, which are said to send out a delicate odour like the purest balsam. On one of these couches reclines King Arthur; and on the other Guenhever, his Queen. Lying also around the fire are his pack of faithful bloodhounds. Upon the table lies his terrible sword - Excalibur - in its sheath, a garter, and a huge brazen horn or trumpet. On other couches in the same chamber also recline the King's faithful courtiers, all equipped, whilst near by are their horses, all harnessed. All are in readiness to start, when the appointed hour comes for them to re-appear in our upper world, and accompany their King in his march to avenge his countrymen, and to reinstate himself in the sovereignty of Britain. To break the spell that has enchanted the King and his court, someone must penetrate the cave, take the sword and cut the garter, and blow the horn or trumpet. This action will restore all to life again. If this feat is not successfully performed - and it has been attempted more than once without success - the King will slowly rise from his couch, so it is said, open his eyes, and lift up his hands and exclaim: -

> "O woe betide that evil day
> On when the witless wight was born,
> Who drew the sword, the garter cut,
> But never blew the bugle horn!"

JANE FRIZZLE:
THE WITCH OF CROOKED OAK.

"Ghosts and witches come in for a share,
Though poor Frizzle has long breathed her last,
On broomsticks, who rode through the air,
And scattered her pins as she past."

Carr. - "The Derwent," an Ode.

To the north of the Sneep is the antiquated farm house of Crooked Oak, with its Jacobean windows indicative of the architecture of the period in which it was built, and the date 1684 and the initials T. and I. R. (the erectors of the house) over its ornamented doorway. The place probably received its name from some distorted oak tree that grew in the vicinity at a former period, and which has now long since disappeared. This place has the reputation of once being the home of more than one individual who during the sixteenth and seventeenth centuries practised the "black art," as witchcraft was called.

One of these was Jane Frizzle, whom the verse at the head of this article commemorates, and this notorious witch is said to have been in the habit of traversing the Derwent Valley by night with a broomstick for her palfrey, and of practising strange spells upon men, maidens, and cattle. Little or nothing, that is definite, is known of her career, or of the approximate time of her death, except that she lived in the seventeenth century, when witches were common in this part of the Derwent Valley, and about the time when they burnt every old woman who had a wrinkled face.

STIRLING OF STIRLING'S BRIDGE.

Between Healeyfield and Muggleswick the waters of the Hisehope and Horsleyhope Burns unite in a deep dene, near what is called Combe Bridges, and a short distance further on the combined streams join the river Derwent. A little above their confluence is the site of Stirling's Bridge, where, according to local tradition, a brave warrior of that name, defended the passage across the river, single handed, against a body of moss-troopers. The bridge in question was only a temporary affair of a couple of large trees laid side by side across the river, and afforded a useful means of passage for travellers on foot from one side of the river to the other and saved much time as the only permanent bridge in the district was at Alansford, further down the river.

These border thieves had successfully crossed the Derwent, and had pillaged and plundered many houses on the south side of the stream, burning the buildings and massacring some of the inhabitants. On their return with their spoil they were seen by Stirling, whose house was one of the many they had broken into and burnt, and he determined to prevent them from crossing the Derwent, and, if possible, to keep them at bay until some of the plundered farmers should be able to come up and attack them. The river was much flooded and was not fordable at the time, and this crossing was their nearest place to escape. He managed to keep them at bay for some time, but at length fearing that he might soon be overpowered and his help being long in coming, he commenced to break down the bridge, and managed after great exertions to dislodge the trees, and escape safe and sound to the northern side. Some of the moss-troopers, seeing Stirling's action, set off to Alansford, and crossing the stone bridge took him in the rear, intending to kill him for his pains. In this, however, they were disappointed, for Stirling, seeing that his retreat was cut off, sooner than fall into their hands and be slain, jumped into the flooded river and was drowned.

THOMAS RAW
THE MOSS-TROOPER

"How rich the wood, how green the grassy mound,
Where sleeps the once indomitable Raw,
And where, asylumed safe, he gazed around,
And, toiling through the scenes surrounding, saw
The coming plunder, or the searching law!
What though unconsecrated memory
May hold a thousand feebler souls in awe?
He slumbers there beneath his chosen tree,
And who wherever laid, may sleep more sound than he?"

Barrass. - *"The Derwent Valley"*

Another famous moss-trooper was Thomas Raw, who lived on the farm at Wharnley Burn, on the south side of the Derwent, above Alansford, and a member of a family who had for several generations lived either at that place or in the neighbourhood. He was a contemporary of Rowley Harrison and they may have gone on freebooting excursions and thieving raids together, though both history and oral tradition are silent on this matter.

He appears to have been one of the last of the race of those desperadoes, who, during the troublous times of the seventeenth and eighteenth centuries in the border counties, lived in contempt and defiance of the law. He managed either to evade the law, or amidst the romantic ravines and mountain retreats in the valley of the Derwent and its tributaries, in the neighbourhood, eluded his pursuers, until the latest day of his life, except that probably he suffered what would nowadays be called boycotting by his more honest or less reckless neighbours. His dishonest occupation, however, brought him under the interdiction of the church, and he was publicly excommunicated, and the prohibition which expelled him from the communion of the church and the Christian fellowship, was read out in all the churches in the Derwent Valley between Hunstanworth and Blanchland, and Medomsley and Whittonstall, and in the district between Hexham and Slaley and Stanhope and Wolsingham, and also in the market places of Hexham, Stanhope, and Wolsingham. Being thus refused burial in consecrated ground, Raw, long before his death, chose a place under a tree in a field on the crest of the hill near his house, and there requested his friends to bury him on his death. This spot, which is on a beautiful promontory, commands a view of all the surrounding approaches, and is said to. have been the place where Raw spent much time in watching the approach of pursuers, or officers of the law, who could easily be detected at some considerable distance, and from whence he could take the best route to elude or evade them.

He died in January, 1714, and his remains were duly interred in the spot which he had chosen, and some time after a neat freestone slab was erected over the grave on which was inscribed, in script letters, the following inscription:

HERE LYETH THE BODY

OF THOMAS RAW OF

WHARNLEY BURN

WHO DEPARTED THIS LIFE

JANUARY 30

ANNO. 1714.

The farmhouse at Wharnley Burn remained as an old thatched dwelling, just as it was when the moss-trooper occupied it, until the sixth decade of the nineteenth century, when it underwent alterations and received a modern roof. There are three rooms on the ground floor, and the central one was the bedroom, or sleeping apartment, of the famous moss-trooper. When at home he slept in a beautifully carved box bed, made of oak, which stood against an oak partition, separating his room from the next apartment, where a doorway led to the outside. The door leading from Raw's room to the adjoining apartment was concealed by the bed referred to, and it is said that he used this secret door as a means of escape from his pursuers. This interesting old bed afterwards came into the possession of Mr. W. J. Scott, of the Sycamores, Rowley, who sold it in the early 'eighties' to Messrs Rushworth and Sons, of Durham, who in turn converted it into a mantel-piece for one of the rooms of Fairthorn, Hampshire.

After the erection of the stone it was carefully preserved, and in later years an old woman named Nelly Wilkinson, who acted as housekeeper to George Raw, a descendant of the moss-trooper, was in the habit of crossing over to the burial place of her master's ancestor, and scrubbing the grave cover every weekend. On this account the stone has yet a smooth polished appearance. In accordance with a wish of George Raw's will this old lady continued to occupy a room at the west end of the house at Wharnley Burn free of rent until her death.

Wharnley Burn, which was formerly the property of the Raw family, passed into the hands of John Emmerson, of Willow Green, near Frosterley, who eventually sold it to Annandale Town, Esq., of Alansford, and previous to parting with the place, he had the headstone removed to his farm at Steeley, near Satley, and inserted in the wall of the western gable of what was the old farm house, now the barn and cartshed, at that place, where it still remains, with the inscription as plain as ever, whilst below is appended, in Roman capitals the record -

REMOVED FROM WHARNLEY BURN, 1866.

A few years before the removal of the stone to Satley, Mr. Frank Bell, at that time tenant of Wharnley Burn, and Mr. George Siddle, butcher, of Castleside, in order to satisfy themselves and others, that Raw was really buried there, opened the grave and found the skeleton, which was in a good state of preservation, probably owing to the dryness of the soil in which the body was deposited.

Thomas Raw's will is in the Probate Registry at Durham, and in it he directed his body to be buried according to the discretion of his executors - his brother Michael and John. To his wife he left an annuity of £4, a bed with the bedclothes, a press, a chest, and a cow; to his son Michael he left the farm of Wharnley Burn, and to his son John the farm of Todd Hills which at his death was to go to his son Thomas. To his nephew Thomas he left the farm of Hollin Hall which was leased from Dr. Oxley. Other legacies were left to his nephews, John and Joseph Marshall, and his niece Hannah Newton. By the inventory of his goods dated 27th June, 1715, his apparel was valued at £5, and the debts owing to him were returned as £114.

Fig. 3 Fawcett excavating Raw's grave in the 1920s

THE WITCHES OF THE DERWENT VALLEY.

The sixteenth, seventeenth, and eighteenth centuries were an age of superstition and a universal belief in the supernatural. Ghosts and goblins haunted every lonely spot and solitary locality, and their weird cries were heard in every storm; and witches and wizards rode through the land on most uncommon steeds, practising their black arts on men, maidens, and cattle, and holding their midnight meetings in the darker nooks of every secluded glen. The district around Alansford, at this time, seems to have been a famous rendezvous for witches. Perhaps it was that in its secluded position in the Derwent Valley, with its many glens, and vales, and haughs, all more or less remote, and almost free from common molestation of human beings, they had a suitable locality in which to live and practise all the arts which appertained to their profession.

Among many of the hidden arts practised by witches in bygone days may be enumerated:- (1) The entering into common communion with familiar spirits, by which they were said to be assisted in their wicked designs; (2) the use of frightful imprecations of wrath and malice towards the object of their hatred; (3) the being able to transform themselves into various animals, such as dogs, cats, hares, moles, rats, etc.; or into various birds, such as owls, swallows, etc., or into insects, such as bees, and in other forms visiting persons and bewitching them so as to cause them trouble, sickness, or death, etc.

Witchcraft in those days was a crime punishable by severe penalties, and those who were alleged to have practised some of the "black arts" as their offences were called, did not always escape being brought to justice. Some accounts of the midnight carousals and weird meetings of witches in the Derwent Valley have been preserved, and from them we learn something of the curious superstitious beliefs which existed in the district a couple of centuries ago. At a trial of certain persons who were charged with the alleged crime of witchcraft, at the Sessions held at Morpeth, on April 9th, 1673, before Sir Thos. Horsley, and Sir Richard Stote, Knts., James Howard, Humphrey Mitford, Ralph Jennison, and John Salkeld, Esqrs., several women from the Derwent Valley district were present as witnesses, amongst whom were Ann Armstrong, of Buksnuke, spinster, who in the course of her evidence said that she attended a meeting of witches on the 3rd of April (1673), in a house at the Riding, and that among the number of persons there she saw "Mary Hunter, of Birkenside, widow, Dorothy Green, of Edmundbyers, in the County of Durham, widow, Elizabeth Pickering, of Whittingslaw, widow, Anthony Hunter, of Birkinside, yeoman, John Whitfield, of Edmundbyers, Annie Whitfield, of the same place, spinster, Christopher Dixon, of Muggleswick Park, and Alice his wife, Catherine Elliott, of Ebchester, Elizabeth Atchinson, of Ebchester, widow, and Isabell Andrew, of Crookedoke, widow," and she also swore that she had seen the same persons holding meetings at various places, and especially "upon Collop Monday last, being the tenth of February," at Alansford, to which she was [placed under enchantment and] "ridden upon by an enchanted bridle by Michael Aynsley and Margaret his wife," and on her arrival there the enchanted bridle was taken from her head, and she resumed her ordinary state of being, and she saw the persons aforenamed dancing, "some in the likenesse of haires, some in the likenesse of catts, and others in the likeness of bees, and some in their own likenesse." They made her sing while they danced, and every thirteenth of them had a "divil" with them in some varied shape, and at this meeting their particular "divell tooke them that did most evil and danced with them first, and called every one of them to an account and those that did most evill he made most of" - a very natural thing for the Satanic being to do.

She then stated that she could remember the confession each made there and then to the devil, and amongst others were the following:-

Mary Hunter (of Birkenside) "confessed to the divill that she had wronged George Taylor, of Edgebriggs goods," and told her protector that "she had gotten the power of a fole (foal) of his, soe that it pined to death. And she had got power of the dam (mother) of the said fole, and that they had an intention the last Thursday at night to have taken away the power of the limbs of the said mare." he also confessed that "about Michaelmas last she did come to one John Marsh, of Edgebrigg, when he and his wife were riding from Bywell, and flew some times under his mare's belly, and some times before its breast in the likeness of a swallow, until she got the power of it, and it died within a week after."

Elizabeth Pickering "of Whittingstall, widdow, confessed that she had power of a neighbor's beast of her owne in Whittingstall, and that she had killed a child of the said neighbour's." Anthony Hunter, of Birkenside, "confessed that he had power over Anne, wife of Thomas Richardson, of Crooked Oak, that he took away the power of her limbs, and asked the divill's assistance to take away her life."

At the same sessions, John March, of Edgebrigg [now Eddy's bridge], yeoman, the person just named, whose horse had been bewitched by Mary Hunter, gave evidence of the loss of his steed. He said "that about a month since he went to a place called Birkside Nook, and there Ann Armstrong hearing him named, began to speak to him, and asked him if he had not an ox, that had got the power of one of his limbs taken from him, and he telling her he had, and enquiring how she came to know, she told him that she heard Mary Hunter of Birkenside, and another at a meeting amongst divers witches, confess to the divill that they had taken the power of that beast, and she not knowing her name, Sir James Clavering and Sir Richard Scott thought proper to carry her to 'Edenbyers', and there to cause the women to come to her there to the intent that she might challenge her, and she challenged one Dorothy Green, a widow, and said that she was the person that joined with Mary Hunter in the bewitching of the said ox. And the ox now continues lame and has no use of his far hinder legg, but pines away and likely to die."

He also said that "Ann Armstrong told him that the said persons (Mary Hunter and Dorothy Green) confessed before the divill that they had bewitched a grey mare of his, and he said that about a fortnight before Michaelmas last (Sept. 29) he and his wife were riding home from Bywell, one Sunday night, upon the saide mare about sunset; and there came a swallow which about forty times and more flew through the mare's belly, and crossed her way before her breast, and he struck at it with his rod about twenty times, and wished to hinder it to so continue, until it went away of it's own action. And the mare went very well home, and died within four days, and before she died was two days so mad that she was past holding, and was struck blind for twenty four hours before she died."

George Taylor, of Edgebrigg, yeoman, the person whose mare and foal had been bewitched by Mary Hunter, also gave similar evidence, as to the loss of his foal and also stated that since that time all his goods had not thrived like those of his neighbours, notwithstanding that he fed them as well as he could.

An amulet supposed to prevent witches taking horses out of the stable and riding them during the night was long preserved at Alansford.

THE DERWENT VALLEY GIANTS

"Up! up with me and from this lofty ridge,
Behold the leagues of undulating shore,
And high o'er-gazing placid Shotley Bridge,
The haunts of whom in old time rivalled Thor
The hammer-wielding god in regions hoar,
Whose awful arm achieved such marvels vast,
And cracked the ribs of Polar gods galore! -
Prone down yon height was CON's huge hammer cast;
Behold, cried eld, behold the prowess of the past!"

Barrass. - *"The Derwent Valley"*

There were in the heroic ages of the Derwent Valley three brothers -
all giants, "great men and tall, and strong beside," named Cor, Ben,
and Con, who are said to have resided each in a cave, at Corbridge,
in Northumberland, and Benfieldside and Consett, in Durham,
respectively, and to have been the possessors, in common, of a large
hammer, which each, at a whistle, could throw nine miles. When any
of the brothers wanted this tool, this was the way it was conveyed to
one another, and on one occasion when Con, who had become blind,
in throwing it to his brother Cor, let it slip and it made a hollow dene,
or hole in the ground, near Consett, which was afterwards called
Howden, and which remains to this day. Con is supposed to have lived
in a cave in Howen's Gill, and is generally believed to have been buried
there on his death. Many and varied are the adventures which might
be enumerated or told of these giants, the whole of which is plainly
fabulous, and has a mixture of the more interesting and elegant classic
mythology.

Dr. Carr, the first local poet in what is the first *Ode to the Derwent*, thus refers to these gigantic brothers:-

> "In elder times giants uprear'd
> Their heads, and affronted the skies;
> Cor, Ben, Con, terriffic appear'd,
> With names of anomalous size.
>
> A hammer in common they had,
> And the use of it easy to all;
> Each whistled, each brother was glad
> To throw it three leagues at his call.
>
> When Con was approaching his end,
> Deaf, blind, and beginning to rave,
> With a ploughman he begg'd as a friend
> To converse at the mouth of his cave.
>
> This ploughman, as prudent men do,
> Held his plough-share, himself to escape;
> Blind Con pinch'd his plough-share in two
> And pronounc'd it the arm of an ape."

There is another traditionary account of the Derwent Valley giants, differing from that already given. In it their names are given as Con, Ben, and Mug, and their names are perpetuated in the place names of Consett, Benfieldside, and Muggleswick. They are supposed to have lived about nine hundred years ago, and to have won great renown in the Palatinate of Durham. Laurence Goodchild, the blind scholar of Sunderland, has perpetuated some of the marvellous exploits and the violent deaths of these cruel giants in a ballad, called *"Durham Giants,"* written many years ago. He thus sings of their eventful career:-

"The first was Con - from him Conside
Is named until this day,
His brother Ben to Benfieldside
Bequeathed his name for aye.

And Mug their mighty kinsman was
A swarthy wight and tall
The name gave he to Muggleswick Moor
Where stood his Castle wall.

Now when their holds these Giants built
They hammer had but one,
They heaved it round from man to man
When each his work had done.

Their size ye well may guess, when in
The boot that Mug did wear,
A greyhound bitch her sucking whelps
Did hide, as men declare.

Their eyes were like the burning coal,
They were bristled from head to heel,
No wight might stand their heavy hand
Though clad in coat of steel.

On Christian flesh they daily fed,
Their drink was Christian blood,
And the delicate limbs of a Christian child
To them was dainty food.

Their teeth stood out like tusks of boar
The bleeding prey to rend,
Their shaggy hair like Norway bear
Did down their back descend;

Their clubs were pine trees strong and straight
Uprooted by their might;
They wielded them, with mickle din,
In many a furious fight.

Whole scores of men, and women too,
By them for meat was slain,
Till Con was with an arrow broad
Shot through at Annfield Plain,

And Ben his brother, void of ruth-
By Launcelot's sword fell he,
Though he waged his fray, the live-long day
On the hill of Medomsley.

And Mug their kinsman, while to sin,
He wooed a beautious nun,
In wassail drowned fell fast asleep
And soon his race was run;

For like that lady in Holy Writ
Who the Paynim captain slew,
That nun with a spike of iron pierced
His temples through and through."

THE DEVIL AT BENFIELDSIDE

Benfieldside is famous amongst other things for one of the first Friends', or Quaker's, meeting houses in England. The Society of Friends, or Quakers, was founded by a George Fox, about 1647, and soon had adherents almost all over England. Within seven years of that date a branch had been formed at Benfieldside, and it was at a meeting of these members that what may be termed a terrible exhibition of fanaticism occurred. According to uncertain history and tradition, we are told that the Devil appeared at the meeting house in great wrath, and attempted to snatch away the key which was destined to imprison him for ever. Some of our country historians have briefly noticed the account, but they have misrepresented the object of his Satanic Majesty's visitation. Details of this strange and unusual apparition are given in at least three different works published shortly after the occurrence, and which are now very scarce. The authors, or writers of the different works, all vouch for the truth of the narrative, and give it as one of the many instances of the strange excitement which possessed the early followers of Fox in their worship. The sect was first called the Society of Friends, but on one occasion when Fox was sent to prison (and he was imprisoned many times) he bade the committing justice "tremble at the word of the Lord," whereupon that magnate applied to Fox and his friends the name of Quakers, by which they were afterwards best known and generally called, though the name was never adopted by the society. This name seems to have described the actions of many members of the sect in its early days, for one of the early writers states that "the monstrous distortions of their whole bodies are very dreadful to the beholders, and such loud and hideous yelling as sometimes frightened dogs, swine, and cattle at a great distance, and set them arunning, howling, lowing, braying, etc."

The outbreak of Satan in the township of Benfieldside occurred on August 19th, 1654, when a grave minister named Thomas Tilham preached to the members of the Society of Friends in the house of one of their own sect. According to the three different narrators, who agree in their separate accounts, when the minister prayed to God, as a Creator, nothing occurred, but when he cried in the name of Christ as a mediator, the Devil "roared" in the souls of those present (about twenty) in a most strange and dreadful manner, causing some of them to howl, and others to shriek, some to yell, and others to roar, and not a few to make a humming, singing noise. "Such a representation of hell," says one of the eyewitnesses, "I never heard of, nothing but horror and confusion." Satan appears to have entered freely into them and caused them to talk as well, for one of the members asked the preacher if he had not come to torment them, and as they left the meeting house one of them cursed the preacher and wished that all the plagues of God might fall upon him. Tradition as well as history is silent as to what followed.

MAD MADDISON

One of the most notorious characters who have lived in the Derwent Valley in the days gone by was "Mad Maddison". He was a member of a local family who for many centuries held lands in the valley and surrounding neighbourhood, and was one of those turbulent characters to whom the unsettled condition of the North of England for centuries previous to the union with Scotland had given birth. His proper name was Ralph Maddison, but as he was a most eccentric and wicked character, his Christian name was seldom given to him. In all the popular traditions concerning him he is called by the most anti-christian name of "Mad," because of its fitness to give some idea of his extremely insane and immoral conduct. Most of his mischievous actions and wicked pranks seem to have been played merely for the fun of the thing, though in many of them he played what can only be termed Satanic malevolence.

He lived immediately opposite the village of Shotley Bridge, on the left bank of the Derwent, in a good plain stone house which stood upon the site of the offices of the present mansion of Derwent Dene, and some venerable trees, which still form a lofty and sombre avenue, may have been planted in his time, perhaps by his own hand.

Maddison was the owner of considerable estates in the neighbourhood, and for some time officiated as a sort of warden of the district, and it may be that in his excursions against the border thieves and moss-troopers he acquired their predatory dispositions and learnt to practise their dexterous villanies. It is evident that a worse choice for the office of warden could scarcely have been made, for, on account of his continuous mischievous habits, he became the constant terror of young and old, male and female, who were forced to go near his residence, or any place which he was accustomed to frequent. His end was quite in keeping with his life, for he died on the gallows in the city of Durham, as will be hereafter told.

Maddison's name has for generations been employed to frighten forward or quieten noisy children on the banks of the Derwent, and such exclamations as "Mad Madison, come and get the naughty bairn," "Mad Maddison will catch you," etc., are often heard on these occasions. His numerous mischievous actions and insane deeds, many of them really horrific, others simply amusing, used to be, and still are, often heard on winter evenings around the hearths in many of the homes and houses in the neighbouring hamlets and villages.

His whole career was so full of adventures that a volume of anecdotes, stories, and traditions concerning him might be collected and written, for as Alexander Barrass, "the Derwent Valley poet", says:-

> " 'T would chill the heart the muse essays to cheer,
> And add encumbrance to a gory verse,
> To count the crimes that crimson'd his career
> And stamp'd him as an impersonated curse;
> That blasted all things with a breath perverse,
> From mortals down to farmer's garner'd hay."

The following are accounts of some of the mischievous exploits of this notorious character –

> "Who wrested frailty with ignoble force,
> Pitched to the waves his unsuspecting prey,
> And with a weird ha! ha! loud-mocking stalked away!"

On one occasion, when the river Derwent was very high and much swollen from excessive rains, and the fords near Shotley Bridge (for the bridge had not then been erected) impassable to any except on horseback, an old woman came to the river bank. She was anxious to get over the stream, but saw that it would be madness to attempt it by wading across. Whilst she was considering what was best to do Maddison rode up. She had heard of his mischievous pranks in the district - for they bad become famed far and wide - but did not know him personally. She told him of her anxiety to get over the river and

60

after he had heard her story he volunteered to take her across behind him, if she dare trust herself on the back of his spirited horse. The woman was quite willing to do this, adding that she was very glad to have met with such a "canny man," as she was afraid of meeting the dreaded "Mad Maddison." Maddison took her up behind him on the crupper with a seeming good-will, and plunged his horse into the river; but when he reached the middle of the stream, he pushed her off into the flooded river, and heartily laughing at his mischievous action, left her to sink or swim. The poor woman after having been carried a long way down the river, providentially gained the shore, by the aid of persons who had witnessed the transaction, and with difficulty recovered from the effects of her unpleasant bath.

Maddison used to amuse himself by doing all kinds of mischief in the night-time, and was addicted to overturning the stacks of hay and corn of the neighbouring farmers, at such time as it was likely to rain, or if the wind blew very strongly. One old man whom he had often annoyed in this way, foiled his malevolence by building his haystack around the stump of an old ash tree in such a manner as to resist being capsized. Maddison, when out one dark night in the performance of such-like capers, went to "cowp ower" the old man's stack, unaware of the presence of the tree stump in the centre. After repeated attempts to over - turn the structure from various sides, he found that it resisted his utmost strength. Dare-devil though Maddison was, he was, like the majority of the inhabitants of the district in those days, very superstitious, and finding that all his tries to turn the stack over were to no purpose, he ran away in great fear, declaring that there was a witch in the stack.

On another occasion, whilst in the village of Ebchester, he saw a couple of webs of linen laid out to bleach, and going deliberately and openly past the old woman who owned them, he picked up one piece, evidently intending to make it his own. As he was carrying it off the old woman protested against such an audacious robbery, saying, "You'll have to pay dearly for what you are doing, some day!" Upon this Maddison coolly returned and seized the other piece, saying, with an oath, "Then I will have both, for it is as well to hang for a hog as a halfpenny," and away he strode with them.

One day when Maddison and his son-in-law had been freely indulging themselves in the cup that inebriates in the Bridge-end public-house at Shotley Bridge, the latter, who had evidently the weaker stomach and head of the two for carrying strong drink, got unsteady on his legs and faltering in his speech. Maddison proposed that they should go home, and that he would himself walk, while the other should ride. This was agreed to, and ordering out his horse, "a wild but gallant dapple grey," of particularly high temper, and the swiftest ever known in the country round, he put his poor helpless son-in-law on the impatient animal's back, with his face to its tail, and placed a bunch of thorns where they caused the greatest irritation. Then the animal was let go, and the infuriated beast darted across the river, with its rider clinging like grim death instinctively to its back. Rushing onward at a most furious speed, it galloped right past Shotley Hall towards Black Hedley, near which place it threw and killed the unfortunate man.

Of this incident Barrass thus poetically writes:-

> "Who may picture with what demon glee
> He viewed his son's distraction on his steed,
> When mad, unbridled, plunging o'er the lea,
> The charger matched Mazeppa's lightning speed!
>
> And when was stretched the rider on the mead,
> No change came over his unaltered eye;
> For his base heart, if heart he had, indeed,
> Felt no fine thrill of sensibility:
> The darker deed the deeper his abnormal joy!"

The widow, who is said to have been a most beautiful woman, of great talent, married again shortly afterwards, and her father, either because he did not approve of the match, or out of some sudden passionate freak, attempted the life of her second husband by shooting at him. Fortunately he missed his mark, or "Mad Maddison" might have come to an earlier end on the gallows.

Innumerable stories are told of the career of this notorious character, and if one-half of what is alleged against him be true, he must have been a consummate villain. In former times a thick wood extended along the north bank of the river Derwent from Espershields to Newbiggen, above Blanchland, but it is said to have been burnt down by Maddison, the owner.

Destruction of property by fire seems to have been a favourite practise of Maddison's. He burned Espershields to the ground, and it is said that when he did this he was in a quandary whether to burn it or Cronkley first. He also burnt a house in Benfieldside in March, 1678 belonging to one John Rawe, and about the same time destroyed by the same means the stable at Nun's House, near Iveston.

In 1661 he was prosecuted by his son-in-law, John Elrington, of Acton for arson and larceny, and was sentenced to be burnt in the hand for the first crime. This only increased the feud between Maddison and son-in-law, and at last Elrington was obliged to petition the Justices of Assizes at Newcastle for protection.

There was indeed no pause in Maddison's career of wickedness, and after innumerable escapades, his life was forfeited on the gallows for murder.

> "'Twould seem that Typhon, Egypt's darkest god,
> Whose baleful eye appalled the pagan Nile,
> Had, housed in this wild heart, the Derwent trod,
> To torture whom he could not render vile!
> But she whose frown ne'er softened to a smile,
>
> The avengeress whom no scheming guilt can shun,
> Great Nemesis was on his track the while,
> Who, when his ignominious course was run,
> Brought to the holy dust the bad Mad Maddison !"
>
> Barrass. - *"The Derwent Valley."*

On the 16th September, 1694, Maddison in a quarrel killed one Atkinson, who was Laird of Cannyside Wood, for which he was afterwards arrested, tried, and found guilty of murder, and hanged at Durham. Where and how the murder was committed, neither history nor tradition has preserved the story. Most likely it was committed under the influence of drink, and it may be that the scene of the catastrophe was the Bridge-end public-house, Shotley Bridge, Maddison's favourite restaurant. After the committal of the deed Maddison, dreading the result of his crime, fled from his residence near Shotley Bridge. As he had declared that he would shoot the first man who ventured to arrest him, it was found impossible to apprehend him in the usual way. A troop of soldiers was therefore sent to protect the civil power. When they arrived in the neighbourhood, Maddison, saddling his famed grey horse, fled westward up the Derwent Valley, past Eddy's Bridge, evidently with the intention of making for the Cumberland wastes and wilds, where he might be safe. On entering Muggleswick Park, however, his favourite and long-tried steed, for the first time, refused to answer either spur or rein, and stood perfectly still. This action was afterwards construed by the country people as an instance of providential interposition, and a proof that the thread of his long ill-spent career was spun, and that the abhorred shears were opened to cut it. Finding that his horse refused to proceed, he dismounted and fled into the adjoining wood, where he hid himself. After a long search the soldiers found him concealed in the hollow trunk of a large old yew tree, from which they dragged him without ceremony and carried him off to Durham to pay the dread penalty of his atrocious crime. At the ensuing assizes, he was tried, found guilty, and sentenced to death, which sentence was duly executed.

Jacob Bee, "the Durham Pepys" as he is called, entered the murder in his diary as follows:-

"*Sept. 16th, 1694. Lord Atkinson, of Cannyside Wood, was killed by Ralph Maddison of Shotley Brigg, which after was hanged for the murder.*"

Bee was probably a witness of Maddison's execution, though he does not record it. He seems to have written the word Lord in mistake for Laird, the north country title of a proprietor of land, no matter how small his estate, or whatever its tenure. Cannyside has been thought by many etymologists and writers to be the same as Conside, now Consett, but there is no proof for such a supposition.

THE EBCHESTER MONEY CHEST.

Near the village of Ebchester, according to a singular traditional belief, there exists a cave in which is concealed a large iron chest full of Roman money, and to which a subterranean passage said to exist under the village is believed to lead. This money chest is supposed to have been left by the Romans when they quitted Britain, in the fifth century, and a large crow is said to be perched on its lid. In the third decade of the nineteenth century an old man who was resident in the village, and who profoundly believed the story, and used frequently to dream about this chest of money and the crow upon the lid, set himself to work, and sunk in different parts of Ebchester a couple of shafts, in which he laboured very hard for several weeks in order to force a passage to where the buried treasure lay. Success, however, did not crown his efforts, and he was obliged finally to abandon the work, more through exhaustion than failing faith in the money being buried somewhere within the, precincts of the Roman station. Joshua Lax, our local poet, in his poem "*Ebchester,*" thus refers to this singular legendary story: -

> "Tradition tells, and I repeat the story,
> That 'neath this village, in some cave, was hid,
> When Rome had boundless wealth and too had glory,
> A chest of money, and upon its lid
> A crow was perched, and some old man to rid
> His brain (whose nightly dreams oppressed him sore)
> Of doubt regarding what the Romans did,
> Worked hard for weeks the treasure to explore,
> But neither gold nor crow to light could e'er restore."

How curiously the fancies of men compound different events and images! In all probability this tradition may have arisen from a belief that the Romans had hid treasures there which their successors, the Danes, whose ensign, by the way, was a raven, or black crow, had secured, but forgotten or left behind:-

> "When Denmark's raven soared on high,
> Triumphant through Northumbrian sky,
> Till hovering near her fatal croak,
> Bade Reged's Britons dread the yoke.
> And the broad shadow of her wing,
> Blackened each cataract and spring."

The discovery in 1727, of a part of the aqueduct that supplied the Roman baths at Ebchester, by Dr. Hunter (the eminent antiquary, who was a native of Medomsley), at the south-west corner of the Roman station, if it was not the origin of the supposed subterranean passage under the village, at least strengthened the popular belief in this singular tradition, for the olden associations of the place, like that of similar spots, readily give wings to the imagination.

THE BURNT ARM:

A TALE OF A BROKEN VOW

"Once again the swift, encroaching night
Steals, lowering, o'er the hermit's home of bowers,
Black mantles spangled mead and shaggy height,
And darklings o'er this dear delight of ours:
Else had the muse sang through the coming hours,
The vow long-broken and the blazing arm."

Barrass – *"The Derwent Valley"*

In the middle of the eighteenth century there lived at Ebchester Hill, a gentleman named Robert Johnson, whose son Cuthbert married without his consent. This action so offended the parent that he made a vow that he would leave nothing whatever to his son, and in the heat of passion he expressed a wish that his right arm might be burned off if he failed to keep that vow.

Circumstances arose, however, that the old man altered his mind and left everything to the son. Shortly after he had made his new will he died, and if we are to believe the superstitious belief and traditions of those days, the wish he had expressed years before was realised. Before the body had been coffined, observing a disagreeable smell, and finding the room full of smoke, the relatives examined the corpse, and found the right arm nearly burned off. The body was slowly smouldering, and the horrified relatives hastily put the remains into the coffin, and nailed it down, from whence immediately afterwards, a noise of burning and crackling was heard to proceed. The coffin was consequently hastily carried to Ebchester churchyard and there buried.

This extraordinary story of a remarkable circumstance of local interest, which has been preserved by oral tradition, is also noticed by the great founder of Methodism - John Wesley, in one of his published works. We know that he believed in ghosts and miracles, for there is abundant evidence in his writings of his being more or less imbued with the belief in the supernatural which prevailed, and was almost universal in the age in which he lived, and in his works he gives credence to very much which would not now-a-days bear investigation.

Wesley adds some minor details to those which are generally given as the tale is orally told, and he states that the body was buried near the steeple in "Abchester" churchyard, which fell down and nearly killed those who attended the funeral. They had observed the steeple to shake, and had luckily got out of the road, just two minutes before part of it fell.

The entries of the burial register at Ebchester for the year of Johnson's death are missing, and thus we have no chance of being able to learn whether anything of more than ordinary occurrence was recorded at the time of his burial.

THE HEDLEY KOW

"In joy-blest homes where calm content immures,
The untold wonder and the huge alarm,
That, whilom,
Hedley Kow bore round from farm to farm."

Barrass – "The Derwent Valley"

The whole world has at one period or another been inhabited, according to superstitious belief, with supernatural beings of one sort or another. Some of them have been good, others bad, and many of them are supposed to have been able to appear at any time and in any place where they pleased, whilst some of these demons were found to inhabit a large area, others frequented only certain localities, and were never found beyond certain limits. Of the many supernatural demons, or sprites, who were believed to have inhabited the North of England, one of the more famous was the Hedley Kow, who is generally believed to have spent most of his time in and about the Derwent Valley. This boggle, to use a local word describing such like beings, was not a terrible creature like some of them, but was mischievous rather than malignant, never doing anybody any serious injury, and merely took a delight in frightening people. Like the Scottish Barquest he usually ended his frolic, and his pranks with a hoarse laugh at the astonishment or fear of those to whom he appeared or on whom he played some sorry trick.

Many are the stories of this mischievous goblin and visionary creature who is believed to have existed about the beginning of the eighteenth century, and who turned up when least expected, and in the most unlikely forms and places, and a volume of strange adventures of the village demon might be collected. Of the many forms and shapes which he used to appear before the people one was that of a bundle of hay or straw, lying in the middle of the road, or in one's path.

71

One day as an old woman was gathering sticks by the hedge side, the Kow appeared in front of her as a bundle of straw on the road. Thinking she had made a lucky find the woman picked the bundle up, and carried it off towards her house. The further she went, however, the heavier her bundle got, until at last she was obliged to lay it down. No sooner had she done this than it began to move, to the great astonishment of the woman, who immediately saw and declared that it was bewitched. Then it stood upright, and began to move slowly away along the road in front of her, swinging first to one side and then to another. Every now and then it would set up a laugh, or give a shout, and finally vanished from sight with a sound like a rushing wind, and a loud farewell ha, ha, ha!

Another favourite prank of the Hedley Kow was to assume the form of some one's favourite cow, and, as he lived in the time when it was the common practise of the milkmaids to have to go into the fields to milk the cows, he often lead them a long chase around the field, before he would allow himself to be caught. When he did stop he would quietly let them come near, put on the tie, and sit down to milk. Then, when they were least expecting, he would begin kicking and "rowting" and perform all kinds of riotous gambols, ending with upsetting the milk-pail, slipping clear of the tie, and galloping away, tail on end, bellowing loudly all the while, and finally disappear, much to the alarm and surprise of the witnesses, and to the utter astonishment of the girl who at last found that she had been a victim of the extremely annoying and mischievous sport of the Kow. As this trick was so common it is the one from whence, by general opinion, he seems to have got his name, - Kow being only another form of cow.

Demon though he was the Hedley Kow was not quite destitute of some sympathetic feeling, and rarely if ever visited the house of mourning. The occasion of a birth, however, was marked for special pranks, and he was rarely absent either to the eye or to the ear. Indeed his appearance at those times became so common as scarcely to cause any alarm. The man who rode for the midwife on such occasions, was, however, teased by him. Sometimes he would take up his position in some lonely place on the messenger's road, and as he came by, cause his horse to take the "reist," or stand stock still in front of him, past whom neither whip nor spur would force the animal, though the rider saw nothing. At others be would allow the messenger to proceed to the house where the "howdie," or midwife, lived, get her safely mounted behind him on a well girt pillion, and return homewards so far with her unmolested. But as they were crossing some rough or lonely part of the road, he would appear and play some prank which caused the horse to kick and plunge in such a manner as to dismount his double load of messenger and midwife. If the Derwent, or some small burn or stream, was in the way, he would play the prank as they were crossing, and cause the riders to be kicked off into the water. Sometimes when the farmer's wife, impatient for the arrival of the midwife, was groaning in great pain, the Kow would approach close to the door or window of the house, and begin to mock her. The farmer, as often happened, would rush out with a thick stick to drive the demon away, but the weapon would be 'clicked' out of his hand before he was aware, by an invisible form, and lustily applied to his own shoulders. At other times after chasing the boggle round the farm yard, he would tumble over one of his own calves, or some other obstruction, laid in the way by the Kow, or perhaps into the 'midden,' and before he could regain his feet or get out of the 'sump,' the demon had disappeared.

The many mischievous pranks of the Hedley Kow caused terror to the whole countryside, and many innocent people, themselves as much afraid as the rest, were often the cause of alarm to others, especially when out late at night, and many cases of mistaken identity with the mischievous spirit occurred. One of the most amusing is the following:-

Late one night a farmer belonging to the north side of the Derwent was riding homeward from Newcastle, and as he approached a lonely part of the road where the Kow was known to play many of his tricks, he observed a person on horseback at a short distance in front of him. Wishing to have company in a part of the road where he did not like to be alone at night, he quickened the pace of his horse. The person whom he wished to overtake hearing the tramp of a horse rapidly advancing behind him, and fearing he was followed by some one with an evil intention, put spurs to his steed, and set off at a gallop; an example which was immediately followed by the horseman behind. At this rate they continued whipping and spurring, as if they rode for life and death, for nearly two miles; the man who was behind calling out with all his might, "Stop! stop!" The person who fled, finding that his pursuer was gaining upon him, and hearing a continued cry, the words of which he could not make out, began to think that he was pursued by some thing unearthly, as no one who had a design to rob him would be likely to make such a noise. Determined no longer to fly from his pursuer, he pulled up his horse, and thus adjured the supposed evil spirit:- "In the name of the Father, and of the Son, and of the Holy Ghost, what art thou?" Instead of an evil spirit, a terrified neighbour at once answered, and repeated the question:- "Aa's Jemmy Broon o' the High Field, whe's thoo ?"

One night about the beginning of the eighteenth century, two young men belonging to Newlands, near Ebchester, went out to meet their sweethearts, and when they arrived at the appointed place they saw, as they supposed, the two girls walking at a short distance before them. They immediately made towards them, but the girls continued to walk onward for two or three miles. The young men followed on without being able to overtake them. Then they made an endeavour to get up to them, and quickened their pace, but, still the girls kept before them. At last, having tried in vain for several miles to overtake the objects of their walk, they found themselves up to the knees in a boggy swamp, where the girls suddenly disappeared with a fiendish and most unfeminine laugh. The young men then found that they had been beguiled by the Hedley Kow who had succeeded in playing off one of his pranks. They then endeavoured to get out of the bog, and as soon as they got clear they ran homewards, as fast as their legs could carry them, with the Kow at their heels, hooting, and laughing, and shrieking, and frightening them as much as he possibly could. In crossing the Derwent between Ebchester and Blackhall Mill, the one who took the lead fell down into the water, and his companion who was close behind tumbled over him. In their great fright each mistook the other for the Kow, and they both screamed loud and lustily with terror as they rolled over each other in the stream . At last, however, they managed to get out, and after a good fright reached home separately, where they told a 'terrible' tale of having been chased and hardly pressed by the Hedley Kow, and of being nearly drowned by him in the Derwent.

Farmers were special victims of the Kow, and he never ceased to annoy them, by alluring them into the most ridiculous situations, by constantly mimicking either them or their servants, by assuming the form of some of their cattle, and pretending to be lame or ill, get them to go to a lot of useless expense and trouble; by playing all kinds of mischievous pranks with their implements or harness, mixing them up promiscuously, etc.

Early one morning a farmer of the name of Forster, who lived at Hedley by the Derwent, wishing to drive to Newcastle so as to be there by the time the shops were opened, went out into the field and caught, as he supposed in the dim twilight, his own grey horse. After putting the harness on and yoking him to the cart, Forster got into the vehicle, and was about to drive away, when to his great astonishment and alarm, the horse, whose form had been assumed by the Kow, for the purpose of having a laugh at the expense of the farmer, disappeared from the shafts and harness, 'like a knotless thread,' and set up a great "nicker" as he flung up his heels, and cleared away 'like mad' out of the farmyard, revealing to the trembling farmer the mischievous Hedley Kow.

The mischievous demon was also a perfect plague to servant girls at farm houses, and played all kinds of pranks upon them. Sometimes he would call them out of their beds by imitating the voices of their sweethearts at the windows. At other times during their absence he would overturn the kail pot, open the milk house door and set the cat to the cream and milk, entangle their knitting by letting down the "loops," or ravelling the yarn, put their spinning wheel out of order, and causing disorder in the farm houses.

The Hedley Kow in the performance of his mischievous pranks assumed all kinds of forms and shapes - like many other European goblins - whether human or animal, as best suited his intentions. As man or woman, horse, cow, ass, sheep, pig, dog, cat, hare, rabbit, and other living forms he could appear, and allure his victim on to be the subject of an annoying but harmless joke or prank.

In 1749 one Thomas Stevenson, of Framwellgate, Durham, made and signed a declaration before Mr. Justice Burdess, that on the 17th of August, 1729, between eight and nine o'clock at night, as he was returning form Hedley, in Northumberland, to Durham, he saw an apparition that looked sometimes in the shape of a foal, and sometimes of a man, which took the bridle from off his horse, and beat him till he was sore, and took his horse from him and misled him on foot three miles to Coalbourne; and a guide he had with him was beat in the same manner; and that the apparition vanished not until daybreak; and then, being on foot, he felt the stripes of the bridle on his body, and found it bound round his waist; and his horse he found where he first saw the apparition by the Green Bank top; and he said that it was commonly reported by the neighbourhhood that a spirit called the "Hedley Kow" did haunt the spot.

THE LOWD FARM MONEY POT

At the commencement of the nineteenth century the farmer who lived at the Lowd or Laud farm, near Catchgate, was named John Taylor. John and his wife Ann, or as they were best known, Jackie and Nannie, were a hard working couple, toiling early and late to earn the necessities of life for themselves and their large family, and to make both ends meets. The farm being a large one a couple of men servants were kept to assist in the work.

One day one spring, at the period above mentioned, having sent the servant men to Running Waters near Coxhoe for lime, Jackie went to take up "furs," i.e., furrows in a tillage field. The land being wet, necessitated his having to place one of the draught horses before the other, tandem fashion, and to have some one to lead the fore, or first, horse. His wife Nannie consented to do the latter task, and as they were going up one furrow the plough caught hold of something in the bottom, which stopped the progress somewhat suddenly.

In the exertion of the horses to pull the plough through the obstacle, it tore off the cover of some kind of vessel, and exposed its contents, at which Jackie called out, "Ho'd, Nannie, ho'd, she's a' here," i.e., Hold, Nannie, hold, she's all here. The trove proved to be a hidden treasure in the shape of an old kail-pot filled with guineas. The discovery was kept a secret in the neighbourhood, and Jackie having some trusty friends in London, sent the old guineas to him, and he getting them changed into the current coin of the realm, returned the same to the finder. After this Jackie Taylor and Nannie are said to have "nivver leuked ahint them," i.e., to have always done well.

Shortly after the discovery they left the Lowd Farm and went to reside at Morrowfield, a farm near Holmside, and from thence to Holmside, where they died, Jackie in 1828, and Nannie in 1861, and are buried at Lanchester.

With a portion of the money obtained from the treasure trove Jackie made himself a landed proprietor, purchasing a couple of farms in the neighbourhood of Cornsay, one North Low Row and the other Hill Top, besides some other property, which passed to his offspring, and have since been sold to different parties.

THE HIDDEN TREASURE OF FRIARSIDE

In a pasture field not far from the farm house of Friarside, about a mile south-west of Rowland's Gill, and visible from the Consett branch of the North-Eastern Railway between Lintz Green and Rowland's Gill Stations, stands the roofless, ruined chapel of Friarside of ancient date and interesting architecture.

Previous to the formation of the Newcastle and Shotley Bridge turnpike in 1836, and the opening of the Derwent Valley Railway in 1867, this chapel stood in a most secluded and romantic spot, and it became the seat of wonderful mystery. Many are the legends and traditions of untold wealth said to be buried in its vicinity, and more than one attempt has been made to find the same.

In the middle of the nineteenth century a man of the name of John Heppell, belonging to Winlaton Mill, a person of a most inquisitive disposition, and a curious enquiring and somewhat poetical temperament, frequently dreamt about the old chapel, and of an immense treasure buried within its walls. When he first dreamt this dream, he thought nothing more about it, but after it had been repeated more than once, he came to the conclusion that it must be true, and he determined to ascertain the reality.

Unfortunately he could not keep his secret to himself. He confided his dream to a trusty friend, who doubtless was to have a share of the result, and together they proceeded to the chapel one dark night, and commenced to dig a large hole in the western portion of this ruin. Their reason for performing this work at night was the double one of not being disturbed by inquisitive and irreverent spectators, who would probably have smiled at their faith in the supernatural revelation, but who would have expected, and perhaps demanded, a share of the proceeds.

They laboured all night, without finding anything, and at dawn left the place with the intention of returning to their work when night again came round. Unhappily, as they were leaving the vicinity of the chapel, with their tools, they met a person who knew them, and he made the result of their night's work known.

A story immediately spread abroad of a large grave having been dug inside Friarside Chapel for the reception of the body of some intended victim, and of how the would-be culprits had been disturbed before they had completed their work, and the day after the discovery the place was visited by numbers of people all anxious to see the grave and the work of some supposed murderer. The story of the grave found its way into the pages not only of the local press, but even into some of the London journals.

The unfortunate meeting with the third individual put a stop to any further search on Heppell's part for the supposed treasure, and the hole was eventually levelled up.

THE BURNOPFIELD MURDER

On the 1st of November, 1855, Mr. Robert Stirling, a young surgeon, twenty-six years of age, assistant to Dr. William Watson, of Burnopfield, was brutally murdered at mid-day, in a lonely road called Smailes Lane, about a mile north of the village of Burnopfield, and in the parish of Winlaton.

He had only been a short while in Dr. Watson's service, having arrived at Burnopfield from Scotland on the 20th of the preceding month. At nine o'clock on the morning of his death he set out to visit various patients, and amongst the rest were some in the village of Spen, and before leaving Burnopfield borrowed from another assistant in Dr. Watson's employ, a silver watch, to which he attached his own guard. In the course of the morning he visited several patients at the Spen, and as he was returning he was shot by some persons lurking near Smailes Lane, the road he travelled, his throat cut, and his head and face frightfully injured, apparently by the butt end of a gun. His watch, money, and lancets were taken from his pockets, and his body dragged through a fence on the south side of the road, and deposited among the bushes in a plantation which covered a steep incline to the river Derwent.

The non-return of Mr. Stirling caused the greatest anxiety to Dr. Watson, as that gentleman had once heard him express a wish to join a Turkish contingent in the Crimea, and he thought it extraordinary behaviour if he had departed for that purpose, without giving any previous warning or notice. He wrote, however, to his father in Scotland, and informed him of his son's absence. A search was made, and on the 6th of November, five days after the murder, the mutilated body of the young surgeon was discovered in the wood as mentioned by Mr. Thomas Holmes, one of a search party of three, including the murdered man's father.

A considerable sensation was excited throughout the counties of Durham and Northumberland, and a thrill of horror was sent throughout the whole country by the atrocious deed, and large rewards were offered for the discovery of the perpetrators. At last, two men, John Cain, better known as "Whiskey Jack," described as a labourer, but known as the proprietor of an illicit whiskey still in the vicinity of Smailes Lane, and Richard Raine, a blacksmith, of Winlaton, were arrested on suspicion, charged with the murder, and brought up at the Spring Assizes at Durham, but the evidence not being complete they were remanded to the Midsummer Assizes. There they were arraigned on the 25th of July, 1856, before Mr. Justice Willis, and pleaded not guilty of the murder.

The trial extended over two days, and created the greatest interest. The prosecution was conducted by Mr. Overend, and the defence by Mr. (afterwards Hon.) J. R. Davison. To this particular trial the latter gentleman, afterwards Q.C., M.P., and Judge Advocate-General, was indebted for his subsequent remarkable success both as a nisi prius and criminal lawyer.

The trial rested upon purely circumstantial evidence, and though the weight of testimony pointed but one way, it failed to bring the crime home to the two prisoners.

The principal witness at the trial was a Cumberland drover named Ralph Stobart, who from the evidence given, was the only person, other than the culprits, who met Mr. Stirling near the scene of his murder. Stobart proved that he had been visiting his sister for a few days, and that on the 1st of November, the date of the murder, he was returning home. His sister set him as far as Derwent Bridge at Rowland's Gill. On reaching an angle of the road he saw a couple of men about two yards from the angle, and not liking their appearance, he passed quickly by, noticing, however, that one of them had either a stick or a gun by his side. Further along the lane be met a young man, afterwards known to be Dr. Stirling, with whom he passed the compliments of the day, and noticing that when he answered, he spoke with a strong Scotch accent. He then went on to the Shotley Bridge road and after getting a short distance along it he heard a shot go off. Stobart upon being pressed by the prisoner's counsel, would not swear positively that the prisoners in the dock were the men he met near the angle of the lane.

Some time after the murder the prisoner Raine was proved to have visited Durham, and to have offered a silver watch to a Mrs Raine, pawnbroker, who would not, however, advance anything on it. Had she done so, an important, link would have been added to the chain of testimony. It was also well known that at and before the time when Raine went to Durham, Cain was seen in that city by several persons who knew him, but this was not deposed to in the evidence. What became of the watch will never be known. After the trial it was more than once stated that it was thrown over one of the bridges in Durham into the river Wear.

The missing link in the chain of evidence in this trial seems to have led the jury, after a deliberation of two-and-a-half hours, to return a verdict of "Not guilty" against the two prisoners, who, each, by the smallest possible chance, escaped the scaffold. At the trial it was never attempted to set up any other motive than that of robbery, as proved by the watch having been taken from the murdered man; but it was well known in the district, both before and after the murder, that both Cain and Raine were lounging about Smailes Lane for an unlawful purpose. The 1st of November - the day of the murder - was also the rent day of the tenants of the Gibside Estate, then belonging to William Hutt, Esq., M.P. and one of the tenants on his way to Gibside had to pass the plantation in which Mr. Stirling's body was afterwards found. It was generally supposed that the murderers were lying in wait for this man, to whom Whiskey Jack owed a grudge, as he had once laid information against him to the Revenue Officer, who escaped by the timely warning of a dream. It appears that the previous night he had a dream, which he told to his wife the next morning, the purport of which was that something would happen to him on his journey to pay his rent. It had been his custom to start from home at a particular hour on the rent day, but that morning he left earlier and probably escaped the fate of the doctor.

Another curious and remarkable incident transpired during the progress of the trial, which was much talked about and commented on at the time. Dr. Stirling's mother had a dream after the murder, in which she saw the murderer of her son. On it being told to some of her friends, it was decided to apply to the Governor of the gaol at Durham, then Mr. W. Green, for admission to the prison in order to test her with regard to the murderer she had seen. This was granted and on a fixed day, a number of prisoners all clad in the same garb, were brought into one of the prison yards, when Mrs. Stirling pointed to Cain, who was amongst them, as the man she had seen in her dream.

Whether Cain and Raine did certainly commit this diabolical outrage must for ever remain a mystery, and the Burnopfield murder, as it is generally called, one of the most cold blooded, dastardly, and foulest murders recorded in our criminal annals must remain as an unpunished crime.

Dr. Stirling's remains were interred in Tanfield Churchyard, where on the south side of the chancel, and on the east of the south entrance, there is a headstone inscribed:-

SACRED
TO
THE MEMORY OF
ROBERT STIRLING,
SURGEON, BURNOPFIELD,
WHO WAS BARBAROUSLY MURDERED
IN THE SMAILE'S LANE
NEAR ROWLANDS GILL GATE
BETWEEN ONE AND TWO O'CLOCK P.M.
ON THE FIRST DAY OF NOVEMBER
A.D. 1855 AGED 25 YEARS.
HE WAS A NATIVE OF KIRKINTILLOCK
DUMBARTONSHIRE
BELOVED FOR HIS VIRTUES,
ADMIRED FOR HIS TALENTS,
AND RESPECTED FOR
HIS UNTIRING INDUSTRY
HIS UNTIMELY END WAS DEEPLY
LAMENTED BY ALL WHO KNEW HIM.
THIS STONE IS ERECTED BY HIS
BEREAVED PARENTS
WHO SORROW INDEED YET NOT AS
THOSE WHO HAVE NO HOPE.

The following somewhat ungrammatical and unrythmetical "Line on the late Mr. Robert Stirling, M.D., who was murdered near Burnopfield, Nov. 1st., 1855," were widely circulated just after the occurrence, in leaflet form, and were often sung by chapmen in the streets of Durham, Newcastle, and other towns on market days:-

"Sad was thy fate, O hapless youth,
Cut down in beauty's bloom;
Who would have thought so fair a flower
Would be shorn down at noon.

He left his home and parents dear
His prospects bright and high
But fate had otherwise decreed,
For doomed he was to die.

'Twas not by foeman's lance he fell
In battle fierce and hot;
But by some prowling ruffians strong
The youth was basely shot.

All day they prowled about the wood
While the sun shone bright and high;
On murder they were wholly bent;
They doomed some one to die.

Crouched beneath a neighbouring hedge
The cringing villains lay;
Like tigers lurking in their lair,
In hopes of some to slay.

By luckless chance young Stirling passed,
His form erect and high;
Poor youth his sun was nearly set,
That hour he had to die.

The deadly gun uplifted was
One moment and no more,
The noble youth, shot in the groin,
Fell down to rise no more.

Then sprang from whence they bad been hid,
Like vultures on their prey;
They finished him straight-way.

Then from the road the villains dragged
Him to a neighbouring wood;
His manly face was battered sore,
And covered o'er with blood.

O God! where was Thy thunderbolts,
Lord, doth Thy vengeance sleep;
When virtue's trampled in the dust,
And friends are left to weep.

O, who can paint a father's grief,
When he found his only joy,
A blackened and disfigured corpse,
And wildly cried - 'My boy.

'Twas not for this you left your home
Your fortune for to try;
For in a lonely stranger's grave
Your body now must lie.'

Now, two men are taken for the crime,
And what more can we say;
Than they who did no mercy show,
Can scarce for mercy pray."

STONEY BOWES

THE FORTUNE HUNTER

One of the most notorious adventurers and fortune hunters was an Irishman named Andrew Robinson Stoney, best known by the additional surname of Bowes, which he afterwards assumed. He was born in Ireland in 1745, and was a younger son of a respectable family. Entering the army, he became an Ensign of the 4th Regiment of Foot, and in 1768 accompanied his regiment to Newcastle-on-Tyne. Whilst there he became acquainted with a Miss Newton, who lived in Westgate Street, the only daughter of a coal merchant named William Newton, who also had a residence at Burnopfield, to whom he proposed marriage. Tradition states that Mr. Stoney persuaded Miss Newton to elope from her father's residence at Burnopfield. This did not take place, however, for they were married at St. Andrew's Church, Newcastle, by the Rev. Nathaniel Ellison, on the 5th of November, 1768. In the "Newcastle Courant" of the period we read:- On November 5th was married at St. Andrew's Church by the Rev. Mr. Nathaniel Ellison, Andrew Robinson Stoney, Esq., an ensign in the 4th Regiment (Brudenell's) to Miss Newton, of Westgate Street, an heiress with a fortune of £20,000.

In 1770 Ensign Stoney was promoted to a lieutenancy in his regiment succeeding, according to the Newcastle Chronicle of January 27th, Mr. Forrest, who had been promoted to a captaincy, and after it was disbanded he retired on half-pay, to the seat of his wife's paternal ancestors, where his wife died, after suffering much cruel treatment at the hands of her husband, soon afterwards, leaving no issue. Not so very long after his wife's death, Mr. Stoney began to have designs on the hand of Mary Eleanor, Countess of Strathmore, a most accomplished young widow, whose husband had died at Lisbon, on the 25th March, 1776, leaving her with five young children, and in possession of immense property and wealth. He commenced his attack on her heart and hand with the most consummate art. At that time the Morning Post was the fashionable society paper, and in its pages there appeared from time to time several articles intimating that the handsome young widow was not leading her life so innocently and circumspectly as to meet with the approval of the more rigorous moralists of the day. These articles led to others being sent defending the Countess and championing her cause. The correspondence led to a duel being fought between the editor of the paper - the Rev. Henry Bate (afterwards Sir Henry Bate-Dudley) - and Lieutenant Stoney, as the champion of the Countess, on the 13th of January, 1777. Four days later the gallantry of the Lieutenant was rewarded by the Countess marrying him, and in consequence of this marriage he assumed by his Majesty King George III's pleasure, the additional surname of Bowes, and became Andrew Robinson Stoney Bowes.

The marriage may seem very much as things should be, but when it is known that the whole thing was a sham, that Stoney himself had sent the articles to the newspaper reflecting on the character of the Countess, and had also written those defending her, that the duel was of a rather equivocal character, and that an understanding existed all the time between the duellists, it puts quite a different light on the affair, and shows what a consummate villain Stoney must have been. He secured his end, and became the husband of the wealthy Countess. Clever as Stoney Bowes had been, however, he found that his cleverest schemes had been outwitted. Soon after his marriage he found that the Countess, just a week before the ceremony took place, had got a deed drawn up and signed whereby she vested in trustees all her property for her sole benefit, but with power to alter and amend the same. He also found that she was considerably in debt. Vexed at what he conceived to be the double dealing on the part of his wife he adopted means far from gentle, to get rid of the obnoxious deed. Whether by fair means or foul, he induced the Countess on the 1st of May, 1777 - less than four months after marriage - to execute another deed, revoking the former, and vesting the whole of her landed property in Mr. Stoney Bowes, who then joined her in a deed granting for the benefit of her creditors, annuities to the yearly sum of £3,000 for the Countess's life, by which measure a sum of £24,000 was raised. In order to secure the payment of these annuities, certain parts of the estates were vested in trustees, who were to receive the rents, pay the annuities, and hand over the residue, if any, to Bowes and the Countess. After their marriage they came to the North of England and took up their residence at Gibside, the paternal seat of the Countess of Strathmore, where they lived in style.

In the same year as he was married he offered himself as a representative of Newcastle-on-Tyne, in succession to Sir Walter Blackett, deceased, but was unsuccessful. His accomplished wife did all she could by an active canvass to promote his return. In 1780 he served the office of High Sheriff of Northumberland and entertained the judges with lavish hospitality. In September of the same year he was chosen a representative in Parliament for Newcastle-on-Tyne.

At Gibside Stoney Bowes commenced his ill-usage of his wife in a similar manner to that in which he treated his first wife, and which was carried on for several years, until the unfortunate Countess had to seek shelter in the Divorce Court. In 1782, owing to his expensive living, his horse racing, his insurances, the expenses of his shievalty, his election contests, his purchase of Benwell Tower, and other matters, Stoney Bowes was obliged to leave Gibside, which during his five years residence had been a scene of continual feasting, extravagance and retreat, but not before he had cut down much of the valuable timber on the fine estate, to raise money, which, however no one would buy from him, and went to Paul's Warden in Northamptonshire, where the Countess was delivered of a son and heir on the 8th of March. This son, the only child the Countess bore him eventually entered the navy, where he died in his father's lifetime. The treatment he showed towards the Countess in the birth of the child was that of a veritable Bluebeard.

About this time Stoney Bowes also commenced a series of stratagems to obtain possession of the Countess's two daughters, by the Earl of Strathmore, who were wards in chancery, in order to obtain more influence over their mother. He did actually get hold of one of the daughters - Lady Anna Maria, who afterwards married Colonel James Jessop - and fled with her to Paris, but in November, 1784, the Court of Chancery brought her back to England, and placed her out of her stepfather's reach.

In the following year 1785, the Countess fled from Bowes's custody, where she had been little better than a prisoner, and began to institute proceedings for a divorce at the Ecclesiastical Court at Durham, on the plea of cruelty. In the evidence which was deduced it was found that Bowes was "a villain to the backbone." It appeared that from a short time after her marriage the Countess had been deprived of her liberty in every respect. The use of her carriage was denied her unless with Bowes's previous permission. Her own old servants were dismissed, and the new ones which took their places were ordered not to attend the ringing of her bell. She dared not send a letter, nor read one sent to her till he had first perused it. She was cursed and sworn at and otherwise treated with foul language. She was assaulted and chastised with blows from his hands and feet, and frequently had black eyes. She was driven from her own table, or forced to sit at it along with Bowes's mistresses and other loose characters, whom he kept about him. At the same Court the manner in which he had obtained the hand of the Countess in marriage came to light.

While the suit for the divorce was pending, Bowes, by a deep laid conspiracy obtained possession of the person of the Countess, in London, and carried her off a prisoner to Streatlam Castle, where he endeavoured to persuade her to become reconciled to him. Hearing that he was pursued he hastily made off from Streatlam Castle, carrying the Countess with him, but was overtaken at Darlington, where the Countess was delivered out of his clutches, and escorted safely back to the Metropolis. Articles of peace were immediately exhibited against him and the Court of King's Bench made an order in the case to the effect that he should enter into security to keep the peace for fourteen years, under penalty of £20,000 - himself in £10,000 and two sureties of £5,000 each.

A charge for a conspiracy against the Countess of Strathmore to assault and imprison her was laid against Bowes and others, and they were tried in the Court of King's Bench on the 10th May, 1787, before Mr. Justice Buller. One of the Counsel for Bowes and his companions was Mr. Erskine, afterwards Lord Chancellor Erskine. Various instances of ill usage were given, and Bowes was subsequently adjudged to pay a fine of £300 to his Majesty, to be confined in the King's Bench prison for three years, and at the expiration of that term to find security for fourteen years, himself in £10,000 and two sureties of £5,000 each. The other conspirators received lighter sentences.

About the same time a suit was instituted in the High Court of Chancery by the Countess against Bowes, charging him with various acts of cruelty and outrage, setting forth that an instrument of revocation was extorted from her by violence and compulsion, and praying the Court to restrain Bowes from recovering the rents of the estates. The case was tried on the 19th May, 1788, in the Court of Common Pleas, before the Right Hon. Lord Loughborough (afterwards Earl of Rosslyn), on an issue directed out of the Court of Chancery. This trial resulted in Bowes being deprived of all the property, and the whole of the rents which he had received were ordered to be given up, and on the 3rd March, 1789, Lady Strathmore was restored to her property, and finally severed from the unfortunate connection she had formed.

As Bowes had spent the whole of the rents he had received, they were entered against him as a debt, and he was cast into prison. There be spent the most of his time in a constant state of intoxication. Whilst there the Countess wrote a very bitter, but just epitaph for him, which she sent to him in his confinement, and which was as follows:

> *Here Rests*
> *Who never rested before,*
> *The most ambitious of men; for he sought not*
> *Virtue, Wisdom, nor Science,*
> *Yet rose by deep hypocrisy, by the*
> *Folly of some and the vice of others,*
> *To honours which nature had forbade, and*
> *Riches he wanted taste to enjoy.*
>
> *He saw no faults in himself, nor any worth in others,*
> *He was the very enemy of mankind;*
> *Deceitful to his friends, ungrateful to his benefactors,*
> *Cringing to his superiors and tyrannical to his dependents.*
> *If interest obliged him to assist any fellow creature*
> *He regretted the effect,*
> *And thought every day lost in which he made none wretched.*

His life was a continual series of injuries to society;
and disobedience to his Maker;
And he only lamented in despair
That he could offend them no longer.
He rose by mean arts to unmerited honours,
Which expire before himself.

Passenger! examine thy heart,
If in aught thou resemblest him;
And if thou dost -
Read, tremble, and reform!
So shall he, who living, was the pest of society,
When dead, be, against his will, once useful to mankind.

In 1790 a sentence of excommunication decreed by the High Court of Delegates - then the supreme Court of Appeal in ecclesiastical causes - against Andrew Robinson Stoney Bowes, for contumacy and for not having paid the expenses of the said court, amounting to £553 8s 6d, in a cause instituted by Mary Eleanor Bowes, his wife, was read in the parish church of of St. Nicholas, Newcastle-on-Tyne.

About the year 1797 Bowes commenced a suit in the Court of Chancery, under the expectation that he was certain of success, but a delay occurred and he was disappointed.

On the 20th of April, 1800, the Countess of Strathmore died, and was buried in Westminster Abbey, dressed in a superb bridal dress, and when this occurred Bowes moved out of the King's Bench prison, the demand of heavy bail having been withdrawn, through application to that Court. His affairs, through his long imprisonment, had become too much involved ever to be settled, so he remained a prisoner for debt. He was, however, granted the privilege of residing anywhere within the rules, chiefly on account, it is said, of his commendable conduct in aiding the prison authorities in quelling the disturbance which occurred during a riot and conspiracy in May, 1791.

He afterwards removed to house in the London Road, St. George's Fields, to await the issue of the law suits, which dragged slowly along, but in 1807 a verdict having been found against him, he was again obliged to remove within the rules of the King's Bench prison, where he died on the 16th of January 1810, and his remains were buried seven days later, in the vault of St. George's Church in the Borough. Stoney Bowes was one of the most notorious characters of his day, and was a compound of baseness and hypocrisy, and his acts, even when in prison, were of the blackest dye. He left a number of descendants by a young lady whom he had seduced in prison, and whom he also treated with cruelty.

If the rooms of Gibside Hall could speak they would tell many tales of Stoney Bowes's cruelty towards the Countess of Strathmore during their residence there from 1777 to 1782, and tradition has not allowed many of these acts to be forgotten, for though a century has passed since the accomplished Countess was laid to rest in Poets Corner, Westminster Abbey, strange stories still linger in the neighbourhood of the violent treatment she received from his hands, of how he locked her up in a closet, and fed her with an egg and a biscuit a day; of how once when in a passion he threw her out of the window of an upper storey; of how she couldn't go into the garden or grounds without his leave; of how she had to take a second place when his mistresses were present, and become their menial; of black eyes, and bruised limbs, of ill-treatment and starvation, and of almost all the cruelties that a villain was capable of.

THE GIANTS OF HOLLINSIDE

Situated on the edge of a steep brow in the midst of picturesque scenery on the south side of the River Derwent, about a quarter of a mile from the river, and within a mile to the east of Gibside, stands the old ruined manor house of Hollinside. It is an interesting place and possesses an interesting history. Standing on the verge of an almost precipitous slope overlooking the Derwent Valley, one hundred and fifty feet above the bed of the river, it occupies an almost impregnable position, its natural security being still further increased by a stretch of marshy ground below, which even after modern drainage affords an unsecure foothold.

Much of the ancient pile has yielded slowly to the destroying hand of time, but from what remains, some knowledge can be obtained of its ancient strength and importance in the days gone by. The walls are of immense thickness, from three feet upwards, and the building measures externally about fifty-two feet in length, and about forty-six in width, and has originally been three storeys in height. It is built in the form of two wings, standing north-east and south-west, separated on the south side by a space about ten feet in width, covered over by an arch, which reaches twenty-two feet from the ground, and on the top of which probably stood a tower or turret. From the water-lines preserved on this we can see that both the main building and the wings were covered by one enormous roof of considerable pitch. As there is no other entrance to the building from any other side this arch or recess has evidently served as an entrance porch, and it is still strong, even in its decay.

If the ruined walls are interesting, the rooms in the building are more so. From its appearance at the present time there appears to have been about ten rooms in the house, of which five have been on the ground floor and the rest above. Appearances also point to the rooms in the basement having been used as store houses for the reception of goods, and, perhaps, of cattle, only, and the upper rooms as dwelling rooms.

When the building was erected and when it ceased to be a place of residence is not definitely known. Judging from its architecture it probably dates from the Thirteenth Century, and was evidently erected at a time when things were quite different from what they are now; when each one had to depend on his own strength and fortress for protection, and when Tynedale reivers, border moss-troopers, and other marauders were often in the field

It originally belonged to a family named Hollinside, who either gave their name to, or took their name from it, from whom it passed to the Bointons, and from them to the Burtons, and thence to the Redheughs, and from them to the Massams, from whom it passed to the Hardings, who after holding it for about three centuries conveyed it to the Bowes, to whose representatives it still belongs.

Like a great many other ruined remains the old Manor house has its traditional history. Local history says that the building, which is very often called "The Giants Castle," was built and inhabited by a family of giants, who, like the rest of their kind were the terror of the neighbourhood.

Tradition says it was built by a giant who wrought the stones in a quarry in Gibside Wood, about three-quarters of a mile from the house, which is still known as the "Giants Quarry", and carried them on his back to the place, and tradition also says that this giant made raids into the surrounding district for cattle and sheep, which he kept in the lowest rooms of his residence, and killed as he required them, and that his favourite place of resort was the roof of the tower, from whence he could view the country far up and down the Derwent Valley, and see where spoils in the form of stock were to be found. The same fickle historian also has it that this giant had an underground passage from his house to the Derwent, in which he stored his treasures, the value of which has never diminished by the telling. This last superstitious belief has under investigations proved to be fallacious.

The tradition of the giant however, has some support in the fact that the majority of the members of the Harding family were men "both tall and strong, and great beside," some of them even attaining to a height of nearer seven feet than six. During the middle of the nineteenth century, whilst some repairs were being made to the vault of the Harding family in Whickham churchyard, a thigh bone of extraordinary size was found, which had belonged to a man whose stature could not have been less than seven feet, and this "find" had at the time a great deal to do with supporting the traditional story of the Giant of Hollinside Castle.

In the Public Domain
Artist unknown

Fig. 4   Hollinside Manor (Castle)

SELBY'S GRAVE

About half a mile north of Winlaton, at the Junction of Barlow turnpike with the road from Snook's Hill farm to Blaydon Burn, is a place called the "Nobbies" or "Nobbys," where there is a large stone quarry. In the corner of the field on the north side of the turnpike at this place is, tradition says, the grave of a suicide, and the site is known as "Selby's Grave."

Who Selby was is unknown, but he is believed to be identical with the "unknown gentleman," recorded by John Sykes in his Local Records, under the date 1660, as having committed suicide near Winlaton.

From him we learn that a gentleman went to reside at Winlaton in the spring of 1660. Who he was or what he was will not now be definitely known. He lived very privately, mixing or making friends with none of the local residents, but he seemed to be very anxious to learn all he could about the abolition of the Commonwealth, and the restoration of monarchy, and daily grew more and more inquisitive after news and every circumstance concerning the restoration of Charles II, which monarch was proclaimed King on May 8th, and entered London on the 29th of the same month. Upon learning of the passing of the Act of Indemnity in the following August, and of the exception of the murderers of King Charles I, he went into a wood adjoining Winlaton and hung himself. This action makes him to be one of the regicides, or one who had assisted in the downfall of Charles I.

According to tradition what is known as "Lands Wood" on the south side of Winlaton was the place where he committed suicide, and the body, being denied Christian burial, was conveyed to the four cross-roads at the Nobbys, and buried at midnight. A stake or stob was then driven through his body, with the then popular double belief of getting rid of the corpse and the ghost. Each passer by, then, in token of abhorrence threw a stone or stones, generally three, on the grave until, in time, a large pile existed. The stake or stob marking the place of burial - but whether the original or one erected at a later date - existed during the first three decades of the nineteenth century, but now all has disappeared. In days gone by a piece of wood from the stake marking a suicide's grave was considered an infallible remedy for toothache, and considerably more than one piece of the stake on Selby's grave made its way into the possession of local residents.

Whether Selby was the proper, or only an assumed name of the man will never be definitely known, for history has left no record of the circumstance, other than a mere note and the parish register of Ryton is also silent with regard to it.

SUBSCRIBERS.

Abercrombie, Joseph;	Leazes, Burnopfield.
Ainsworth, George, Esq., J.P.;	Consett.
Anderson, Miss W.;	Leazes, Burnopfield.
Andrews, William;	Royal Institution, Hull.
Archer, Thomas;	Blackhill.
Armstrong, Richard;	Burnopfield.
Arrowsmith, William J.;	Edward Pease Public Library, Darlington.
Askew, Joseph;	Blackhill.
Batey, R. T.;	Dipton.
Bell, William;	Consett.
Bellam, George;	Consett.
Bewick, Abraham;	Castleside.
Biggs, J.T., journalist;	Annfield Plain.
Blackhill and District Naturalists' Field Society;	
Bowes, John;	Dipton.
Boswell, S.;	Hare Law, Annfield Plain.
Bourn, William;	Whickham.
Brock, A. H.;	Durham.
Bryant, J. W.;	Stockton-on-Tees.
Bulman, Mrs.;	Guardian Office, Consett.
Burdess, John;	Hebburn.
Bustin, A.;	Gibside, Burnopfield.
Butt, Joseph;	Chester-le-Street.
Carr, George;	Crook.
Carr, James;	Blackhill.
Carrick, J.J.;	Consett.
Caygill, James;	Consett.
Chatt, J.;	Benfieldside.

Cheesman, Mrs.;	Tow Law.
Clarance, Lloyd;	Consett.
Collinson, William;	Consett.
Colpitts, Robert;	Blackhill, 2 copies.
Cooper, John;	Dipton.
Craggs, Mrs.;	Tow Law.
Cummings, W.;	Consett.
Cuthbertson, Thomas S.;	Blackhill.
Daglish, W. T.;	Dipton.
Darlington and Teesdale Naturalists' Field Club;	
Davison, John;	Consett.
Davison, J. R.;	Consett.
Davison, B., Jun.;	Marley Hill.
Dipton and District Naturalists' Field Club;	
Dixon, Miss;	Ebchester.
Dixon, Miss;	Dipton.
Dixon, John;	Blackhill.
Dobson, L.;	Shotley Bridge.
Dover, Thomas;	JCrook, 2 copies.
Dowson, Jacob;	Blackhill.
Durham City Field and Research Club;	
Durham Historical Society;	150 copies.
Eales, William;	Consett.
Edgell, George;	Guardian Office, Consett.
Edgell. G.T.;	Guardian Office, Consett.
Egglestone, G.T.;	Consett.
Ellison, James;	Blackhill.
Eltringham, E. E.;	Blackhill, 2 copies.
English, Henry;	Blackhill.
Errington, Joseph;	Blackhill
Evans, Thomas;	Blackhill.
Featherstonhaugh, Rev. Walker;	Edmundbyers, 2 copies.

Foster, William J.;	Consett.
Frost, Robert;	Newcastle, New South Wales.
Fryers, William;	Blaydon.
Gardiner, John, Jun.;	Blackhill.
Gatiss, Thomas;	Annfield Plain.
Gibson, Rev. J. G.;	Ebchester.
Gilmour, Alexander;	Consett.
Gledstone, Frederick Farrar;	Consett.
Gledstone, Herbert Reginald;	Consett.
Gledstone, Thomas Liddle;	Consett.
Greedy, Edwin;	Guardian Office, Consett.
Gregory, William;	Blaydon.
Hall, Jonathan;	Blackfine.
Hall, William;	lackhill.
Hancock, W.J.;	Burnopfield.
Harrison, Anthony;	Tow Law.
Harker, Thomas;	Durham.
Henderson, Thomas;	Dunston-on-Tyne.
Henderson, T. N.;	Blackhill.
Herdman, N. R., ;	Burnopfield, 3 copies.
Herdman, Robert R.;	Annfield Plain, 2 copies.
Hogg, Thomas;	Dipton.
Hogg, Richard;	Consett.
Holmes, William, Esq., J.P.;	Tantobie.
Hooper, W. H.;	Blackhill.
Huggup, Miss;	Acklington.
Hutchinson, James;	Blackhill.
Hyden, Geo. T., Esq., J.P.;	Blackhill.
Jack, John A.;	Blackhill.
Jackson, Robert;	Gateshead.
Jackson, Robert, Jun.;	Guardian Office, Consett.
Jamieson, J.;	Blackhill.
Jennings, John;	Dipton.
Joicey, Edward, Esq.;	Blenkinsopp Hall, Haltwhistle.

Johnson, James;	Burnopfield.
Johnson, William;	Byer Moor.
Jessop, Thomas; 1,	Flint Hill.
Jessop, William;	Flint Hill.
Kell, Jasper;	Durham.
Kirkup, J., G.;	Blackhill.
Lamb, E. J.;	Consett, 2 copies.
Laws, J. L.;	Catchgate, Annfield Plain.
Lee, Miss;	Burnopfield.
Lee, Miss F.;	Gateshead-on-Tyne.
Lee, Miss R. M.;	Gateshead-on-Tyne.
Leybourne, John;	Sunderland, 3 copies.
Leybourne, J. W.;	Consett.
Leybourne, S.;	Blackhill.
Little, J. W.;	Consett, 2 copies.
Longworth, T.;	Consett.
Lovett, James, Junr.;	Blackhill, 3 copies.
Lowes, William;	Waskerley, Darlington, 2 copies.
Lumley, Francis;	Blackhill.
McQuillen, William;	Dipton.
Middleton, William;	Marley Hill.
Mitchinson, Robert;	Catchgate, Annfield Plain.
Morison, Dr.;	Catchgate, Annfield Plain.
Mounsey, Alfred;	c/o Consett Iron Co., Ltd.,
Muir, J. T.;	Blackhill.
Naylor, Miss A.;	Dipton.
Nicholson, C. W.;	Blackhill.
Nicholson, J. M.;	Consett.
Nicholson, R.;	Beamish.
Nicholson, S. R.;	Blackhill.
Norton, Henry;	Blackhill.
Nutt, F. A.;	Blackhill.
Ord, G.;	Marley Hill.

Ornsby, Robert;	Consett.
Osborne, Mrs.;	South Shields.
Palmer, Henry, J. P.;	Medomsley.
Parnaby, Christopher;	Blackhill.
Pattinson, John Burton;	Fulham London.
Pattinson, Joseph;	Mainstique, Michigan, U.S.A.
Pattinson, William;	Castleside.
Peacock, Nathan;	Blackhill.
Pegge, J. T.;	City Surveyor, Durham.
Pickering, G. A.;	Newcastle-on-Tyne.
Poole, John;	Consett.
Proud, John;	Derwent Crest, Castleside.
Public Library;	Newcastle-on-Tyne.
Public Library;	Heaton Park Road, Newcastle-on-Tyne.
Public Library;	Sunderland.
Raine, Rev. Foster;	Appleby, 2 copies.
Raine, John E.;	Consett.
Raine, J. G.;	Castleside.
Raw, William;	Blackhill, 2 copies.
Reay, John;	Whittonstall, R.S.O.
Reed, Thomas;	Blackhill.
Richardson, Henry;	Literary and Philosophical Society, Newcastle-on-Tyne, 4 copies.
Robinson, J. G., J.P.;	Blackhill.
Robinson, William;	Leadgate.
Robinson, R.;	Shotley Bridge.
Robson, Miss;	Blackhill.
Robson, Miss A. M.;	Swalwell.
Robson, Edward;	Consett.
Robson, Nicholas;	Consett.
Rogerson, John;	Lintz Green, R.S.O., 2 copies.
Ross-Lewin, Canon G. H.;	Benfieldside.
Rouse, S.;	Dipton.
Rule, Geo.;	Gateshead.

Rutter, John;	Castleside.
Saunders, Edward, Jun.;	Marley Hill, 2 copies.
Scott, C. F.;	Leadgate, R.S.O.
Sisterson, John;	Consett.
Sloane, E. J., Mus. D.;	Blackhill.
Sloane, John;	Consett.
Smith, John Bowey;	Castleside, 2 copies.
Spinks, Joseph;	Burnopfield.
Strathmore, Earl of;	Streatlam Castle, Darlington.
Strong, G.;	Consett.
Surtees, Miss;	Hamsterley Hall, Lintz Green, 2 copies.
Surtees, John;	Blackhill.
Swales, George;	Blackhill
Taylor, H. E.;	Whickham.
Thompson, A.;	Consett.
Thompson, Bentham;	Snow's Green.
Thompson, T.;	Lintz Green.
Tones, John;	Catchgate, Annfield Plain.
Turnbull, George;	Blackhill.
Turnbull, T.;	Burnopfield.
Turner, George;	Blackhill.
Turner, Robert;	Blackfine.
Usher, Thomas;	Rowland's Gill.
Vale of Derwent Naturalists' Field Club; Burnopfield.	
Vickers, F.;	Consett.
Waite;	Durham.
Ward, Richard;	Leadgate
Wardhaugh, Edward;	Shotley Bridge.
Wardhaugh, H. F.;	Taringa, Brisbane, Queensland.
Wardhaugh, J. H.;	FShotley Bridge.
Walton, John;	Castleside.
Walton, William;	Acomb. 2 copies.
Walton-Wilson, J. W., Esq.;	Shotley Hall.

SUBSCRIBERS

Weardale Naturalists' Field Club;	Stanhope.
Wells, Richard Garr;	Consett.
Whitehead, Ernest A.;	Consett.
Williamson, John;	Brandon Colliery.
Wilson, Rev. R. W.;	Shotley Bridge.
Wood, George;	Consett, 2 copies.

PART TWO

The Extraordinary

Mr Fawcett

INTRODUCTION

Researching a Life

We hope you've enjoyed the Tales and we're sure you'll agree that they bring to life the rich history of the Land of Oak & Iron. Each story has a history of its own, but the man who set them down has a history richer than any of them.

When the original Tales of Derwentdale was printed in Consett in 1902, Fawcett was only half way through his life. And what a life it turned out to be! He had just returned from mysterious foreign adventures which may or may not have involved the Intelligence Services and Lord Kitchener. He was already well-known as a naturalist, historian and writer in Australia as well as the north-east.

In the second half of his life, his reputation grew: he researched and wrote an enormous number of works on a huge range of subjects. At heart, he was a chronicler and antiquarian, noted for preserving the family records of local churches, so it was a tragic irony that he was to be buried in an unmarked grave.

Thanks to Ray Thompson, whose campaign in 2009 brought Fawcett to the attention of the newspapers and succeeded in raising funds to erect a gravestone in Satley Churchyard, a Google search immediately brought results. I contacted Ray, now 87, and was thrilled to find that he had a folder of articles he'd transcribed from cuttings that his uncle, Harry Dent, had taken from Fawcett's house after his death in 1942. He also told me that John and Rosemary Gall, respectively deputy director and senior keeper of Beamish Museum, had been involved in the project, so I lost no time in contacting them.

We were onto something. It was time to approach David Butler, archivist of Durham County Record Office and fellow Gibside researcher, whose knowledge of local history and expertise in searching the archives would be indispensable. In what seemed like no time at all, David had produced an extensive document listing Fawcett's family records and published works.

It was through Facebook that I was able to contact someone who put me in touch with Chrissie, the warden of Satley Church, and when I met her and she mentioned that the book Fawcett had published about the church contained information about a drama that he'd been involved in with a corrupt vicar, I was hooked. She had also arranged for the current owner of Fawcett's family home to meet me and show me round Satley Grange.

David brought in Terry Coult, who was able to tell us about a spat that had taken place in the Newcastle Chronicle between our man Fawcett and a noted naturalist. Not only that, but he could provide photographs of the articles. One of them mentioned that Fawcett had sailed to Australia.

It was a surprise to see that Fawcett had published extensively in Australia and was evidently an expert on Aborigines. I knew from my training as a librarian that Australian libraries and archives are wonderfully accessible, and once I had some dates for Fawcett's stay there, I was away: the Queensland Archive and the National Library of Australia's marvellous Trove website were particularly rich goldmines.

In the material world, we are blessed in this area for research of this kind: Les Jessup introduced me to the Lit and Phil's collection of the Proceedings of the Society of Antiquaries; Howard Cleeves helped with the SANT archives at the Hancock Museum; June Holmes and Peter Quinn suggested Bewick illustrations for the Tales.

Thank-you all: we couldn't have done it without you.

There were so many strands to the research that sometimes I felt like one of those dog-walkers you see with twelve hounds on tangled leads! This 'Life and Work' section is just a start. I never did get to the bottom of the Kitchener connection, but I have an intriguing theory; I don't know how to find out whether he was really shipwrecked three times or picked up in a gunboat; I can't go to Australia to read the fragile records from a part of his life that will really surprise you; the National Archives is bound to have information I haven't found; if you're a genealogy buff, you might be able to find him on more passenger lists, and you might even be able to find out whether he has any living relatives; you might have documents or photos in your loft... The possibilities are endless.

If you fancy picking up one of these strands of research, please get in touch. If you need any pointers, there's a list of resources on the Land of Oak & Iron Local History Portal to help you get going.

There are endnotes in this Life & Works: I've listed the resources we used and included transcriptions of articles. You'll also find more information in the Appendices.

Let's find out everything we can about James William Fawcett: not only does he deserve it, but we'll also find out more about our own history along the way.

Val Scully

THE LIFE AND WORKS OF
JAMES WILLIAM FAWCETT

SATLEY AND BUTSFIELD

The modern visitor to this picturesque corner of County Durham should have no trouble at all imagining how it looked a hundred and fifty years ago, when our hero was born. The quiet curved main street with its soft sandstone cottages is largely unchanged, though the local black thatch that Fawcett would have known has long since been replaced by slate tiles. Beyond the picturesque churchyard where he lies buried, the gentle hills rolling away into the distance would

Photo Courtesy of John Gall

Fig. 5 Satley Main Street

once have been far more wooded, but during the First World War, he will have witnessed the loss of many of the trees that once clothed them. Loving the place as he did, he would be comforted to see how beautifully peaceful Satley still is.

He once wrote: 'The village of Satley occupies a pleasant situation in a narrow vale between Lanchester and Tow Law. It was originally part of Lanchester, but became a parish in its own right in 1868. Steeley Burn flows through a deep, wooded ravine to join the river Browney below the village… On top of a ridge on the north side of the river are two ancient hamlets of East and West Butsfield, lying on the south side of the township of Conside-cum-Knitsley, at the head of … Butsfield Burn in north-west Durham.'

He tells us that 'there were several ganister quarries and a freestone quarry at Woodburn where stone slates and flagstone kerbstones were worked,' but this was always farming country, the few outcrops of coal above the millstone grit having been found to be worthless: 'The soil and subsoil are clay, and the chief crops are wheat, barley, oats, potatoes and turnips.' [1]

In July 1998, Ray Thompson transcribed an old newspaper cutting from the Consett Guardian which he had come across in the belongings of his late uncle, Harry Dent. Under the title 'Butsfield Sixty Years Ago - An emigrant's memories,' [2] the unnamed writer described the characters he remembered from his home village when he was a child in the 1860s, the decade of Fawcett's birth. Their fathers clearly knew each other: 'My father's dear old friend – one of God's own gentlemen – lived at Satley Grange.'

The article paints a lively picture of the inhabitants of the two villages, with illicit whiskey stills in the woods, 'buzzom makers, drunken wastrels,' and the 'laughable farce' of a frenzied old lady throwing her best china out of an upstairs window to save it from a fire started by a pyromaniac who went on to burn down his next house in the same manner!

It seems that Fawcett and the anonymous writer were not the only Satley natives who had made lives for themselves in distant countries: 'Young Willie Langton [who had] served his time at Consett to be a joiner, afterwards emigrated to South Africa and made good in Natal.' Willie Suddes' illegitimate son, 'George I think was his name,' went to America and 'wrote from the United States, where he was a farmer in good circumstances with a wife and family.'

> *Jacob Hopper lived at one of the farms at East Butsfield and William Bulman at the other. The latter afterwards became a steward to the last squire of Woodland, who bought the estate after we had left the district, and later on emigrated to British Colombia. He left behind him, however, his eldest son, the only child of his first wife, and Jack ("Poor Jack") has led a wandering life about the farms, Consett Works and the workhouse. Jack was driven to this by the ill-usage of an abominable stepmother. I met him, one day, with an old sack on his back, tottering along the road to the Butsfields, to the farmhouse of some kindly farmer. We were lads together, and I felt heart-sorry for poor old Jack.*

We'll be hearing more about 'poor old Jack' later.

THE FAWCETT FAMILY

William Fawcett [3] was a Satley man through and through: born at South Broomshields in 1830, he had taken over the family farm when he reached his majority, and in 1860 had moved to Wooley Close, Brancepeth, where in 1866 he married Margaret Sarah Charlton. [4] James William was their first child, born on 14 April 1867, and that year the small family moved to Satley Grange Farm: by the time the census was taken four years later, James had two little sisters, Susannah and Eleanor.

The family steadily grew; by 1891, when it was complete, there were seven children: James William (1867), Susannah (1869), Eleanor (1870), Catherine (1873), Harriet (1875), John (1878) and Joseph (1882).

Fig. 6   Satley Grange

Photo: Ray Thompson 2009

Satley Grange is now a simple double-fronted stone farmhouse with a slate roof. A paving slab walkway still dissects the downstairs rooms, running from the front door straight to the back. Just inside the front door there used to be a steep open ladder for access to the first floor: the holes for the bottom of the ladder are still visible, and a neighbour remembers it still being there, though very rickety, in the mid 1960s.

William Fawcett farmed his 54 acres and took an exceptionally active part in the running of the village and the church. As well as being Satley's first People's Churchwarden (April 1870 to April 1878), he was by all accounts a pillar of the community. One of his many parish roles was 'Waywarden for the Township of Butsfield (1876-1888) and Rate Collector for the same (1876-1888).' His son James was later to refer to himself having had the latter role at the age of twelve: the busy father no doubt delegated some of his duties.

A Mentor for Our Young Hero

The land farmed by the Fawcetts had once been part of Satley Fell, formerly an area of Lanchester Common. 'In 1773, it was formed into five fields by enclosures of stone walls and thorn hedges and brought under cultivation.' [5]

One of his father's oldest friends, and a frequent visitor to Satley Grange Farm, was the famous archaeologist Canon Greenwell (1820-1918). The Greenwell family had been prominent in Durham life for three hundred years, and their family seat was not far from Satley, at Greenwell Ford, Lanchester, near the ancient Roman fort of Longovicium.

William Greenwell was a polymath: originally a lawyer, then a theologian, librarian, antiquarian, archaeologist, collector, historian, numismatist. Despite all his achievements in academia, it is as a fisherman that his name is most widely known nowadays: Greenwell's Glory, the trout fly he is credited with inventing, is still in use.

In 1875, when James was eight, a Bronze Age stone hammer was found in one of the fields. [6] Canon Greenwell will have been there like a shot, and we can imagine what an impact this powerfully intelligent and charismatic man had on the academic little lad: librarian of Durham Cathedral (1863-1908) and editor of *The Boldon Buke* for the Surtees Society, of which he would become vice-president (1890 – 1918). The Bronze Age hammer may well have been one of the many artefacts he sold to the British Museum between 1879 and 1907, where his items form one of the foundation British collections.

Portrait Courtesy of Durham Cathedral

Fig. 7   Canon Greenwell

In 1885, William Fawcett made a much more exciting discovery, and many years later, his son wrote an account for Newcastle's Society of Antiquaries:

> *In one corner of this field there was, and had been since memory of man, a mound or heap of soil. By most persons it was called an old 'Whicken Heap,' or place where 'whickens' - couch grass, sods, weeds, etc. - had been carted to when ploughed lands were cleaned. [William Fawcett]*

*carted the heap away, and when he reached the level of the
adjoining land found a large flagstone in what had been
the middle of the heap. This was raised and it was found
to cover a cavity some three feet by two and about two feet
deep. The hollow was empty, except that in one corner
lay an earthen pot. There were signs of the place having
contained water at one time. The late Canon Greenwell,
who was an old friend of the finder and a frequent visitor
to his house, saw the cavity soon after the opening and
declared it an ancient British burial.* [7]

Three years later, in 1888, another burial cist was found in a
pasture field between the hamlets of East and West Butsfield, and this
one contained the skeleton of an adult, lying on its right side, 'which fell
to dust on exposure to the air.' Again, Canon Greenwell was present,
but our hero was not: young James was already off on his adventures
and did not return to England until the following year.

In 1890, when he was back at home in Satley, a stone road was
uncovered. Thoroughly excited by the find, he wrote a paper and
presented it to the Society of Antiquaries of Newcastle upon Tyne. 'On
the remains of an ancient road near Satley' [8] was the first piece of work
by the enthusiastic young academic that was read to the Society, and
his youth and excitement are clear to see:

> *'On the writer of this note becoming informed of what
> was going on, he paid several visits to the place and saw
> the operations. He saw at once that the long narrow stony
> strip was none other than a portion of an ancient British
> road and as perfect as it was in the time of its builders...
> The direction of the road northwards seems to me to be to
> meet the ancient British road which ran down the Derwent
> Valley on the south or right bank of the river, traces of which
> are visible between Muggleswick and Allensford and also
> near to Lintz Green. The opening out of this long-hidden*

antiquity verifies the etymology of the name of the village of Satley near to which it lies. The prefix SAT- is derived from the British word "sathe" signifying a trampling or a treading; a place beaten down by the continued walking over of men or animals; a well-worn track. If I read the old British language correctly; the affix -LEY is from the termination of the same language signifying a woodland clearing, grassland, an open space in the forest. Putting the two syllables together we have Sathelle, since corrupted into Satley and signifying pastureland near the well-trodden road in the clearing by the main road.'

We can imagine he must have been quite crestfallen when he read the response of one of the sage members of the Society after hearing this paper read out: 'Mr Hedley thought the road in question could not be ancient British as the known roads of the Britons were not paved and are now merely hollow ways. The portion of the paved road ascending a bank near Muggleswick appears to be medieval.'

Satley Church

The ancient rural church of St Cuthbert had once had a black-thatched roof 'exposed to all winds and weathers,' [9] like many of the houses in the area. By 1793, 'it had again become very bad, cracks and crevices and gaping holes let in the daylight and the rain and snow.' Funds had been raised by public subscription to provide the beloved building with 'a new roof of grey slates fastened by means of sheep shanks.'

In the churchyard once stood an even more ancient cross of millstone grit, older than the church itself; how this cross came to be destroyed shall be revealed shortly. The church and its graveyard are as picturesque as they ever were, and the modern visitor might imagine it as perennially peaceful and unchanged since the Fawcett family worshipped there. That would not be strictly true. The story of the drama that unfolded behind those sturdy stone walls and Fawcett's role in it shall be saved until later.

Photo: Val Scully 2019

Fig. 8 Satley Church

SCHOOLING

Fig. 9 Village Green & School House

Next to the church stands a pretty schoolhouse which had been built by one of Canon Greenwell's relatives in 1846. Miss Elizabeth Greenwell lived at Broomshields Cottage, in the grounds of Broomshields Hall, 'a neat modern mansion a little to the south-west of Satley... [occupying] a pleasant position, overlooking a well-wooded gill, through which flows the Pan Burn, a truly sylvan streamlet.' [10]

The little boy destined to be this school's most illustrious pupil will have been enrolled at the age of five, in 1872. The surviving log book records admissions after 1874, and shows his younger siblings Catherine, Harriet and John joining him and the other seventy students of all ages. Of James the only record is the date he left: 1 April 1881, at the age of fourteen, having passed the sixth standard. [11]

In the nine years he spent at Satley School, he had several teachers: George Moses until 1876; Thomas Graham for ten significant months from 1786-7; and then William Heaviside, who had returned to the position for a second time, having previously been Satley's

Photo Courtesy of John Gall

schoolteacher from Sept 1863 to May 1867. Heaviside had been educated at Blue Coat School, Durham, and he had six sons and five daughters, one of whom was destined (in the distant future) to be Fawcett's wife. Heaviside stayed at the school for two years and was succeeded by Elizabeth Proud, the first female teacher Satley had ever had.

On 25 April 1881, at the age of fourteen, James was admitted to Bede College Model School in Durham. We know no more than that: after this, things get mysterious.

GIFTED LINGUIST

By all accounts, young James was extraordinarily precocious at learning languages, and it seems his schools were unable to provide the tuition such a prodigy needed. Quite how he accessed all the learning he managed to amass is a cause of wonder and admiration. Half a century later, he wrote an account for the *Consett Guardian* of how he acquired such a breadth of learning at such a young age, and the determination it took:

> *I had got a good grounding in Latin at my old school in Durham… my knowledge of the classics did me good…I had, by self-study at home, learnt the ancient Greek language, and could read the Greek classics and the Greek testament with ease, before I was 15…Before I left England I knew the Hebrew. Many a time I had tramped over the hills by Consett to Whittonstall to the residence of the Rev. J. J. Low, the then Vicar, who was a good Hebrew scholar. He had been Hebrew Prizeman at Durham University in his graduate days, and whilst he was at Whittonstall (1872-1888) was secretary of the local society for the study of the Hebrew language and the Hebrew scriptures, and it was my privilege to be the only lay member. I had also many and many a time tramped to Durham and back (24 miles) in order to have half-a-day, or a few hours, talk in Hebrew with Canon Fowler, then Professor of Hebrew at Durham University. I once walked from my parents' home to Newcastle and back (32 miles) in order to buy a Hebrew dictionary, which I knew was for sale there….* [12]

Photo Courtesy of Whiting Society

Fig. 10   Canon Joseph Thomas Fowler (1833-1924)

Philology, or the study of languages, was to prove a lifelong interest of Fawcett's: it is said that he could speak thirty-three languages by the age of twenty-five. [13] We mere mortals doubt that such a thing is possible, and clearly this sense of other people's incredulity is something he was aware of. In 1927, in another article for the *Consett Guardian* [14] he addressed this uncanny ability:

> *It is not everybody who is successful at mastering languages. And one is inclined to think that there is a linguistic facility, something more than a powerful and retentive memory, which absorbs language-forms like a sponge absorbing water. And when those who realise keenly their linguistic failings, remember that they can only write and speak one language, and possess a very poor smattering of several others, they stand in awe of the man who is master of half-a-dozen. But what shall we think of the man who can speak fifty languages?*

Somewhat surprisingly, he left the Model School after only one year: it was 1882 and he was fifteen years old.[15] At this point, young James disappears from the records, but wherever he went, by 1889 he was back in Satley, ready to bring down the vicar!

130

No-one knows for certain where James William Fawcett got to between the ages of fifteen and twenty-one: accounts vary, and his name does not appear in any formal records between 1882 and 1889 that have so far come to light.

In later life, he spoke of having spent two years on a natural history survey of Queensland. Although he never specified when that was, and we haven't been able to track down any records in Australia, it would have to have been before 1891. In that year, when he left England again, Fawcett was definitely bound for Australia and he told people that he had been there previously for two years on a botanic survey of Queensland. [16] When he was in his fifties and a respected member of Newcastle's Society of Antiquaries, he twice put on record the fact that he had left England for Australia in 1886, 'having sold a large number of deeds, documents and wills pertaining to Durham and Northumberland.' [17]

One possibility is that his father's friend, Canon Greenwell, who had founded the Tyneside Naturalists' Field Club in 1846, provided the contact that saw the gifted young man sent to the Antipodes on the first of his many adventures. There are other theories, however: Henry Baker Tristram (1822 – 1906) was a Canon of Durham Cathedral and curator of the city's museum. A noted ornithologist, geologist and author of several books on the natural history of the Holy Land, Canon Tristram had travelled extensively, beginning with a two-year stint as secretary to the governor of Bermuda and then exploring the near east, China and Japan. Durham was noted for its naturalist-scholars, several of whom were also clergymen. A prodigiously talented young man like Fawcett would be sure to come to their attention one way or another. If an opportunity arose to go off on a foreign adventure, our hero would no doubt have seized it with both hands.

It is widely believed that this linguistic prodigy was plucked from his school to be recruited by the government in the Intelligence Services. When he came to record his own life for posterity in 1914, he listed an astonishing array of places he had worked in the service of the Intelligence Department: 'Gibraltar, Malta, Italy (Naples and Rome), Egypt, (from Alexandria to Khartoum), Aden, Ceylon, Java, Australia, and China, between 1886 and 1899.' [18]

Fig. 11   Canon Henry Baker Tristram

Photo in public domain

To date, no official evidence for any of this can be traced. The difficulty lies in Fawcett having apparently been a government employee rather than a military man: the National Archives have plentiful records of army personnel but of their civilian colleagues, particularly those in the intelligence services, records are scarce and secretive.

In later life, he spoke often of his adventures in Egypt and the Sudan, particularly having been one of the first white men to have entered Khartoum after the murder of General Gordon. He is said to have rescued a neglected rose bush from Gordon's garden and sent it home to be planted by his parents in the garden of Satley Grange.

Drypoint etching by George Joy, 1895.
Courtesy of the Council of the National Army Museum.

Fig. 12   General Gordon's death at the hands of
the Mahdi's followers 26 January 1885.

Certainly the years in which Fawcett was absent from England correspond with the events taking place in Egypt and the Sudan; and although the evidence at present is only circumstantial, the war records of three other men give credence to the story of his early adventures.

The most important of these is Field Marshall Garnet Joseph Wolseley (1833-1913) who was one of the most decorated, influential and admired British generals there has ever been. Significantly, he is credited with having created the Directorate of Military Intelligence. In April 1882, Wolseley was appointed Adjutant-General to the forces: four months later, he was given command of the British forces in Egypt. After seizing the Suez Canal, he quickly defeated the Urabi Pasha at the Battle of Tel el-Kebir. For this significant victory, he was raised to the rank of general and given a peerage.

Also in Egypt at that time was a British soldier who was to become even more famous than Wolseley, and one whose name is indelibly linked with that of James William Fawcett: Horatio Herbert Kitchener (1850 – 1916). On 4 January 1883, Kitchener was promoted to captain, given the Turkish rank bimbashi (major), and dispatched to Egypt, where he took part in the reconstruction of the Egyptian Army.

It cannot be mere co-incidence that another Satley lad was also with the army in Egypt in 1883. Harold George de Pledge, the third son of the vicar, was four years older than James Fawcett and at the start of a long, illustrious military career which would later be commemorated on a marble wall tablet in St Cuthbert's Church:

> *In loving Memory of Harold George de Pledge, Colonel Commanding 19th (Alexandra Princess of Wales's own) Hussars, third son of the late Reverend Joseph Price de Pledge, sometime Vicar of the Parish, who entered into rest, January 2, 1908, aged 46 years, and is interred in Kensal Green Cemetery. He served in Egypt, 1883, the Nile Expedition 1884-5, South Africa 1899-1902, assisting in the Defence of Ladysmith. Mentioned in the Despatches. He was awarded the Brevet of Lieut.-Colonel for gallantry in action. A brave soldier, a staunch friend, and a dear brother. 'Faithful unto death'.* [19]

The National Army Museum's website contains a good deal of information and several photographs of de Pledge's regiment: 'During the 1882 Egyptian expedition, the 19th Hussars fought at Tel el Kebir on 13 September 1882 as part of the Cavalry Brigade. They then pursued the defeated forces of Arabi Pasha towards Cairo.'

Photograph by Edouard Eugene Dulier.
Courtesy of the Council of the
National Army Museum..

Fig. 13   19th Royal Hussars (Queen Alexandra's Own)
formed up in front of a pyramid at Giza,Egypt, 1882.

On 1 September 1884, General Wolseley was called upon to command the Nile Expedition for the relief of the garrison besieged at Khartoum under the command of General Gordon. The Dictionary of National Biography tells us that Kitchener acted as an intelligence officer in that relief expedition. [20]

> *Wolseley's relief column set off from Cairo in October 1884. Realising that his infantry, travelling in boats up the Nile, might not reach Khartoum in time to save Gordon, he detached a desert column to travel overland by a faster, but more dangerous route. This force, commanded by Brigadier-General Sir Herbert Stewart, was composed of four regiments of camel-mounted troops formed from the various units in Egypt and a detachment of the 19th Hussars. The column finally reached Khartoum on 28th January 1885, two days after Gordon had been killed and the town had fallen. [21]*

Harold George de Pledge was in the detachment of 19th Hussars who were sent racing across the desert on camels in a desperate attempt to rescue General Gordon. It is entirely possible that 'various units' included Intelligence personnel and among them a talented eighteen-year-old interpreter called James William Fawcett…

Fig. 14   Sir Herbert Stewart's column crossing the Bayuda Desert, 1885

Oil on board over photograph by unknown artist, 1885. Courtesy of the Council of the National Army Museum.

MALTA

Later that year, Fawcett won a hotly-contested position working as an interpreter for the British government in Malta, a significant posting for the military because of what was to become known as the 'Mediterranean Command' – the vital 'chain that linked British bases in Gibraltar, Malta, Cyprus, Crete and Egypt.' [22] In this exalted role, which he wrote about many years later, he mixed with the great and the good, learnt law and expanded the range of languages he was able to speak. In the account he gave to the *Consett Guardian* many years later, he clearly remembers his excitement at his sudden propulsion to a position of real status: we learn of a young man hungry to make the most of the opportunity he had been afforded:

> *My official appointment made me a somebody on the island. In my official capacity I occupied a seat at the Governor's Council and attended to him when on State duties. I also took a place on the staff of the Chief Justice, occupied a seat near the judicial bench when the Civil and Criminal Courts were sitting, and accompanied his Lordship when on judicial tours. Moreover, I gained the friendship of all the learned and scientific gentlemen on the island, had access to, and was present at, as many scientific meetings as I could get. At those places my seat was never vacant. Besides, there was a seat for me at the officers' mess on the island, and when the Admiral of the Mediterranean Fleet stayed in the harbour, there was a place for me at the officers' table.*
>
> *The director of Public Education on the islands also claimed my services, and I was a frequent visitor to the schools, which were similar to the Board schools in England, where the English language was taught. The University, founded by the Knights of Malta in 1768, also*

claimed me, and I gave special addresses both in English and Maltese to the students, who numbered over 800, at the request of the Syndics. Those were happy days, and I look back with pleasure on days that are gone, never to return, when a humble learner out to learn all he could, spared neither pains, time, nor trouble to gain knowledge.

Though I had gained two promotions in six months, and had become first Spanish, and then Maltese Interpreter, I was out to learn more languages. I had got a good grounding in Latin at my old school in Durham, and was out to learn the Italian, which was considered only modern Latin. In this matter my knowledge of the classics did me good. I learned the book knowledge from grammars, and I made the best of my spare time in mixing with the Italian residents to get the colloquial and oral speech. I had, by self-study at home, learnt the ancient Greek language, and could read the Greek classics and the Greek testament with ease, before I was 15. In Malta I had an opportunity of acquiring modern Greek. My colleagues on the staff of interpreters were mostly Greeks – all fine fellows, out to make the best of their opportunities of life like myself. They

Portrait by Giuseppi Cali. Public Domain.

Fig. 15   Sir John Simmons, Governor of Malta.

welcomed me into their midst, and I fraternised freely with them. I was the only Englishman on the staff of interpreters and held the highest position. They wished to improve their knowledge of pure English, and I desired to acquire modern Greek. We all gave and took, taught and learned, and were really private tutors to and with each other.

Another language I set myself out to learn was the Arabic. [This is where he tells us about learning Hebrew from the two scholars, Rev. J.J. Low and Canon Fowler.] *And I have nothing but kindly remembrances of these two good men and true, who were ever ready to help a young student in the Hebrew tongue, forty years ago, and who spared nothing in doing so. Our friendship only ceased when death intervened.'*

Confusingly, from this point on, Fawcett writes in the royal plural: we can speculate on the reason for this later.

'We once walked from our parents' home to Newcastle and back (32 miles) in order to buy a Hebrew dictionary, which we knew was for sale there. We still have that volume and money would not buy it from us. How many boys of the present day would do these things?

The Arabic has been called modern Hebrew, and as the Maltese language contains some seventy per cent of Arabic, the acquisition of this tongue was made easier. There were several pure Arabs on the island, and we did not forget to seek them out, and from them obtain that oral pronunciation which grammars and book learning does not give. Suffice it to say that before we left Malta we were master of five languages spoken in and around the Mediterranean region – Spanish, Maltese, Italian, Greek, and Arabic, to which could be added French, which we knew before we went there. And even these did not suffice us.'

MEANWHILE, BACK IN SATLEY

Wherever he had been, we imagine that when he returned home to Satley in 1889, it would have been a relief to settle back into the peaceful life of a rural village. Rural it was: peaceful it wasn't.

There were ructions in the church, and none of it appears to have reached the newspapers. The world wasn't to hear about the events in St Cuthbert's Church until Fawcett himself wrote a full account twenty years later. [23]

In the *Satley Registers* (1914) the story of what had happened to this ancient church in Fawcett's lifetime emerges slowly over several pages: it is clearly one in which he was personally involved and which he finds painful to relate. When he gives us a pen-portrait of the church as it looks at the time of writing, the reader senses that there is something wrong: 'with the exception of a portion at the west end, opposite the south door, and the aisle, the floor is boarded. The walls are bare and devoid of plaster... built into the west wall of the nave near the font are portions of two Thirteenth Century grave-covers... these with eight others were unfortunately destroyed by orders of the then Vicar.' [24]

Aha! Here we have it. We don't have to read on very far before we learn that said vicar, who is never directly named in connection with the charges, had been in Fawcett's view, a destroyer who had presided over an 'iconoclastic spoilation.' Not only was that ancient cross gone, but also the original church floor, made of gravestones hundreds of years old.

In 1870 and 1871 the church underwent a thorough "restoration" – in some matters a wilful and deliberate destruction of almost all that was ancient belonging to the church. The floor of the ancient chancel was covered with ten ancient grave-covers all inscribed with Calvary, floreated and other crosses, and bearing symbols of Communion cups, shears, &c. The whole of these were ordered to be taken up by the iconoclastic incumbent, and broken into fragments for "filling in." Fortunately, two of the grave-covers were saved by the appearance and order of the People's Churchwarden whilst the destruction was going on – and they are now preserved in the internal wall at the west end of the nave. The old three-decker oaken pulpit was cast out and desecrated by being partly made into a dog kennel and partly into a chicken coop; the old font was cast aside, and the box pews removed.

It is worth noting that the heroic Churchwarden who had saved the two grave-covers was none other than William Fawcett, father of the writer, whose position is recorded on a brass plate on the north side of the newly erected chancel arch: 'This chancel was reseated and embellished by voluntary subscriptions A.D. 1870. J.P. De Pledge, Vicar. George Alder, William Fawcett, Churchwardens.'

James would have been only four years old at the time of the 'iconoclastic spoilation': forty years later he was to get his revenge by recording the desecration for posterity.

But the parish record book was not to be the only role little James was to play in the future of the destructive vicar: none of them could have suspected that the warden's toddler son was to grow into the nemesis of Reverend de Pledge.

SCANDAL AT THE VICARAGE

You may recall that the pretty stone school building which had provided an elementary education for James and his siblings had been built by Miss Elizabeth Greenwell of Broomshields Cottage in 1846. In addition to paying the £100 it cost to build a school for eighty children, 'she also by indenture of 17 December 1846 gave £350 three per cent consolidated bank annuities to be placed at interest for its repair and the free education of four children.' The vicar of Satley was the trustee of the fund, which came to be known as the Greenwell Charity.

In 1867, De Pledge was appointed and things started to go wrong. Here is Fawcett's account of what happened:

> *From 1870 to 1891 the income was received by the incumbent of Satley, who retained the same, and refused to carry out the conditions of the trust. The present writer called the attention of the Charity Commissioners to the misapplication of the income, and they demanded a full account of the same, and the production of all deeds, &c. These were refused, and legal notices were immediately served. During the process the Incumbent suddenly died.*

For the record, Fawcett also recalls other financial irregularities, notably the funds which had been raised in 1886 'for the purchase either of a new or a second bell…to a total of £7, which intention was not carried out.'

Shockingly, particularly for a natural antiquarian and historian like James Fawcett, 'While the matter was under consideration the whole of the parochial records of Satley from before 1797 to 1890 inclusive, except the parish registers, and all the School records, except the Log Book, were destroyed by the Incumbent – after August, 1890 and before 9 February 1891.' As that is the date of the vicar's death, we can presume that the destruction was not discovered until after the event. When he destroyed all the parochial records, De Pledge made sure evidence of financial irregularities was erased: 'all trace of the money in the hands of the Vicar was wiped out when the Account Books were destroyed.' [25]

All was not lost, however: 'Copious extracts had been made by the writer in August 1890, and these are the only records of the parish now extant for that period. Some of them have been incorporated in this work.' We can only speculate as to what had made Fawcett create his copies: did he suspect that De Pledge was not to be trusted?

In June 1891, the Charity Commissioners appointed Fawcett sole trustee of the Greenwell Charity. It was to be another twenty years, years packed with adventure in foreign climes, before James William Fawcett would sit down to preserve the story in a book. Although he was careful not to use de Pledge's name in the same sentence as the various allegations – he is always referred to as 'the incumbent' or 'the iconoclast' – it doesn't take Sherlock Holmes to work out the name of the evil-doer.

Fig. 16   Rev. Joseph de Pledge
Photo by Val Scully from Satley Church

143

OF VICARS AND ZEPPELINS

There is a curious Australian connection to the story of Satley Church. The vicar who succeeded De Pledge in 1891 was Thomas Lewis John Warneford, [26] Associate of King's College, London. The story goes that Warneford and Fawcett had met previously in Australia:

> *During the time that he lived at Queensland, Australia, Mr. Fawcett, who was a warden at St. Peter's Church, entertained a visiting preacher to lunch. The preacher had returned to Australia after completing 25 years' service as a Church missionary in India. Some years later when he returned home to Satley Mr. Fawcett met the Vicar of the church, and to his surprise discovered that he was the missionary he had met at Queensland. He was the Rev. Thomas Lewis John Warneford, whose grandson, Lieut. Rex Warneford, V.C. [27], of Satley, brought down a German Zeppelin during the Great War. [28]*

We'll be hearing more about this war hero from Ray later on.

illustration courtesy of Ray Thompson.
(Public Domain)

Fig. 17   Zeppelin

Flight Sub-Lieutenant Warneford VC bombs and destroys Zeppelin airship 1915, from 'The War Illustrated DeLuxe', published in London 1916 by English School

PRODUCTIVITY AND REPUTATION

In the extraordinarily productive two years between 1889 and 1891, Fawcett established his reputation. By this point, he had not only written and published his *Birds of Durham* and *History of Tow Law*, but also written many and various learned articles on a staggering range of subjects for a variety of societies and magazines such as the *Society of Antiquaries, The Naturalist, A Monthly Illustrated Journal of the North of England* and *The Monthly Chronicle of North Country Lore and Legend*.

He quickly gained a high profile as a regular contributor to the *Newcastle Weekly Chronicle*, and when he answered a correspondent's enquiry about his background, his reply is clearly intended to publicly establish his place among the pantheon of other notable Fawcetts:

> *This is a question I care little about answering, yet I feel certain that if I don't, the querist will not gain his, perhaps anxious aims, and the query will be one of the many which unfortunately never gain an answer. The Fawcett family of Corbridge, of which I am a cadet, is a branch of an old North Country family, remarkable for the number of its scions, and the distinguished members of them, including doctors of divinity and medicine, clergymen, lawyers, legislators, barristers, men of science & etc.*
>
> *Besides the Corbridge branch there are the Fawcetts of Lambton, now represented by the city of Durham family; the Fawcetts of the West India islands, one of the descendants of whom is, if I mistake not, Superintendent-Director of the Kingston Botanical Gardens, Jamaica; the Fawcetts of New South Wales, of whom William Fawcett, late puisne judge, after whom the town of Fawcett, on the Richmond river is named, and Charles H. Fawcett, M.L.A., F.L.S., are members; the Fawcetts of Kirby Lonsdale,*

Westmoreland, from whom sprang the late Henry Fawcett, LL.D, Professor of Political Economy, Cambridge, and Postmaster-General, and several others. Wherever they are found they all seem to carry with them the one family expression, broad high foreheads and open countenance, and "true sons of the North" constitutions. The writer may state, though it matters little, that on several occasions he has, from his resemblance to the late postmaster, been taken as his son by entire strangers to him, though old friends and acquaintances of the P.M., but who had not seen him for many years and were not cognisant with his family. I have many pedigrees of this and numerous other families, and may be able to give J.T. the information he requires, should he write to me at the below address, making matters plain. J.W. Fawcett, The Grange, Satley. [29]

Fig. 18   Postmaster-General Henry Fawcett

One extensive article of particular interest to tree-lovers in the Land of Oak & Iron was written for the English Arboricultural Society, who published it in their *Transactions* in 1896. 'Dendrological Notes from North-West Durham' is printed in full as Appendix A. It would be interesting to hear from anyone who knows the trees he describes, at least some of which will by now be the 'sturdy giants of the future' that be envisaged.

Fawcett had also established his own magazine, the title of which gives a clear indication of his breadth of interests: *The Durham Magazine and County Historical Record. Comprehending Antiquity, Biography, Dialect, Folklore, Genealogy, History, Legend, Natural History, Song, Superstition, Topography, Trade, &c, &c.* But it is his 'Introductory Address' which reveals the truly breath-taking ambition that this twenty-three-year-old had for his project:

> *Every book, Journal, magazine, Newspaper and Periodical that is born into the world of Literature is issued for some intention, reason, and scope, and the principle and motive for casting upon the waters the Durham Magazine and County Historical Record is an interesting and important one. Summed up in as few words as possible, it is the collection and preservation, by putting into permanent form, of all facts and matters of interest connected with the history, past and present, of the County of Durham.*
>
> *Durham, small though it be in size, comprehends a very wide and important history – one of the most important of the British Isles – and though she has had several recorders, historians who have left elaborate compilations, much of the past yet remains untold, whilst of the modern history little or nothing has been written. Our old compilers in their works (which are now very expensive and rare, and consequently beyond the means and reach of the general public) have given brief accounts of the various parishes in the county, but owing to the limited extent and size of the books, the authors have been obliged to curtail the contents of many of the important documents which passed through their hands. Of the contents of the greater number of these and many other old manuscripts, which*

ought to be placed in a more permanent form than that of writing-ink and parchment, we are yet in the dark, and it is greatly to be regretted, for it is a serious loss to our county annals, that since some of these old documents were perused and partly transcribed by the older compilers of our county histories, several have either been destroyed or lost.

That the scope and general character of the Durham Magazine is intended to be a valuable work, by giving an enduring worth to the records of the county, cannot fail to be acknowledged, and these will be better indicated and understood when it is known that amongst the more important subjects which will appear within its pages are the publishing in the original tongue and their translation into English of the various hitherto unpublished chapters, documents, grants, inquisitions, manuscripts, public instruments, records, tenures, &c., &c., connected with the ecclesiastical and general history of Durham; the printing of the contents of the various parish registers, many of which are annually losing their legibility; the transactions contained in the Halmote Court Rolls of the Prior and Convent of Durham, the only true historical records of life in their respective periods; the contents of the various surveys of the county; the origin, history, and present position of our county charities; and matters of similar interest, together with other items dealing with the history, ancient and modern, as far as can possibly be fully and comprehensively given of the city of Durham, and of every town, village, and hamlet within the county; the biographies of men and women of rank, title and note, deemed eligible of the name of a "Worthy of Durham"; the antiquities, ballads, commerce, customs , dialects, genealogies of our old county families, geology, industries, lore and legends, manners, natural history, poetry, songs, superstitions, trade, traditions, ancient and obsolete words and phrases, &c., &c., - in fact all and every matter connected with the county of Durham, with occasional illustrations, when possible, of the places described, and portraits (if any exist) of the persons whose careers are sketched.

Such, then, being the aims and purposes of the Durham Magazine, it is hoped that it will meet with a hearty response of the appreciation and support of its readers and subscribers, and that one and all will endeavour to promote the valuable work it has taken up and the noble end it has in view.

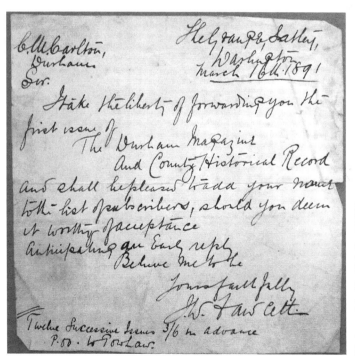

Fig. 19   Fawcett's Note to Subscribers

Photograph by David Butler. DCRO

NATURALISTS' FIELD CLUBS

The first Naturalists' Field Club was founded in Berwickshire in 1831 and Fawcett's mentor Canon Greenwell founded the Tyneside Naturalists' Field Club in 1846. The fashion soon spread across the country, [30] and when Darwin published his Origin of Species in 1859, it caused an explosion in interest in the natural world: naturalists' field clubs sprang up where people could meet, discuss his ideas, go on field trips to study the wonders of nature, and listen to papers presented by scientists, both professional and amateur. The Derwent Valley, being particularly rich in interest, had many such clubs, and they were unusually egalitarian: women could participate on an equal footing; miners could be friends with professors of Geology, and a man like Fawcett could be in his element.

The Vale of Derwent Naturalists' Field Club was founded in Burnopfield in May 1887 by James F. Robinson, who was to become a great friend of Fawcett. The Society's objectives were as follows:

1. *The practical study of Natural History in all its branches.*
2. *The annotation of the various Natural Products of the Derwent Valley.*
3. *The preservation of Rare Birds and Plants from wanton destruction.*
4. *The study of Local History and of the Antiquities of the district.* [31]

photo courtesy of Joe Mallon.

Fig. 20   Vale of Derwent title slide

These clubs usually had an annual meeting to elect a committee and decide membership fees – 'Gentlemen (over 21) 2 shillings (under 21) 1 shilling., and Ladies 1 shilling per annum.' It gladdens the heart to see women encouraged to join, and Fawcett seems to have been a great supporter of their accomplishments in natural science. In his essay 'Women as Students of Nature', [32] he celebrates the achievements of female scientists the world over, one of them particularly close to home. You can read the full essay in the notes at the back, but here are a few extracts to give you a flavour:

> *Man, standing as he does at the head of all created nature, the crowning piece of organic life, endowed with varied mental qualities, and possessing the most ambition and perseverance, peers further into the deep unfathomable depths of science, and working with more unwearying energy, attains greater results than the opposite sex; yet in all these works of research, how often is he assisted and cheered in his labour by the feebler yet far-seeing help of a weaker though sometimes firmer mind?*

> *Dame Nature [is] man's great teacher, and because she is man's great teacher, she is also woman's great teacher, for are not we one of another? Besides the many who have given the result of their labours to the public at large, there are others who have rendered great help to the botanical world by their discoveries of various plants. These are found more frequently in our colonies, and especially Australia.*

> *But we need not look so far away for female botanists of note, for in the county of Durham - amongst others - two deserve especial notice. One is Miss Deborah Wharton, of Old Park, Durham, whose hortus siccu, or collection of British plants made in the county of Durham, A.D.1760-1802, is now in the University Museum, Durham ; the other is Mary Eleanor, Countess of Strathmore, of Streatlam and Gibside.*

At the annual meetings, the clubs planned their programme of talks and excursions: Gibraltar Rock, Shotley Bridge, Lanchester Roman Camp, Ebchester Woods… the Derwent Valley provided plenty of options, and sometimes trips went further afield, to Alston, Nenthead, Corbridge, the Hancock Museum, Jesmond Dene. The members are often described as 'travelling by brakes' but accessing some of the points of interest, the caves and waterfalls and promontories, would also have required stamina, particularly for the women, hampered by their skirts and corsets.

Photograph by Billy Costello, courtesy of Joe Mallon.

Fig. 21   Vale of Derwent Field Club Group

Fawcett was to be a well-known speaker at many of these clubs for fifty years. In July 1901, the 'First United Meeting of the Naturalists' Field Clubs in the County of Durham' was held at Shotley Bridge. Members of the Field Clubs of Bishop Auckland, Blackhill and District, Dipton and District, Durham City, Gateshead, Vale of Derwent, and Weardale attended. Of the five lectures read aloud to the assembly, two were delivered by Fawcett: a paper on 'The Swordmakers of Shotley Bridge' was read 'in the grounds of Shotley Hall'; then an ambitiously wide-ranging 'address' on 'The Derwent Valley, its History, Biography and Legendary Lore' was delivered 'on the lawn of Shotley Hall by Mr J.W. Fawcett of Satley.'

That year, 'Miss Surtees, Mr J.W. Fawcett and the Rev. J. Magill were elected [as] Honorary Members ... Ladies and Gentlemen distinguished for the attainments in the Study of Antiquaries or Natural History, to whom the Club may be indebted for communication of papers or specimens, or for Lectures.' [33]

The talks were often illustrated by lantern slides: in recent times, those belonging to the Vale of Derwent Club were retrieved from Leadgate Tip! Images made from them can be viewed on the Beamish Photographic Archive as the 'Leadgate Tip Collection' but sadly they don't include the ones Fawcett used for his lecture 'to a full house' on 'The Aborigines of Australia – their Customs and Habits – illustrated by lantern views.' [34]

Billy Costello was a contemporary of Fawcett: he was a miner who possessed a good camera and a fine eye. Billy had a particular interest in geology, which brought him to the attention of eminent academics Professor George Alexander Louis Lebour (1847-1918) and his student Dr David Woolacott (1872-1925) both authors of many seminal works on the geology of the north-eastern coalfields. Thanks to the work of his descendant, Joe Mallon, Billy's photographs and notebooks have survived.

In the photograph on the next page, taken at Gibraltar Rock at the source of the River Derwent beyond Blanchland, possibly on 2 August 1909, [35] Professor Lebour is pictured on the far right; next to him Dr Woolacott, and it is perfectly possible that the man next to the two academics is Fawcett.

Photograph by Billy Costello, courtesy of Joe Mallon.

Fig. 22   Gibraltar Rock - group including Professor Lebour.

Fawcett's *Birds of Durham* was published in 1890, and in the introduction, he sets his stall out, not as an expert on birds, but a chronicler, an altruist and a person proud of his local area and keen to record its distinctive character:

> In compiling this List of the Birds of Durham my chief reason for doing so is to benefit, as far as I am able, my fellow ornithologists. In previous lists Durham has generally been joined to Northumberland, and the occurrences of many Birds which have appeared in only one of the Counties have been appended to both Northumberland and Durham, and this, to many persons, has been rather misleading... For some of the occurrences of the rarer birds I am greatly indebted to brother ornithologists, and must herewith thank them for whatever information I have culled from their works or correspondence, and especially to the following: - Mr R. Calvert, of Bishop Auckland, author of "Geology and Natural History of the County of Durham, 1884"; Mr J. Hancock, the talented curator of Newcastle Museum, and author of a "Catalogue of the Birds of Northumberland and Durham, 1874"; Mr T. Grundy, Burnopfield, one of the vice-presidents of the Vale of Derwent Naturalists' Field Club, a person who furnished Mr Hancock with several rare and unique specimens for the Newcastle Museum, and with whom I had the pleasure, conjointly, of writing out "Notes on the Birds of the Derwent Valley" for the above club; and Mr T. Tinkler, Leadgate, author of some valuable notes on "Ornithology in Weardale," which appear from time to time in the Consett Guardian. Also to Messrs. Cambridge, Gurney, Gornall, Nelson, and others whose names are appended to records. Persons forwarding imperfections and

additions to the author will be thankfully acknowledged in any further edition which may be made.

Woodcut by Thomas Bewick

Fig. 23   Heron

The essay *'Notes on the Birds of the Derwent Valley'* [36] which he refers to here was later published by the Vale of Derwent Naturalists, and in it we learn more about the main source of his information, retired gamekeeper Thomas Grundy:

> *In compiling the following contributions towards the ornithology of the Derwent Valley, allow me to say a few words by way of introduction. The greater portion of the information given to me for the above purpose is that by Mr Thomas Grundy, who for many years was gamekeeper for gentlemen in the Valley of the River Derwent. Mr Grundy was born at Ravensworth in 1815, where his father was gamekeeper to Sit Thomas Henry Liddell, sixth Baron of Ravensworth, in the County of Durham, in whose service and that of his son, he acted as such for sixty years.*

In 1836, when twenty-one years of age, Mr Grundy went into the service of Mr Walker of Bradley Hall, west of Crawcrook, adjoining the River Tyne, as gamekeeper, and after residing there for eleven years returned to Ravensworth, in 1847, where he acted in the same capacity for seven years, until 1854.

Mr Grundy, who is now advanced in years, in his boyhood was, like many other of the children of that period, unable to obtain that great benefit to mankind, which is now so common, i.e., education – thanks to the various Education Acts; hence he was unable to commit to paper any of the important items of ornithology which he came across. Knowing that Mr Grundy wished someone to write these notes down, and so preserve them, the writer, for that reason, and the great importance of which he considers such to be, undertook to do so, feeling that, by so doing, he is rendering an important benefit to the ornithological world.

The knowledge which Mr Grundy has of the birds of the Derwent Valley is unrivalled, and from what short notes he has given to me – thanks to his wonderful and retentive memory – I must say he has been a close and keen observer of the birds, and quite different from many of the gamekeepers in the county.

In the following list the writer has, for various reasons, kept Mr Grundy's notes intact, and whatever additions have been made to them will be found at the completion of his (Mr Grundy's) list.

A list of 130 species is reproduced at Appendix E.

In conclusion, Fawcett writes: 'If any reader could add occurrences of birds in the Derwent Valley not mentioned above, or could add any further knowledge of their range in that district, the writer would feel greatly obliged if they will kindly do so. In order to make the list as complete as possible, it is extremely important that all collectors of bird notes should co-operate and add to each other's knowledge.'

Woodcut by Thomas Bewick

Fig. 24   Magpie

This paper was recently useful to the Natural History Society of Northumbria in clarifying the lives of two naturalists, both called Thomas Robson, who lived in the same area and both recorded birds. Thomas Robson (1871-1944) of Winlaton is the author of the definitive *Birds of the Derwent Valley*: 'In 1993, when *Birds of Gateshead* was published (Bowey *et al.* 1993), Robson was described as "Undoubtedly the most important ornithologist of the area" his book being "one of the principal reference documents on which this present work draws."' [37] When Fawcett set down the gamekeeper's entry for Redwing *Turdus iliacus,* he mentions an entirely different Thomas Robson: 'Two or three eggs of this bird were obtained on the Bradley Hall Estate about 1836, by Mr Thomas Robson, at that time clerk for Crowley, Millington and Co., Swalwell. They were lying on the grass and had probably been dropped by the birds while feeding.' In another incidental detail of interest, when this 'lesser' Thomas Robson was baptized at Ryton in 1812, his father was registered as an anchor-smith and would probably have been employed by the Crowley family at Swalwell.

It seems clear from this that Fawcett saw himself not only as an observer but as a chronicler, a gatherer of information from others. As the editor of a 'Natural History Department' column in the *Supplement to Newcastle's Weekly Chronicle,* he made it clear again how he saw his role:

> *'The Naturalist' will be happy to receive contributions of interest from our wide circle of correspondents…West Durham differs greatly from other districts where many other notes similar to these might be made. Who will begin, each in his or her near neighbourhood, to do the same? Surely there are some? I carry my naturalist's note book with me wherever I am, and note down every naturalistic item worth noting.* [38]

Whether he always credited the sources of his information is a moot point: as you will see, this trust in others led to damage to his reputation among certain naturalists.

Woodcut by Thomas Bewick

Fig. 25   Curlew

OF BREAM AND BUTTERFLIES

In the *Newcastle Weekly Chronicle Supplement* on 31 Oct, 1891, a letter appeared from an authoritative naturalist of great standing in the North East: John Emmerson Robson (1833-1907), F.E.S. and Editor of *The British Naturalist.* In a tone of polite disdain, and simultaneously congratulating himself on his own restraint, Robson derided Fawcett's reliability:

> *Some months ago Mr J.W. Fawcett, The Grange, Satley, published in this column a list of the fishes of Durham. In this he included the black bream, as one that had occurred on the Hartlepool coast. Residing here all my life, and taking a great interest in our local fauna, I was surprised at a statement like this, for I had never heard of the supposed occurrence of this rare fish. I made enquiry at once, through you, for Mr Fawcett's authority for the statement; and no reply being made, you most kindly permitted me to ask the question a second time. Up to the present no reply has been given, and I would respectfully submit that, apart from the want of courtesy displayed in thus ignoring an important inquiry, that it is extremely unscientific to make a statement like this, and neither acknowledge the error, if one have been committed, nor give the evidence on which the statement was based, if there be any.*

It seems grossly unfair that Robson is choosing to ignore the fact that in that list, Fawcett had made it clear where he got his information:

> *Owing to the study of the saltwater fishes of this country being greatly neglected, it is a dubious matter to give a full list. I shall be glad if every fisherman and fish merchant would give, either through this column or by*

forwarding them to me, lists of the saltwater fishes in their neighbourhoods, with dates, if possible, or the rarer species. All sent to me will be duly acknowledged. I return my sincerest thanks to W.H.W., Newcastle and also to Mr T.R. Clay, of the same city for addendae to Part 1 in the issue of October 25th.[39]

Fig. 26   Black Bream

Robson's letter continued in sarcastic vein:

> *Mr Fawcett has now favoured your readers with a list of "Butterflies of Durham."* [40] *On this subject I claim to be an authority, and I venture to assert that it would be scarcely possible to publish a list more full of the grossest errors than that Mr Fawcett has sent you. I challenge him to produce the slightest evidence for the occurrence, within this county, of the following three butterflies, the first of which he marks as "frequent", and the other two as "common": 1. High brown fritillary (Argynnis adippe); 2 Frizzled skipper (Pyrgus malvae); 3. Small skipper (Pamphilia linea) If he can produce such evidence I will confess my error and apologize, but I feel perfectly certain none of them were ever taken within the limits of the county of Durham. Of minor errors and omissions, I forbear to speak, but if a correct list of the butterflies of Durham would be an acceptable contribution, I will be very pleased to furnish it.'*

Robson was indeed to go on to compile the definitive List of British Lepidoptera which was published after his death.

In a letter published two weeks later, James F. Robinson of the Vale of Derwent Naturalists' Field Club leapt to Fawcett's defence and provided an explanation for his silence:

> *I note in the Weekly Chronicle a letter from Mr Robson, editor of the British Naturalist, on Mr J. W. Fawcett's statement about the black bream as having occurred on the Hartlepool coast. Mr Robson complains of Mr Fawcett's want of courtesy in not answering his inquiry as to his (Mr Fawcett's) authority for the statement. I am quite certain Mr Robson will excuse Mr Fawcett when he learns that he sailed for Australia on September 14th. I note from today's (October 31st) shipping news that the vessel in which Mr Fawcett sailed is reported as having arrived off Brisbane. Mr Fawcett has gone to Australia to fulfil a scientific appointment under the Government of Queensland. He was two years in Australia formerly as assistant botanist in the botanical survey of Queensland.*
>
> *From my knowledge of Mr Fawcett, I am certain that if he had been here he would willingly have supplied Mr Robson with the authority on which he made the statement that the black bream had been caught off Hartlepool, or would have acknowledged that he had been misinformed. He would have done the same also with regard to the butterflies. Mr Fawcett is not the man to make statements without authorities, or what he thought were authorities. I know Mr Fawcett's address in Australia and will probably send him Mr Robson's paragraph. Mr Fawcett will in all likelihood reply.' James F. Robinson, Burnopfield.* [41]

Whether Fawcett ever did reply is unlikely. Only two months after he had been assigned sole trustee of the Greenwood Charity in Satley, he had applied his 'power to appoint three trustees': in August 1891, he handed over to Robert Hedley of Satley Villa, Reverend Thomas Lewis John Warneford, and his father, William Fawcett.

He sent letters to all the subscribers of his *Durham Magazine*: 'The proprietors of the Durham Magazine regret that owing to the unexpected recall of their acting editor to Australia they have to discontinue the issues of that publication.' Having only produced three of the projected twelve editions, the subscribers received a refund of 2s 7½d.

Then he sailed for Australia.

QUEENSLAND

One of the difficulties in pinning down Fawcett's whereabouts with any certainty is his prolific use of the postal service. The journey to Australia will have taken just over a month, so if he sailed on 14 September and Robinson reported that his ship had arrived off Brisbane on 31 October, he was certainly in Australia in December when the *Newcastle Chronicle* carried his item about buffaloes.

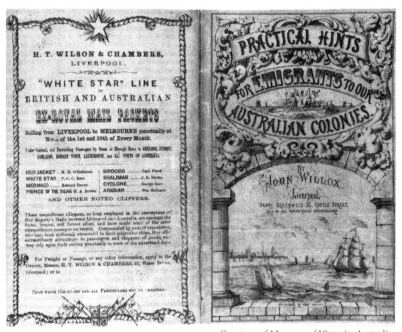

Courtesy of Museum of Victoria, Australia.

Fig. 27   Advice to Australian Emigrants

Likewise, while we believe he was at home in Satley in the previous October, wrestling with the troublesome priest, an article appeared in the Mackay Mercury, Queensland on Tuesday 28 October 1890, under the title 'An Australian Pioneer' and credited to J. W. Fawcett, The Grange, Satley. [42] So we can never assume that he was in the country (or even the hemisphere!) where he was currently being published.

The subject of the article was Robert Towns (1794-1878) a fellow north-easterner born in Longhorsley, whose meteoric rise had begun by being apprenticed on a collier sailing out of North Shields. By the time he gave his name to a settlement in the colonies, he was a hugely successful shipowner, trader and civic leader.

Queensland had been declared a state separate from New South Wales in 1859. Townsville, on the north-eastern coast of Queensland, is where Fawcett was apparently to live, or at least be based, from 1892 until he returned home at the end of the century.

An English explorer who was there a decade later wrote: 'Townsville is now the chief port for North Queensland. It has a population of over 25,000 people. Its trade and importance are rapidly growing. Located 748 miles nearer the Equator than Brisbane...rich tropical belts running north and south of it...in the same latitude South as Bombay North. Its average rainfall is 47 inches. It is a tropical city... Flinders Street is in summer one of the hottest streets in the world.' [43]

He describes the 'ever-blue, ever-bright' seascape looking towards Magnetic Island, 'the pleasure-place of Townsville....A hazy coast-line, covered in dense jungles, where wild pigeons call, and little marsupials hop cautiously along shaded, well-worn paths known only to themselves....Across the bay, one sees the funnels of shipping... pointing a passage to that Northern Sea-road which rolls away to Papua, the Dutch Indies, China and Japan.'

It seems to have been a place where worlds met and adventures began: he describes the delights of sitting for hours in the public areas of the Queen's Hotel 'to lounge in the spacious smoke-room and listen to stories of the North. There one meets men who grow sugar along the littoral, men who grow fine wool on the treeless Western plains, men who control copper mines in dusty, distant Cloncurry...'

The Lit and Phil has several books on early Australia, many of them by gentleman explorers, naturalists and visitors. William Lavallin Puxley was an Allied Warship Commander and a V.C., but even he was moved to raptures about this 'New Eden':

> *I shall never forget my first morning in the bush...I cannot imagine a happier feeling for a naturalist than to find himself in a new wild country, free to go where he wishes with the certainty of finding something new at every step. At any rate I can think of nothing in this world for myself to compare with it for pure happiness. That first afternoon I counted over twenty varieties of eucalyptus, many of which were coming into flower, and everywhere the pretty grey and yellow soldier-birds flew round me.*

> *Have you heard the magpies calling in the dew time cool and clear*
>
> *When the bush is stirring softly in the breeze?*
>
> *Have you heard the waters falling where the timid wild things peer*
>
> *And the hills and vales are murmurous with trees?*

> *Have you heard the curlews crying when the dusk is over all?*
>
> *Have you heard the mopoke calling 'neath the moon?*

Have you heard the tender music of the mountain waterfall?

Have you heard by night the ocean's endless croon?

Have you heard the bell-birds tinkling in the fragrant mountain glens –

Ah! The beauty and the greenness of those dells!

Where the wild wood is a refuge for the wagtails and the wrens

And the air is full of chiming silver bells? [44]

If Fawcett had indeed been part of a natural history survey of Queensland, one of Puxley's anecdotes gives us a flavour of the kinds of experience he will have had:

> In 1883, a party of explorers, who had determined to survey the northern coast from the sea, landed in the middle of a mangrove swamp and made their way painfully through the deep, evil-smelling ooze. For miles they went, passing flocks of spoonbills, cranes, and wild duck, until they reached higher land and found themselves in scrub country with all the denseness of the tropics. Through this they forced their painful way, at the rate of a few miles a day, until at length they emerged into open plain country. [45]

Whether or in what capacity Fawcett was employed by the government has so far proved impossible to ascertain, but what is certain is that from 1892 until 1899, he established an unassailable reputation as a natural historian and writer in Australia.

AN EXPERT ON AUSTRALIAN ABORIGINES

In reading the work of some of these Victorian colonialist explorers, modern sensibilities can be quite shocked: the attitudes and assumptions of the white settlers and their treatment of the indigenous people is alien to us now. James Fawcett, as a student of languages and natural history, found the original inhabitants of Australia completely fascinating and wrote about them with a respect that was unusual at the time.

Having arrived in Townsville in early November, he wasted no time at all in writing letters to newspapers all over Australia announcing the inception of the Australian Aborigine Association, which he appears to have created and of which he was president. These were published in papers such as *The Queenslander, The Australian Town and Country Journal, The Melbourne Argus, The South Australian Register, The West Australian* and *The Western Mail.*

Further proof that he had already spent considerable time in Australia lies in the expertise he had already acquired in the language of the Aborigines. In the month before he left England, an extremely knowledgeable article appeared in *The Queenslander* [46] and was then syndicated around the region. It is quoted in full so that you can see the level of detail and the range of research that Fawcett had conducted: he credits no-one else.

> *At the last monthly meeting of the newly formed Field Naturalists' Club of Townsville, some interesting notes were read by Mr. J.W. Fawcett, the president, on the numerals of the Australian aborigines: 'In the mental power of counting the Australian aborigine is deficient, having no comprehension of numerals. Many tribes have only two numerals, which by combination they are enabled to count to five. Several have three numerals, a few four, and*

an occasional one five. In general they can only count to four or five, after which the number is expressed by a word signifying many or a great number. It is very interesting to know that the equivalent for the word two is very much alike amongst the different aborigine tribes, and in some of the tribes there is a word for ten.

The numerals of the aboriginal tribe inhabiting the district around Mount Elliot, in our immediate vicinity, are woggin (one), boolray, (two), goodjoo (three), munwool (four), and murgai (five); and this is one of the few who do possess five numerals. The tribe inhabiting the Upper Herbert, about 120 miles to the north-west, possess only three numerals, yongul (one), yakkan (two), and karbor (three) ¡ numbers over and above these are expressed by the word taggin (much or many). The Moreton Bay tribe possess only two numerals, which by combination are increased to four. Ganar (one), burla (two), burla ganar (two-one = three), and burla burla (two – two = four; after which the numbers are expressed by the word koramba (much). The Purapper tribe, living near the River Murray, in South-east Australia, have only two numerals, by combination making four; kiarp (one), bullait (two), bullait kiarp (two-one = three), and bullait bulliat (two-two = four).

Three of the numerals of the Boraipar tribe of Western Australia, who possess three numerals, and by combination four, have a close affinity to those of the Burapper tribe:- Keiarpe (one), pulette (two), pulekvia (three), and pulette pulette (two-two = four). The tribe living near Adelaide have only three numerals,and by combination, four:- Kumande (one), pulaitye (two), marnkufeye (three), and pulaitye pulaitye (two-two = four) ; and one of the tribes of the now extinct Tasmanians had a distinct word for four, but none for three; marra va (one), I pualih (two), and wullyava (four.)

Whilst most of the New Guinea tribes can count to hundreds and thousands, some of the tribes inhabiting the islands of Torres Straits count no higher than two or three. The Machik on York Island have only three numerals, one of them being a combination: Urapun (one), kusa (two), and kusa urapun (two-one=three); and the Erub or Darnley Island tribe have only two numerals - netat (one) and neisa (two). As showing the sameness of some words, and the natural affinity between the dialects throughout the continent, the numeral two is represented by the following equivalents in various parts of Australia : Bollo win, bolita, boolray, budelar, bular, bulara, buled, bulicht, bulli, buloara, pollai, pualih, pular, pulette, &c. In the tribes possessing an equivalent for ten the word or words so used literally mean two hands. This is a remarkable parallel, which exists in many other languages or dialects in Melanesia, Malaysia, and Africa.

Two years later, in a small item on 'Native Art' which appeared in *The Queenslander* on 2 June 1894, he is cited as an expert on Australia's native people:

Rude drawings found in caves, on smooth rocks, and on trees in various parts of Australia show that the aboriginal inhabitants were not altogether without appreciation of the beauties of art. Though the drawings are of the roughest they are sufficient to place the authors far above the animals with which it is the custom to compare them. Art, such as it is, is even yet practised in some parts of North Queensland. The specimen we give on this page is a facsimile of a set of drawings found in a cave on the Upper Herbert River, and a copy of which was sent us by Mr. J. W. Fawcett. The figures are scratched with a bone or hard stick, and charcoal and ochre have been rubbed into the marks thus made. What the hieroglyphic design in the lower corner signifies is a mystery, but the others are easily identified as representations of the aboriginal conception of the human form, of a kangaroo, an opossum, a boomerang and shield, and a native wooden sword; all objects with which the artist would be familiar. There is merit in these drawings when it is considered that they are the work of savages of so low a type as the aborigines of Australia unquestionably are. [47]

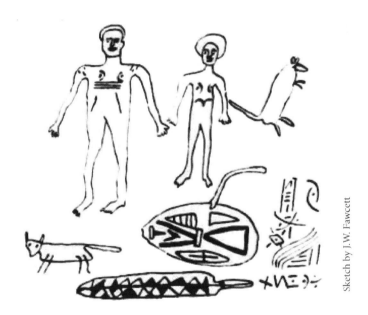

Sketch by J.W. Fawcett

Fig. 28   Aborigine Cave Drawings

FAWCETT IN PARADISE

Fawcett clearly loved Australia: he found freedom and wonder there which he expressed with unbridled passion in the first of his regular columns, 'The Naturalist in North Queensland by J.W. Fawcett, Townsville', which were syndicated from 1894. In his introductory article he wrote:

> *He who would study Nature well*
> *Must seek her in the forest dell,*
> *Where knowledge, unadorned by art,*
> *Pours forth the fullness of her heart,*
> *Imparts to man that "better part",*
> *And breathes on him a holy spell.*
> *Full of precious deeds and gifts,*
> *Thoughts and imaginings.*

> *The land of Australia is a paradise to the student and lover of Nature, for as one wanders in her vast wilds, a charm of strange and exhilarating novelty meets the view at almost every step. She possesses such a wealth of animal and vegetable life that every moment the attention, whether of the scientific scholar or of the casual observer, is attracted by fresh forms, each entirely different, it may be, from one another, and as curious or strange as they are variant.*

> *Having journeyed over a considerable portion of North Queensland, north and south, east and west, principally on foot, and being an ardent observer of Nature (and Nature in her untrammelled wildings is my delight), it has been mine to observe in many forms and attitudes and localities various of the customs and habits, characteristics and peculiarities, of the many denizens and members of Nature's vast family in this, part of the Australian island-continent.*

As the collection and publication of particulars of some of these observations may be interesting and instructive to fellow naturalists and students and worshippers in the one vast temple, I have been encouraged to gather my notes together and present them to public criticism. As the various objects of Nature in Australia are of promiscuous kinds, almost peculiar to the island-continent, and admit of different methods of arrangement, I have not in the following articles followed any system.

It is when I traverse the solitary wilds of the Australian "bush" - whether it be in the thick scrubs or dense jungles, if I may so call them, of the northern coastal rivers, on the vast rolling prairies of the west, amongst the gullies, gorges, or crevices of the coast ranges, or by the seashore, with the wide expanse of blue sky overhead, the burning sun kissing me with his torrid rays, or the breezy air buffeting or fanning me, that I feel borne in upon me that God is in Nature, and that through sympathy with Nature we approach closer to Him who is the Great Designer and Creator of all. [48]

This ecstatic contemplation of creation is uplifting, and it is rare to find such transports of delight expressed so movingly by a scientific Englishman of the period. It also gives us an insight into his faith: he is clearly what we would now call a pantheist.

Like many explorers, Fawcett travelled on foot or on horseback, and it seems from something shortly to be revealed that he was in the habit of sleeping in a tent of a particularly Australian kind: Aboriginals often slept in a 'humpy', which was a small temporary shelter built around a standing tree. We can imagine that this would enable Fawcett to travel light and blend in to his surroundings, the better to observe the birds and mammals of the bush.

Thanks to the *Police Gazette* of 1896, we know that Fawcett had a house on the southern outskirts of Townsville:

> *Stolen from an unoccupied house at Cluden, the property of J.W. Fawcett, a resident there, during the month of April last, 1 English pigskin saddle with the initials "J.W.F." inside flaps, 1 single-rein bridle with "J.W.F." on it, 1 Martini-Henry rifle and cartridge belt, 1 telescope with the object-glass broken across centre, 1 gold chronometer Rotherham watch with "Presented to J.W. Fawcett, 1892, by his fellow naturalists J.C. and J.F." inscribed inside back case; 1 gold band ring with two marks on each side; also 1 opossum-skin rug, ½ dozen cups and saucers, and ½-dozen table knives and forks with white handles: value £15.* [49]

Drawing in Public Domain

Fig. 29   Aborigine Humpy (Shelter)

His regular columns embraced a wide range of Australian fauna: the kangaroo, the dugong, exotic bird species like the Green Oriole and the Blood Bird, snakes, insects. For a complete list of these columns, see Appendix B.

The landscape and flora regularly evoked in him transports of delight:

> *Here's a bunch of April grasses,*
> *Lately plucked from off the plain,*
> *Where they grew with many fellows,*
> *All in browns, and greens, and yellows,*
> *Both in the sunshine and the rain,*
> *Moved by every breeze that passes.*

> *Prominent amongst the stars of earth are the beauteous nodding grasses which deck the mountains and the plains and clothe the hills and dales with a mantle of living green. Linnaeus, the great Swedish naturalist, once exclaimed, "Thank God for the green earth," and, with a heart full of that fellow-feeling which sympathises with those who love and appreciate Nature in her untrammelled wildings, I re-echo that sentiment, ay, with a thousand times a thousand thanks. Grasses are universal members of the great vegetable kingdom, and are as varied in size and colour as in form and species. Of the numerous members of the family the continent of Australia possesses an abundant share. Their forms and habits are as variable as the shades of their many hues, and a beautiful sight it is to see miles of flat country a few weeks after the wet season with its stretches of waving verdure, rolling in green and gold, like the billows of the ocean, beneath the light of a waning sun.*[50]

He soon had a fan club: in a letter to the editor of The Queenslander, 8 December 1894, Mr B.P. Chrichton of Herbert River wrote:

Sir - I have been greatly interested with the articles which are appearing in your paper by Mr. J. W. Fawcett, of Townsville, entitled "The Naturalist in North Queensland." They are simply unique in their way, and it is to be hoped that when they are concluded in your paper Mr. Fawcett will do all the Nature-loving readers and others who are interested in such a noble science a favour by having them printed in volume form. What say you, Mr. Editor? Are they not worthy of such? From what items of knowledge are therein presented it is evident that Mr. Fawcett is a born naturalist and a most careful observer, and judging from what has already appeared may be called the Gilbert White of North Queensland. My request that the articles be reprinted in book form is shared by many of my friends and others in this and the adjoining colonies, and may I be allowed to ask if the writer intends to do as I have wished?

The Editor appended a reply to this suggestion: 'We are not aware what is Mr. Fawcett's intention in this matter. Certainly the articles are well worthy of republication, and it is to be hoped in the interest of those who have been unable to read the whole of his interesting Naturalist papers that the author may be able to make arrangement for their appearance in volume form.—Ed.'

Woodcut by Thomas Bewick

Fig. 30   Kangaroo

This high profile continued into the first months of 1895, with articles on Entomology, Botany, and further 'Birds of Queensland': he was clearly particularly interested in raptors such as the White Breasted Eagle.

But then in May 1895 came shocking news. It appears in only few of the smaller papers - notably not *The Queenslander,* whose editors kept quiet on the sudden arrest of their esteemed nature correspondent!

Under the incredulous headline 'Missing Books – Extraordinary Charge', *The Telegraph* of Monday 20 May 1895 reported that, 'A man giving the name of J.W. Fawcett has been arrested at the Herbert River on a charge of stealing books from the Townsville School of Arts. Recently several books, which have been missing for years, were found in a humpy stated to belong to Fawcett and situated off the road leading to Stewart's Creek.'

A few days later, he appeared in court, and the sentence was shocking: 'J.W. Fawcett, a contributor to various newspapers on the subject of natural history was at Townsville sentenced to six months hard labor for the larceny from the School of Arts of books on natural history.' [51]

The nature of the extreme punishment meted out, for what could be considered a victimless crime, implied that there had to be more to it than a couple of library books: scrutiny of the *Police Gazette* provided the answer. The books in the humpy, which might have been discovered by any passer-by, were only the tip of the iceberg. They must have led to a search of the culprit's home and the subsequent discovery of an extensive library of stolen books: 'James William Fawcett has been arrested by Detective Grimshaw for the larceny of 120 books (recovered) from the School of Arts, Townsville. 15th July 1895.' [52]

Even worse, it wasn't his first offence. *The Police Gazette* for April of the previous year recorded the following: 'Stolen from the School of Arts, Stanley Street, Townsville, between 1888 and the 1st instant, the property of the School of Arts Trustees, 2 books by J. Gould on natural history, with "Townsville School of Arts Library" written on outside of covers: value, £15. Identifiable O. 1356. 27th August, 1894.' [53]

The news of Fawcett's disgrace was reported in several smaller papers such as *The Gympie Times* and *Mary River Mining Gazette*, *The Western Champion and General Advertiser for the Central Western Districts*. *The Queenslander* stayed silent on the matter: their correspondent clearly wasn't sufficiently disgraced to be banned from print: his column on 'The Eagle Family' went ahead two days after he was sentenced, and more of his *Ornithological Jottings* were printed at the end of June, by which time Fawcett will have been in Her Majesty's Penal Establishment Stewart's Creek, which at least had the benefit of being a relatively new prison, having been built only fourteen years earlier.

Fig. 31 Townsville Prison

If anyone reading this ever feels moved to visit the Queensland Archive, the prison records (which are delicate and have not been digitised) could prove fruitful for further research into the enigma that is our man Fawcett!

DISASTER HITS TOWNSVILLE

By the beginning of 1896, when Fawcett would have been just released, disaster struck Townsville. On 26 January, Cyclone Sigma hit the town. Nature caused terrible destruction and the newspapers turned to their natural historian to record the momentous event and explain how such a thing could happen. Fawcett was commissioned to produce an extensive and detailed eyewitness account of the disaster, and he produced a marvellous, vividly written, knowledgeable, compassionate record of the devastation wrought on the town and its inhabitants. Eighteen people lost their lives.

It was published by local bookseller and stationer R.H. Thomas in a small hardback book entitled *Narrative of the terrible cyclone and flood in Townsville, North Queensland, January 25th, 26th, 27th, 28th, 1896 compiled by J.W. Fawcett from personal observations, Townsville Daily Bulletin and Townsville Evening Star; with illustrated supplement from Blocks supplied by Northern Miner Newspaper Co.* Copies are extremely rare and fragile but the Queensland Archive was kind enough to send photographs of the pages. Here are some extracts to give you a flavour:

> *Saturday, Sunday, Monday and Tuesday, the 25th, 26th, 27th and 28th days of January 1896, will long remain, like memorable landmarks, on the minds of the residents of Townsville, as the period of the most terrific of all cyclones and floods which have occurred in this city. So strange are the powers that be in Australia, whilst the people of Southern Queensland, New South Wales and Victoria were suffering from the effects of a terrible heat wave which claimed many victims as its own, the inhabitants of Townsville, in North Queensland, and adjacent districts, were visited by a most terrific hurricane accompanied by an equally terrific rainstorm and flood.*

On the evening of Friday, January 24th, a telegram was received in Townsville from the officer in charge of the Meteorological Bureau at Brisbane as follows :-"Considerable indications of tropical disturbance named 'Sigma' to N.E. of Cardwell; please wire tonight, eight o'clock, any fall in barometer;" and the weather forecast for the 25th contained the intimation that "Sigma" was making southwards.

The warning was timely, but no human preparation could have avoided the dire effects which followed the violent disturbance of the forces of nature, nor ensured preservation from the appalling outcome of so terrible a cyclonic visitation.

...great trees, some four, five and six feet in circumference, and how old it is impossible to say, were either torn up by the roots or broken off close to the level of the ground...Strong men were blown down by the wind, and all who braved the weather had to manoeuvre adroitly in order to get along, and to pause frequently for breath. The drifting rain stung one's face like hail, and the noise of the atmospheric tumult was almost deafening. Sheets of iron torn from roofs flew before the wind high in the air or skimmed along the street or were tossed about like sheets of paper; and telegraph wires torn from insulators whipped wide areas until they became twisted and plaited around the poles. Along Flinders Street the wind stove in shop windows leaving valuable goods exposed, and in several *instances sheets of iron were driven through the plate-glass that had been left unprotected by shutters. So many houses were damaged, and the disturbance so unremitting in its attacks that few could have been buoyed up by the hope that theirs would be fortunate enough to escape. Momentary dread of being rendered homeless and exposed to the pitiless fury of the warring elements must have been almost universally felt, together with pity and sympathy for less fortunate neighbours and friends.*

Ross River overflowed its banks about midnight and flooded the whole of Cluden ... an expanse of country some three miles wide was one stretch of water, over which the waves of no ordinary size rolled, tossed and foamed, like the billows of an angry sea...The town was in a terrible state, being deprived of telegraphic communication, railway service, the water supply and the customary visits of the baker, butcher and milkman.

It is the most calamitous visitation that has ever befallen Townsville, and the general and widespread desolation which followed its visit was something enormous. To attempt to give details of the damage, destruction and loss effected by this most terrible calamity is an almost impossible feat, for every portion of the entire city, suburbs and district suffered, and almost every inhabitant was a sufferer, some way or another. The following particulars will give some faint idea of the extent, devastation and havoc committed by the storm fiend 'Sigma.'

He goes on to give a detailed description of the damage to each ward of the city, to the suburbs and the islands, then the harbour works, the multitude of wrecked vessels, the railway station and track, the telegraph.

Of the people - apart from one 'Pitiful Case of Mental Anxiety', about a mother separated from her infant for the duration of the worst day - he can barely bring himself to tell their stories:

> *It is impossible to chronicle the self-denying acts of the many who rendered assistance to the destitute, or of those who put off in boats on Sunday and Monday to convey to safer places those whose houses had already been demolished, or were in a state of insecurity, or those who made homeless neighbours welcome to such comforts as houses subject to the beating rain could afford.*

Most poignant of all is 'The Death Roll', giving the names of the eighteen dead and the manner in which they died:

> *Frank Rawley, a sailor on board the schooner Lavinia, was struck by a heavy sea and his head dashed against a pump, killing him instantly; Gertrude Viola Rowe, aged 10, and Mary Dora Rowe, aged 14, daughters of Charles and Mary Rowe; two female aborigines were drowned in attempting to swim over Ross River; Robert Baker, aged 60, and Jessie Baker, aged 56, husband and wife, who lived in a cottage opposite the North Star Hotel. Their cottage collapsed, and they drowned.*

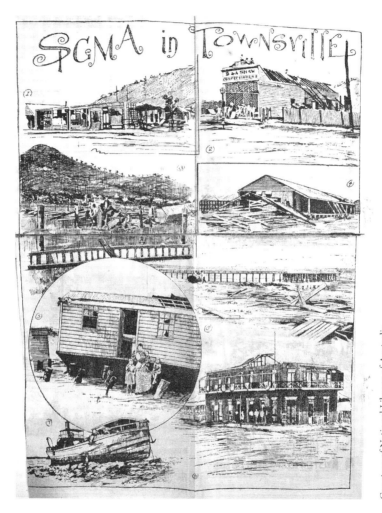

Fig 32   Sketches of Cyclone Damage

Fig, 33   Sketches of Cyclone Damage

Fig. 34   Sketches of Cyclone Damage

Fig. 35   Sketches of Cyclone Damage

Fawcett seems to have stayed in Australia for four more years, towards the end of which he appears to have lived in Brisbane. Whether he had any source of income other than his journalism cannot be ascertained. Certainly, given his prison record, it is extremely unlikely that he was a Chief Stipendiary Magistrate, as was later claimed. It is certain he was never MP for Kennedy, which is also part of the mythology surrounding him: there is a complete list of Queensland MPs dating back to 1860 and his name does not appear.

In addition to his work on the cyclone, he was compiling a collection of poetry: the *North Queensland Register* reported on 9 September that they had received 'a book of Australian verse edited by J.W. Fawcett of Townsville', which was later to be published locally by D.W. Hastings & Co as *Songs and Recitations of the Australian Bush.*

It seems that he carried on travelling, researching and writing on nature. At the Royal Society of Queensland's monthly meeting in March 1898, the honorary secretary read 'Notes on the nests and eggs of some Queensland birds of prey, by J.W. Fawcett, which gave the results of the writer's observations on the subject made whilst travelling from Cape York to the Tweeds Heads, and from the eastern coast-line to the South Australian border.' [54] Later that month, he was nominated for membership

FAWCETT THE CONSERVATIONIST

Fawcett had established his belief in conservation years before, when he contributed to the Vale of Derwent Naturalists' *Notes on the History, Geology and Botany of the Vale of Derwent* in 1891. The Society had made a point of exhorting their members to:

> *discourage the practice of removing rare plants from the localities of which they are characteristic, and of risking the extermination of rare birds and other animals by wanton persecution … use their influence with landowners and others for the protection of the characteristic birds of the country, and to dispel the prejudices which are leading to their destruction; and that consequently the rarer botanical specimens collected at the field meetings be chiefly such as can be gathered without disturbing the roots of the plants, and that notes on the habits of birds be accumulated instead of specimens, by which our closet collections would be enriched only at the expense of nature's great museum out of doors.* [55]

Ten years after his 'Dendrological Notes on North West Durham', and on the other side of the world, the *Warwick Examiner and Times* published Fawcett's article on 'Giant Trees' and the following year another paper published in two parts an article Fawcett had originally written for the *Queensland Agricultural Journal* on 'The Uses of Forests: a plea for forest conservancy.' [56] In it, Fawcett writes an impassioned and well-informed argument for the conservation and enlightened management of trees, citing the evidence of climate change that their destruction brings. It is as persuasive now as it was then.

A question of great importance, one which is growing in importance daily, and yet one of which very few individuals ever dream or think, is that of the conservation of our native forests, the protection of our valuable native-timbers, and the provision of supplies for the future. Man is a destructive being, and his destroying power is perhaps nowhere so well shown as in the wholesale cutting down of large tracts of timber in various parts of the world. Thinking only of himself and his present wants, and reckless of all consequences, the timber has been, and is being, wantonly and wilfully destroyed. It is sad, very sad, to think what mischief and what desolation has been wrought in the fairest countries of the world by the reckless, wanton, wilful, destruction of forests.

Persia, the whole Indus valley, the valley of the Euphrates, Palestine, and, above all, Lesser Asia, have each of them suffered grievously from this waste. Lesser Asia, which the ancient Greeks looked upon as the garden of the world, is now subject to droughts like that which not so very long ago spread death throughout whole provinces. It is the same everywhere: in Europe, Asia, Africa, America, and Australia. In many countries the evil effects of this clearing of extensive tracts of timber has been followed with direful results, and strenuous efforts have been, and are being, made to try and remedy the serious consequences of such wanton folly. France, India, and the United States, amongst other countries, all have made extensive forest clearings on the spur of the moment, and without the least thought of what might follow.

Let me tell you something of the use of forests in their effect on climates. Forests have a four-fold effect on climate and rainfall, as follows:

Firstly.   There is the chemical action of their leaves which decompose the carbonic acid of the air, fixing the carbon in their woody tissue, and liberating the oxygen.

Secondly.   There is their physical action in hindering evaporation and stopping currents of air, and in covering the ground with a vegetable mould which holds water like a sponge.

Thirdly.   There is the organic action of the leaves, which, in breathing, restore to the air a part of the water which the roots have drained from the soil.

Fourthly, and lastly.   There is the mechanical action of the roots, which at once prevent the earth from being washed away by rain, and also enable the water to filter down deep into the ground.

From these four actions we can see that forests ought to make a country cooler, by withdrawing the carbon from the air; for the heat that is set free when wood or timber is burned is the very heat that was being absorbed while the tree was growing. A forest may thus be looked upon as one vast condensing apparatus for storing up the heat of the atmosphere. This is what theory says and experiment confirms it.

What I advocate is forest conservancy, whereby the following different matters should be attended to :

The wanton wilful destruction of our useful timber trees should be stopped.

That a system should be adopted by which only certain trees should be cut down, and that this should only include such as are of no value commercially.

That noxious trees should be cut down and replaced by valuable species.

The planting of indigenous timber trees on our timber reserves and waste lands.

The introduction and planting in forests or plantations of valuable timber trees of other lands which will thrive in this colony.

That laws be promulgated setting out the sizes over which certain timber trees now becoming scarce should only be cut, and that such laws be strictly carried out.

To these others could be added.

The wanton destruction of our valuable native timbers, in many instances the wholesale and unnecessary wiping out of certain species in certain districts, is a grievous shame and . disgrace to each individual Queenslander as well as to the colony. Not only is it a useless, but a wicked, waste to denude this fair land of ours of the trees which are (though looked upon by most people as useless encumbrances) placed here by a greater and far-seeing Power than is given to such poor mortals as we are to understand. Trees are living things, working for the good of the common weal, and if we recklessly destroy them we lessen the sum of national life, and therefore the amount of national power.

It is easy to make a place treeless, but oh! so hard and difficult to re-clothe it. Let us, then, as a people be not so wasteful with our forest wealth; it will not last for ever. It was here when we came as interlopers into this country, and we have had, and are having, the use of it. But it will have an end. Our children and their children require it, and how can we hand it on as a legacy if we do not plant and strive to keep up the supply, equal to the demand. Forests did not grow in a year; but trees, once they start, grow till they die. The great question now is: "Will the supply of timber here at present last until a new supply (planted now) is ready to take its place?" I think not. I trust that our legislators will look at once to the formation of a Forestry board and the establishment of forest conservancy, and let each one who has land not forget the old Scotch motto: "Be yo aye sticking in a tree, Jock; it'll aye be growing when ye're sleeping."

Fig. 36   Great American Chestnuts

Photograph in Public Domain

He also continued to write about history, particularly of religious institutions: in 1897, The *Launceston Examiner* published 'A History of Wesleyanism in Tasmania by J.W. Fawcett of Brisbane.' And in 1898 a Brisbane company published a book called *A Brief Life of the Rev. John Cross, forty years a chaplain in the Colony of New South Wales.*

In the Australian *Town and Country Journal* of 29 January 1898, writing on 'The Last Resting Place of Governor Phillip,' he mentions that he was in England between 1889 and 1891, during which time he wrote several articles on the Governors of New South Wales: it was amongst these items that he wrote about Robert Towns.

On the subject of Governor Phillip, the following week a letter appeared in the *Sydney Morning Herald* which gladdens the heart of all who are fond of this remarkable, if flawed man. We shall leave it as the epitaph on his years in Australia. In it, he is described as 'one of the best-informed gentlemen of the history of our continent, and especially of its early days – a gentleman whose very heart and soul have been set to study the early days of these colonies.' [57]

HOME TO HIS CALF-YARD

Every man and woman who claims to be a patriotic Britisher should take some interest in the history not only of their native country but of their native county, and not only of their native county but of their native town, village, hamlet or parish. To many there is no place on earth so dear as one's calf-yard – one's birthplace. [58]

Fawcett's father passed away in April 1900: whether that was the reason for his return to England, we do not know, but on the first day of the following year, 1 January 1901, he founded the Durham Historical Society. When the next census took place, on 31 March 1901, he was at Satley Grange with his mother, who was fifty-six. The only other person in the house was his sister Catherine, who would marry and leave home six years later.

You will remember that when he had left England ten years previously, there was a slight shadow over his status as a naturalist. Having established such a strong reputation in Australia in the intervening years, it was strange to find that in 1901, he won The Hancock Prize. [59] This had been set up by Canon Tristram five years before in memory of John Hancock (1808-1890). It was a naturalist essay competition intended 'primarily and essentially for the benefit of those whose opportunity had been ... restricted and who, working to some extent in the dark, needed the encouragement of a helping hand.' Unfortunately, there is no record of the subject of Fawcett's winning essay or whether he chose for his prize a medal, books or 'instruments suitable for the pursuit of [his] subject,' but the fact that he won seems to indicate that he was regarded as being in need of encouragement or assistance.

The early years of the twentieth century saw Fawcett concentrating on local history. During this period, he wrote pieces for local newspapers which he then compiled into books: *Historic Places in the Derwent Valley* (1901), *Tales of Derwentdale* and *Annals of the City of Durham* (1902), *A Brief History of the Township of Chopwell* (1907), *A History of the Parish of Dipton* (1911) . He published these books himself, sometimes having received contributions from subscribers to fund the printing, which he often had done at the Advertiser offices in Saddler Street, Durham. On Page 105 you can see the list of subscribers who enabled the publication of *Tales of Derwentdale*.

He transcribed and published the records of churches, starting with *Blanchland Church with List of Incumbents* (1904); *Durham Churches, Descriptive and Historical with Lists of Incumbents* (1904); and *The Church of St John the Baptist, Newcastle upon Tyne* (1909) notable for the fact that this was the first time he had claimed any qualifications: 'B.A., LL.B.' Where, how and when he had acquired a degree in Law is another mystery that might never be solved.

Then he moved on to meticulous records not only of the church buildings, memorials and ministers, but also who had been baptized, married and buried there: *The Parish Registers of Muggleswick containing Baptisms, Marriages and Burials from 1784 to 1812, transcribed, annotated and indexed by J.W. Fawcett* (1906). When he did the same for Lanchester in 1909 the records he transcribed went all the way back to 1560!

Finally, in 1911, he turned his attention to the church that was closest to his heart.

ST. CUTHBERT'S CHURCH, SATLEY

In 1908, the Secretary of the Durham Historical Society was forty-one years old and living with his mother at Satley Grange. She had not long to live and war was coming. It was time to set the record straight and record his life for posterity: he would write the definitive history of his own church, and in doing so he would ensure that the future heard about the desecration that had been done. He would record his own life and those of his forebears; he would also set down the truth as he wished it to be known.

It took six years to write and compile *The Parish Registers of St Cuthbert's Church, Satley: containing the Baptisms, Marriages and Burials from 1560 to 1812, Gravestone Inscriptions, Local Pedigrees &c. Transcribed, Annotated and Indexed by J.W.Fawcett, B.A., LL.B.*

Fig. 37   St. Cuthbert's Church, Satley

Photograph in by Robert Graham

By the time it was published, just before the outbreak of war in 1914, his mother had joined her husband in the grave in Satley churchyard. Only 150 copies of the work were printed, 'of which nearly one-half go abroad to Canada, the United States, South Africa and Australia.'

The parochial records had of course been destroyed by De Pledge in an effort to cover up his financial shenanigans. In writing the book between 1911 and 1914, Fawcett was able to draw on 'a transcript of 1797-1812 which had been made by the Rev. John Hodgson in or about 1812.' As well as recording the history of the church and as many of the names of the people of Satley, the names of sub-curates and chapel wardens were 'rescued from oblivion.'

He worked in London and Durham as well as in his home, and in his introductory notes he wrote: 'The best part of this prefatorial notice is to express our grateful thanks to the many kind friends who have gladly and willingly tendered assistance, in one way or another, towards making the work as full as it is, and we would especially mention the kindness of the Hon. Sidney Hobart (London), and his talented sister, the Hon. Lady Pearl Ruby Dacre Hobart, whose unstinted assistance as amanuensis for a while in London, &c., is gratefully remembered.' [60]

He also extends his thanks to 'Miss M. Heaviside of Consett,' for acting as his 'present amanuensis.' That's all she gets, so in view of the fact that she was shortly to become his wife, we have to wonder about the rather more heartfelt tribute he pays to his other assistant, a forty-year old schoolteacher who lived on a Satley farm with her father: 'Particular thanks to Miss S. Walker (Satley) to whose assiduity, constancy, and fidelity, as our amanuensis, when stricken with illness at the beginning of 1912, we owe more in the way of literary assistance than pen can tell.'

The bare facts about De Pledge's incumbency are dutifully presented in the chronological list of church official: 'Joseph Price De Pledge, M.A., of Durham University, presented by Dr Maltyby, Bishop of Durham; instituted 15th November, 1867; died at Satley, 9th February, 1891, aged 64 years; buried at Satley; headstone there; also memorial window.'

In his carefully objective recording of the facts, it must have stuck in Fawcett's craw to dutifully describe without comment all the memorials to De Pledge: not only the plaque recording the church "restoration" which included his own dear father's name, but 'a memorial window was placed in the church in memory of the Rev. J. P. De Pledge, Vicar from 1867 to 1891, at a cost of £40 raised by public subscription; and a new set of three communion vessels costing £21 was also purchased as another memorial.' Later, after the death of the vicar's widow, a brass plaque was affixed to an oak screen 'by their eleven sorrowing children.'

In an interesting aside and another unexplained link between Fawcett, Egypt and Australia, it is curious that in 1908 the Right Rev. N. Temple Hamlyn, Bishop of the Gold Coast, a city in Queensland, preached in Satley Church on behalf of the Gold Coast Mission, and unveiled and dedicated the marble wall tablet commemorating the Egypt and Sudan veteran, Henry de Pledge of the 15th Hussars.

In detailing all the Satley scions of the Fawcett family, the author recorded his own life in these words:

> *Fawcett, James William, eldest son of William (d.1900) and Margaret Sarah Fawcett (d.1912); was born at Wooley Close Farm, Brancepeth, 14th April, 1867; baptized in St.Cuthbert's Church, Satley, 4th August, 1867; was in the Imperial Service (Intelligence Department), and a resident at Gibraltar, Malta, Italy (Naples and Rome), Egypt, (from Alexandria to Khartoum), Aden, Ceylon, Java, Australia, and China, between 1886 and 1899; B.Sc, D.Sc, B.A. (bis), M.A. (tris), LL.B., Ph.D., &c. Resident of Satley; Freeholder of Satley since 1900, and of Corbridge since 1912; Author or Editor of a large number of works on Biography, Ethnology, Genealogy, History, Natural History, &c. (including the present work).*

We learn more about him from what he chooses to include in his writings about other Satley residents. It was the teacher who stayed for the briefest tenure in Fawcett's young life that he was to memorialise in emotional terms in the book:

> *Thomas Graham, who had left Satley on 29th March, 1877 to work at Falloden Church of England School, Northumberland until his retirement in June 1899, whereupon he retired to Heaton, Newcastle upon Tyne and died suddenly at 16, Roxburgh Place, on 23rd December 1908 aged 69 years, being buried in Heaton cemetery.*

What is clear from the rather emotional eulogy that follows is not why this teacher in particular held such a special place in the writer's heart, but that in writing about the old man, Fawcett has another, rather more self-serving purpose ….

The Editor of this work would like to pay a tribute of respect to the departed worth of this one of his old schoolmasters. It was under him that, when only ten years of age, he won the first, and, up to date, the only (Queen's) Scholarship ever won by a scholar at Satley National School, and laid the foundation of a knowledge which enabled him nine years later to head the list of over 2000 competitors, in open competitions, for a position in the Imperial Service. Since then he has added academical honour to academical honour, and before he was 30 years of age had become the possessor of not less than seven degrees, all with one exception granted in honora causa, by English, Colonial and Foreign Universities or Colleges, which include B.Sc, B.A. (bis), and LL.B.; M.A. (tris), D.Sc., and Ph.D. Ever ready to give honour where honour is due, and to acknowledge his indebtedness to those who have helped him along the road of learning, one of his first visits, after his return from the colonies a few years ago, was to his old schoolmaster, who had helped him to plant his foot on one of the rungs of the ladder, and to lay down at the old man's feet the honours he had won. The joyous twinkle in the tear-berimmed eyes of the old master, and the heartfelt grip of his hand told of greater thanks than words could express. When the old master was laid to rest – "till the day dawns, and the shadows flee away," – in Heaton cemetery on 24th December, 1908, there was no more sorrowing pupil among the many old scholars who had assembled from various parts to pay their last tribute of respect to the teacher each one owed more or less, than the old scholar from Satley. [61]

It is easy to assume that because Fawcett's writing was so prodigious in this pre-war period, between his return home in 1900 and the outbreak of war in 1914, that he was in England the whole time. It's already been noted that apart from the nights when a census was taken or he is on record as having attended a meeting, we cannot know for sure where he was.

The connection with Lord Kitchener has always been the most mysterious aspect of Fawcett's life and no concrete evidence has yet come to light for his having served as an aide-de-camp for the great general. There is, however, one piece of circumstantial evidence, and it centres on Java. Kitchener biographer Trevor Royle explains that Kitchener's tour of Australasia and the Far East in 1909 was at the invitation of the governments of Japan, Australia and New Zealand, who wanted him to inspect their home defences.

Photograph in Public Domain

Fig. 38   Lord Kitchener

On Tuesday 28 December 1909, Lord Kitchener arrived at Port Darwin in northern Australia aboard the Dutch Steamer *Van Outhoorn* to commence a tour of Australia during which he examined the defensive capabilities of the harbours. In the newspaper report - which you can read in full at Note [62] - we learn that he had travelled there from Java:

> *Interviewed by a press representative, Captain Fitzgerald, A.D.C., stated that Lord Kitchener arrived at Singapore after his visit to Japan in the steamer Assaye, and stayed there only one day, joining De Carpentiere at Singapore. They voyaged to Batavia, where they landed, and were the guests of the Commander-in-Chief of the Dutch forces in the East. After spending one day in Batavia, Lord Kitchener proceeded to Buitenzorg, where the Governor-General was residing, and there he was welcomed and entertained by the Governor-General. Leaving Buitenzorg, but still the guest of the Governor-General, he was taken by rail and motor to all the most famous beauty spots in Java, and finally, after six days in Java, joined the Van Outhoora for Port Darwin on the 11th inst. The stay in Java was thoroughly enjoyed by Lord Kitchener.*

Postcard in Public Domain

Fig. 39   Buitenzorg Palace, Java

Almost twenty years later, on 18 March 1927, Fawcett wrote a piece called *Javanese Memories: Buitenzorg* for the *Consett Guardian*:

> *Forty odd miles to the south-west of Batavia lies the town of Buitenzorg, where is the country residence of the Governor-General of the Dutch East Indies, and also many of the more opulent petty Javanese rajahs and business merchants. The road between the two places is a good macadamised one, bordered by a fine avenue of tropical trees for part of the way. By the side of the main road runs a narrower one. The former is for vehicular traffic - open carriages each drawn by a couple of diminutive but spanking Junior ponies – not much larger than big dogs, driven by Malay coachmen who wore large inverted punchbowl hats during the day when the sun is hot, and European headgear at night-time; two-wheeled carts which excellently well-arranged light wicker tilts, or covers (wherein sat the passengers), drawn by small but docile oxen, or bullocks, having fine limbs and fetlocks and small hoofs. The side-tracks, or footways, are for foot passengers. "En route" you passed dozens of pretty wooden cottages with overhanging roofs, the homes of Malays, and surrounded by sufficient cultivation to satisfy all the owner's wants. On the eminences and rising grounds are many fine country residences belonging to the better class residents of Batavia. The low-lying patches, and the swampy lands form extensive rice fields irrigated by a most carefully and ingeniously managed water carriage. Here and there at regular intervals are good rest houses or accommodation houses for travellers – hotel-like buildings with bedrooms and refreshment rooms for travelers and stabling for horses. One which we called at had accommodation for 40 horses.*

> *The country travelled over is undulating and very picturesque, and the air from the mountains, which lie on the right, was very bracing. Many rapid streams are*

crossed by substantial bridges, most of them carefully roofed in. Here and there groves of cocoanut (sic)trees stud the landscape, and with the wooden cottages nestling in their own wooded groves, and the tree-clad mountains, chequered with the most marked effects of light and shade, make the whole journey one of beauty and pleasure.

About three miles from Buitenzorg you arrive at a tall white obelisk, and then you entered a magnificent avenue of umbrageous trees, through the luxuriant foliage of which the soft air soughed gently. At the end of the avenue lies the stately country palace of the Governor-General of Netherlands India. A short distance beyond it is the town itself – the country retreat of the richer people of Batavia. The place is a collection of houses erected in every style of architecture, and peopled with human beings of every colour of the human race, dressed in the various colours of the rainbow, and their component parts.

The palace of the Governor is a spacious building with capacious wings, fine Ionic colonnades and imposing terraces. One day I was the guest of His Excellency, who after hospitably entertaining me, was kind enough to personally show me over the house and grounds. It occupies the site of an old castle which was founded in 1744, enlarged in 1809, restored in 1819, and damaged by an earthquake in 1834. The principal buildings of the town were a new church which served for both Protestant and Roman Catholic services, a Mohammedan mosque, barracks, and a prison, a regent's mansion, and a bathing establishment. The palace stands 830 feet above the level of the sea and has a most salubrious climate. The place is connected with Batavia by a railway, opened in 1872, but we preferred travelling hither and thither by road on account of the magnificent scenery passed through.

In the neighbourhood of Buitenzorg is a sacred wood called Batton-Toulis-Cocabaton – which is held in high veneration by the Javanese. Near here, too, are some ruined Hindu remains. They are in two groups, a few paces apart, and both covered over by roofs, and railed in. One consists of three upright blocks of stone, two of which seem to be markless, but the other bears a cross-legged figure rudely carved in relief. The other group consists of a stone slab set up perpendicularly and bearing a sharply and long legible inscription in Sanscrit – the sacred language of the Hindoos. Unfortunately, it has been much injured, either by violence, time, or the weather. Nearby was another stone slab lying flat, on which were said to be, and what really resembled, two human footprints, which the superstitious natives believed were those of some god whose name I forget.

NO LONGER A CONFIRMED BACHELOR

In 1916, at the age of fifty, Fawcett married. We cannot know why he chose to do this at this point in his life: it might have been because after the death of his mother, Satley Grange had to be sold and the proceeds split between the children; it may simply have suited Mary Jane as well as him. His bride was forty-seven, and they will have known each other since school, as her father William was one of Fawcett's teachers at Satley. At the point when she was acting as one of his amanuenses for the Satley Registers, Mary Jane Heaviside was listed in the 1911 census as a 'fancy draper and confectioner at 9, Harvey Street Consett'. The year after their marriage, they were living at 57, Constance Street [63], and in 1920 they moved to Templetown House. [64]

What is not known is at which point they separated. By 1930, Fawcett was living alone in Holly Cottage, back in Satley. [65] It is not clear whether he actually owned the house. One story has it that the cottage's owner had gone missing in the Argentine and Fawcett's occupation was initially only a temporary measure. In an interview with the *Daily Herald* in October 1938, he claimed not to be sleeping there, possibly to avoid paying rates. The article, by 'Our Special Correspondent' was published under the headline 'Kitchener's Assistant Forgotten.' Whoever told the journalist Fawcett's age was five years out.

> *Seventy-six-year-old James William Fawcett – brilliant antiquarian, author, holder of 13 honorary degrees, and a man who knows 33 languages – is today trying to eke out his old-age pension with historical research work which brings him in just enough for mere existence.*
>
> *In his stone cottage at Saltley (sic) he is transcribing old British university charters for a northern antiquarian society, wondering when fortune will smile again.*

When he was 18 Fawcett was chosen from 2,000 candidates for the post of Army Interpreter. He travelled the world, was shipwrecked in the Mediterranean, the Indian Ocean and the Red Sea. Later he became aide-de-camp to the late Lord Kitchener.

No Army Pension

In New South Wales, Australia, he studied law and became stipendiary magistrate for Kennedy and represented the town in the Legislative Assembly.

But in spite of his colourful career, Fawcett has been forgotten by the world. He does not grumble, except to say with gentle emphasis that the Army has treated him "rather shabbily."

"I was looking forward to an Army pension," he told me today. "I have never received one. I don't know why. If only Lord Kitchener had been alive my circumstances might have been different. Now I manage as best I can on the old-age pension. I work here and sleep at the home of a friend in Headley Hill."

Fig. 40   Holly Cottage, Satley

ALTER EGOS

Because he is recorded on every census between 1900 and his death in 1942, we might assume that he stayed home, but as has been pointed out previously, he could well have accompanied Lord Kitchener on his visit to Java in 1909. He might have continued to travel throughout his life: intriguingly, a J.W. Fawcett is recorded arriving in Townsville by ship on 28 September 1931.[66]

A number of observers have wondered whether our J.W. Fawcett was also the architect who won a competition to design Flinders Street Station in Melbourne in 1899. Our man was apparently still in Australia at that time, and because he was a polymath and particularly elusive, it did not seem beyond the bounds of possibility that he could also design a building. However, a determined search of the Australian newspapers scotched that myth: the Melbourne Herald of 5 September 1934 reported the death of the retired chief architect of Victorian Railways at his home in Camberwell, Melbourne after a long illness. He was a prominent member of the Masonic Lodge and was survived by a wife and daughter. The synchronicity of the two men's lives is clear: this man had been born in England just four years before our Fawcett, and he'd arrived in Australia in 1887, around the time that our man's whereabouts are uncertain. But the obituary confirms that he'd been admitted as an associate member of the Royal Victorian Institute of Architects ten years before he won the competition with his partner H.P.C. Ashworth.

Another intriguing possibility that might merit further investigation is a certain William L'Estrange Fawcett, who, as an acting Clerk of Petty Sessions (CPS) was effectively assistant registrar of births, deaths and marriages at several different regional locations in New

South Wales in the early 1890s. One position in the Registrar General's Office in Sydney can be seen in the New South Wales Government Gazette of 4 May 1893, when a man by that name was appointed to 'the District of The Macleay, at Bellingen, from the 15th April ultimo, vice Mr F.B. Treatt, absent on leave.' [67]

In a co-incidence that makes this man even more intriguing, William L'Estrange Fawcett had enlisted for Sudan on Friday 20 Feb 1885 in Sydney. Three days later, as a private in the 4th regiment, his name is in the list of volunteers boarding the ship to Egypt. [68] Small world.

Another J.W. Fawcett, a civil engineer of St Kilda near Melbourne, is likely to be the passenger recorded as having passed through Albury on an express train heading for Melbourne on Saturday 25 February 1888. On 5 July 1888, a J.W. Fawcett arrived from Hong Kong on the 1406-ton vessel Catterburn captained by J.W.B Darke, travelling 'to Melbourne via Port Darwin.' As far as we know, our man never went to Melbourne, but who can tell?

And so it goes on: *The South Australian Register* of 1 June 1893 records that someone under that name submitted an application to register a patent for an improved means of regulating rays of light passing through photographic lenses; *The Mercury Hobart of Tasmania* on 15 March 1906 lists a J.W. Fawcett having been installed as a Freemason at Zechan Lodge; and *The Sydney Morning Herald* of 3 July 1915 tells us that someone named J.W. Fawcett appeared before the registrar, Mr F.H. Salisbury, to have a creditor's petition read against him: it was dismissed without costs.

There are certain newspaper items where we can be much more confident that the J.W. Fawcett is the hero of our tale. On 25 January 1917, the *Australian Worker* published an enigmatic and poignant short piece entitled The Old Garden. [69]

"It is a lovely old garden," they said.

"It is a shame to spoil it."

But business marches like other plagues, and so they set about wrecking the tiny paradise of blossoms.

Rose and lilac, hollyhock and phlox, sweet pea and bachelor button; all fell before the vicious spade.

The soft velvet of the lawn was swept away, and at last the plough was brought in to complete the havoc.

The cold, bright steel of the share sank greedily into the long-untouched loam, and tore from its sacred rest the skeleton of a little child.

"It was a lovely old garden," they said.

NEWCASTLE SOCIETY OF ANTIQUARIES

The 'northern antiquarian society' of which the *Daily Herald* reporter spoke did indeed receive innumerable papers from Fawcett between 1917 and 1942. They are listed and sometimes transcribed in the bound copies of *The Proceedings of the Society of Antiquaries of Newcastle-upon-Tyne*. From the first, 'Notes on the Chantry Chapel and Cantarists of Alnwick Castle, 1362-1548', to the last to be read in his lifetime, 'The place name Satley, and some coin finds there,' which was read on 27 August 1941, they are all on the kind of learned subjects we have come to expect. You can read a complete list in Appendix D.

Fig. 41   Seal of Society of Antiquaries

There are a few surprising items, such as 'Sheepmarking on the Fells', in which he not only entertains his learned colleagues with the details of the practice, but also ensures that his own grandfathers are preserved forever in the annals of the esteemed Society: he still has the branding irons belonging to them both– James Fawcett of South Shields (originally South Broomshields), Satley, 1824-1861, and Wooley Close, Brancepeth, 1860-1875 (died 10 September 1879, age 83); and James Charlton of the Grange Houses and Bavington Mount, Stamfordham (died 2 September 1864, age 50) [70]

It is from these Proceedings that we can glean more snippets about his life:

> *The following is a list of deeds, documents, wills, etc., connected with people and places in Northumberland and Newcastle-upon-Tyne, which were in my possession*

in, and previous to, 1886. In that year I left England for Australia and sold them to a gentleman interested in the history of the above counties. He, as I learnt afterwards, disposed of them. In 1889, 1890 and 1891, and occasional subsequent years, 1899, 1900, etc, in searching the collection of documents, deeds etc in the Public Record Office, London, for historical records connected with the north of England, I made a calendar of the deeds relating to Northumberland and Durham, which I came across. As this was before the days of printed descriptive catalogues, the work was not so easy as it is now. As the publication of this calendar of Northumbrian deeds may be of interest to fellow antiquaries, I have pleasure in passing the same on to others... some are now in the possession of the public library of Newcastle-upon-Tyne. [71]

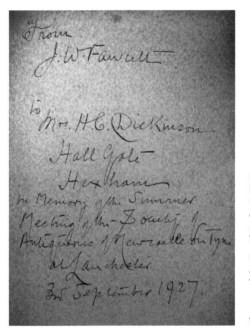

Photograph by David Butler DCRO

Fig. 42 Note from IWF to Society of Antiquaries

A PRODUCTIVE OLD AGE

Fawcett remained busy researching, writing and giving talks until the end of his life. (Appendix C provides a list of his English publications.) His articles for the local newspapers, particularly the *Durham Advertiser* and the *Consett Guardian* in the 1920s and 1930s were particularly wide-ranging, prolific and popular. Sometimes this journalism was published as 'Copyright' so that he could sell them elsewhere. It was a widespread practice at the time for regular newspaper columns to be published under cryptic pseudonyms: *Annfield Plain Notes* were written by 'Lintley'; *Burnopfield Notes* by 'Stand-Easy' and *Dipton Notes* by 'Scrutator.' Fawcett wrote under his own name, but also under pseudonyms. He is certainly 'A Lover of Nature' and 'Rambler', and it is possible he was also 'Nomad.' Given his interests, he probably wrote 'Queer Place Names' but probably not 'The Allurement of Alliteration'!

For a new generation, he recycled articles and stories which he'd published decades previously, including *Tales of Derwentdale*. As a postscript to his retelling of the Blanchland Bells on 5 February 1926, he wrote a sweet note to his readers: 'I sincerely thank the many correspondents who have written lately in connection with these "Derwent Stories" and am pleased to know how much they are appreciated. The questions some of these readers ask will be dealt with in due course, and any additions our readers can give will be gladly welcomed. It's the little bit you know, and the little bit I know, and the little bit someone else knows which makes the story.'

But on 19 March, his postscript to another tale was of an entirely different nature: 'NOTE – It has come to my knowledge, from various sources, that certain unscrupulous persons are circulating reports that they are the writers of these "Stories," some of which they have copied and sent to other papers as their original contributions. It would be better for the latter if they stated that they were taken from the "Consett Guardian." If they are called on to produce the original documents, they might find themselves in "Queer Street." – J.W.F.

FAITHFUL FRIENDS

Harry Dent of Partridge Close was a great friend of James Fawcett, and on some of his visits in the 1930s, he used to take along his young nephew Ray, a bright lad who loved to listen to the two men talking. None of them could have suspected that that little fellow was to play a pivotal role in securing the legacy of the great man.

Ray Thompson remembers those visits well: 'They were good friends and shared an interest in local historical and archaeological matters. I used to be fascinated because the whole house was packed with books; there was nowhere to sit because all the chairs were stacked with them. Nevertheless, I remember him as a kind and dignified old gentleman who always made time to have a joke with a little boy. If he and my uncle were gabbling on and he could see I was getting bored, he'd go out the back and return with a handful of raspberries.'

There were piles of books everywhere and the staircase was narrowed by the boxes of index cards on each side of every step: twenty-six boxes in all, one for each letter of the alphabet. Many years later, Beamish curator John Gall spent time with Harry Dent, after which he wrote about the 'vast card index Fawcett had worked on over his long life… and for which he had cut up anything to hand: proofs of his books, church bazaar receipts, bills etc.' The cards, one of which John still has pasted into his commonplace book, revealed the tremendous detail of Fawcett's work. [72]

Other locals remember the kindly old gentleman who was so generous with the produce of his garden: Nora Dent also recalls how he used to give the local children fruit. James Fawcett had grown up in the timeless village and had been at school with many of their grandparents. Tom Gibson's maternal grandfather, Tom Rippon, had been a schoolmate of Fawcett's. 'He had been far ahead of my grandfather because he was so clever.'

Photograph by Val Scully, courtesy of John Gall

Fig. 43 One of Fawcett's Index Cards

Now, after a lifetime of travel and adventure, 'Major' Fawcett was a well-known, striking figure, striding about in his cape-like black trench coat and trilby hat. Every Saturday he'd walk to Consett to do his shopping, even in his seventies, returning with his walking stick over his shoulder and the carrier bag swinging from the end. When he became more frail, his friends Harry Dent and Harry Raine took him out and about on a motorbike and sidecar.

No hermit, he still gave talks, produced learned articles for the Society of Antiquaries, and continued his prolific work on genealogy, gaining a reputation as a source of information on family history, particularly for people living in other countries.

Photograph courtesy of Ray Thompson

Fig. 44   J W Fawcett with his niece, c1940

POOR JACK

We gain some insights into Fawcett's life at this time, as well as his kindness, from a piece he wrote about the life of poor abandoned Jack Bulman, whom you may remember from the start of this piece. In early April 1932, shortly after Bulman passed away in the workhouse after a life 'on the road', his old friend wrote:

> *There died in the Poor Law Institution at Lanchester at Eastertide, three months after attaining his eighty-fifth birthday, John (or Jack) Bulman (alias Johnnie or Jackie Bulman) , one of the best-known characters of North-West Durham (Consett, Knitsley, Lanchester, Butsfield and Satley districts chiefly) a "wander kind" of the last seventy years or more.*
>
> *He belonged to one of the best-known and most respectable families of the mid-Derwent Valley. His grandfather was a well-known agriculturalist of his day, for many years farm bailiff to Robert Smith Surtees Esq., the sporting novelist of Hamsterley Hall, and, if the writer mistakes not, forms the subject of one of the characters in one of those novels. Jack's mother was a member of the yeoman family of Greens, who were quondam residents of Whittonstall Hall farm, and died soon after giving birth to her only child. Jack was born on the last day of the year 1847, and his upbringing was left to the cruel jealousy of a hard-hearted stepmother, whose treatment of a stepson was neither motherly, womanly, nor natural.*
>
> *When a young lad his father left the Hamsterley district, and became a farmer at East Butsfield, where he resided seventeen years till he went through Jack's patrimony,*

which accrued to the orphan lad from his mother. Then he entered the services of the late W.B. Van Haansbergen of Woodlands, [73] and acted for some years as his farm bailiff.

In the late seventies of the last century he, his (second) wife, two sons, and four daughters migrated to British Columbia. One of these sons – half-brother of Jack the wanderer, is an employee on the present Prince of Wales's farm in Alberta. When the family went abroad Jack was left behind to sink or swim.

Jack went to Satley School and received his education from Alexander McDonald, "little Ellick", or "little Allick, the Satley skeynmasrer", as he was generally called; and his successor, William Heaviside. Very few of Jack's old schoolmates are now left in the land of the living.

When he left school his parents gave him employment on their farm, but as there was "nee pay" and "little meat" and "little to eat", Jack betook himself off to the Castleside district where he worked for a few years in the bark woods, and it was said that he soon became an adept at stripping the oak trees of their skins, and was looked on as the champion barker of the district.

Jack was also a great sprinter and won many a bottle of whisky, which was always the first prize at that time for foot-racing. It was the custom for the winner to have the first "swig", and then to pass the bottle on to the loser, who, after having a sup passed it on to the principals and the supporters. When Jack won the race, which occurred most times, there used to be very little left in the whisky bottle after he had first "swig".

When not employed in the bark woods at Castleside, he used to work for the late Ralph Hedley of Satley – one of his schoolmates, either in his water sawmill at West

Butsfield, which stood on the site of the present ganister quarries, or travel with Hedley's steam thresher, then a horse-drawn affair.

Jack travelled seventeen seasons with the thrasher and then joined the "thresher gang" of Tommy Hunter's thresher, of Medomsley. In between times and of later years he worked at odd jobs for farmers, stutting whins in the winter months, spreading muck, setting "taties", hacking "taties", hoeing turnips, hay-making, binding corn, following the reaper etc.,etc and generally sleeping among the hay and straw in the barn, byre, stable or loft. Jack had a hard life, and as the years rolled on he found it rougher and harder to live. As his old schoolmates, who all had a warm place in their hearts for Jack, died, the number of his friends lessened. Many and many a time Jack had to sleep out, "back of a wall" with only an old sack over him,

The writer, who knew Jack since a boy, once found him fast asleep behind a wall, in a rainstorm, the rain peltering down on him and his clothes sodden. More than once he has found him in a similar position in the winter months, covered with hoar frost. Many a time he has given him a shelter at his own fireside, allowing him to sleep on the mat in front of a good fire. One dare not give Jack a bed, for he kept company that no cleanly person cared for.

At one time Jack got a barrel organ and travelled the North of England. It is hard to say to what part he did not get into with it, "making musick" as he called it. The writer has known him with it on the north side of the Tweed and the Cheviots as far south as Northallerton, and as far west as Carlisle. Jack was a good cadger, and if he could only get "a bit of bait" and a "sup of tea" was all right. If one treated him kindly, there was no kinder friend than Jack. With all his failings and foibles Jack was a harmless fellow, and the writer does not remember in the past fifty years that he knew him, ever to have seen Jack in the hands of the police, or known him to be in their clutches.

Jack was many times advised to go into the workhouse, but life and liberty outside is sweet, and Jack preferred to roam about picking up a bite and a sup here and there, to a caged existence. Besides, Jack and fresh water did not always agree, and once, when he was ill (which was not often) the writer advised him to go there, but Jack's answer was – "No, d'ye knaa that they mak a fellow hev a wesh when yen gans there?" Jack's last days, however, were spent there and he was well cared for.

The writer saw him at Christmas, just a "wriggle of bones" but with a memory second to none in the world, and he recounted deeds of fifty years ago with a freshness, and described men and women known to him personally to the writer as if they were still alive and moving about.

Fig. 45 Woodcut by Thomas Bewick

THE END

Ten years later, James William Fawcett was to follow his old friend to the grave, and we learn about the circumstances of his passing from the obituary written for The Society of Antiquaries by Madeleine Hope Dodds. [74] There are inaccuracies in the dates, but there is no mistaking the tone of utmost respect and affection from members of Newcastle's esteemed Society:

> By the death of James William Fawcett of Satley our Society has lost one of the most remarkable of its members; one who, starting without any advantages of wealth or position, devoted a long life to private study and public service. He was born on 14th April 1867, at Brancepeth, where his father was a farmer. Here his schooling began, but at the age of 12 he also began to be a wage-earner, collecting rents at Butsfield in Lanchester parish, for which he received 30s. a year, out of which he had to pay postage.
>
> When he was fourteen he passed an examination which gave him admission to the Model School for boys in Durham. He had an extraordinary gift for languages, and, while at school in Durham, he used to walk to Newcastle for private lessons in Hebrew and Latin, which were not in the school curriculum. When he was nineteen he qualified for the position of Spanish interpreter at Malta in the Intelligence Department of the Imperial Service, winning the post for which there were 2,000 competitors. At twenty-five he could speak thirty-three foreign languages. He remained in the Government service for seventeen years and acted as interpreter in the High Courts of Justice in Spain, Italy and Egypt. During his Egyptian service he worked for Lord Kitchener personally for seven years, having the rank of bimbashi or major.

He married on 20th August, 1915 (sic) but had no children. He retired from the Government service in 1895, and spent seven years in Australia, where he was member of parliament for the Kennedy district of New South Wales in 1897 and later Chief Stipendiary Magistrate at Kennedy.

In 1902 he returned to England and to the district of his birth, living first at Consett and later at Holly Cottage, Satley. He was a devout churchman and his other interests were many. As a naturalist he promoted field clubs at Blackhill, Dipton and Burnopfield. With his wide knowledge of languages he took some interest in philology, but it was chiefly the spoken tongue which interested him.

The greater part of his time and energy he devoted to local history and genealogy. He was secretary of the Durham Historical Society and made himself thoroughly acquainted with local records by constantly indexing those he read; these indices, with his remarkable memory, enabled him to reply to genealogical inquiries from all parts of England and the U.S.A. Wherever he went he contributed to the local press, and it is not possible to list all his articles and pamphlets. The following are his principal works:- Tales of Derwentdale, 1902. The Church of St. John the Baptist, Newcastle upon Tyne, 1909. The History of the Parish of Dipton, 1911. Life of Bishop Westcott. Historical Places in the Derwent Valley. Birds of Durham. History of Tow Law. Life of Charles Attwood, founder of Tow Law. Parish Registers of Satley, Muggleswick and Lanchester.

He joined the Society of Antiquaries of Newcastle-upon-Tyne in 1917, but his first contribution to Proceedings was in 1890, and from that time forward he frequently sent in notes on local antiquities, sometimes recording those which were in process of being cleared away. His last contribution is printed on another page. Although his health had been failing for some time, his last illness was brief. He was taken from his home in Satley to hospital at Consett and died there on March 20th, 1942. Mrs. Fawcett, who survives him, has generously given his papers and indices and many of his books to the Black Gate Library and to the Society of Genealogists of London.

After the Society had visited the house at the invitation of Mary Jane, friends of Fawcett were invited to help themselves to the remaining books, papers and mementoes. Harry collected several loads of documents in his sidecar, and the residue was either pulped for the war effort or destroyed. Due to the shortage of paper, his large collection of nineteenth century newspapers was taken to Lanchester Fish and Chip shop, where it was found that they were too brittle to be used, and so they were burned.

The greatest loss was the vast card index Fawcett had worked on all his life. Having to be frugal with paper, he had snipped up anything to hand: proofs of his books, church bazaar receipts, bills... The indexes contained a tremendous amount of detail across his vast range of interests: family history, cuttings, obituaries, medieval charters, natural history notes. It's a tragedy it was lost: researchers can hardly bear to think about it.

The combination of marital estrangement, lack of funds and the fact that there was a war on must account for why Satley's most esteemed son was laid to rest in an unmarked grave.

Photo by Ray Thompson.

Fig. 46   J W Fawcett grave marker, 2009

THE CONSETT CHRONICLE OBITUARY

Under a triple headline, *The Consett Chronicle* [75] recorded the life of its most illustrious and prolific contributor in style and at great length. Again, the facts are a mixture of truth, hearsay and mythology, but the respect and the reputation are so vast and so warm that it hardly seems to matter.

PASSING OF A COUNTY HISTORIAN

———————————————

JAMES W. FAWCETT OF SATLEY

———————————————

WITH KITCHENER IN THE SUDAN

In the little churchyard of the rural village he loved so well, there was laid to rest a few days ago the remains of a man who, although he may have died in obscurity, was one of the most outstanding personalities in his day in our northern district. In the last two decades or so, little was heard of or about James William Fawcett of Satley, but nevertheless his life had been one full of interest, and he has left behind monuments of his work and ability. He is the last male member of a family that has had association with the district since 1956.

For some years he lived in Consett, but he preferred his little cottage in Satley, where with his books he loved to delve into ancient history. His book upon the Derwent Valley is one. He wrote many other histories, and all have stood the test of time, and will continue to do so. He had a wonderfully keen insight, and loved to delve into the past, tracing records and old manuscripts. In his cottage at Satley he had round him many valuable old records and much valuable data. He was indeed a wonderful personality and is worthy of no mean tribute not only from this district but the whole county, for it is through the indefatigable industry and skill of such men as he that much of our history is known and kept alive. He was a remarkable naturalist too, and lectured on all branches of natural history to local clubs. The writer had vivid memories of him coming to lecture at Dipton well over 30 years ago, a striking figure in his cape and big muffler.

HISTORY OF DIPTON

He would walk from Satley, many miles away, and after a lengthy lecture he always found it difficult to stop, so much had he to tell. He would have supper at the house of one of his friends and then set off home irrespective of the lateness of the hour.

He loved to tramp and seemed happy to be alone with nature. To his many naturalist friends in Dipton he paid a fine tribute by compiling a history of the Parish of Dipton which, although out of print, remains in the proud possession of several old members of the late club. This well-stocked book was published in 1911, and in his foreword the author writes: 'Every man and woman who claims to be a patriotic Britisher should take some interest in the history not only of their native country but of their native county, and not only of their native county but of their native town, village, hamlet or parish. To many there is no place on earth so dear as one's calf-yard – one's birthplace. Until of late years, however, interest in local history has been very small indeed but it is gratifying to know that there is a growing interest in the matter among the general public.

The History of the Parish of Dipton given in this work was undertaken at the wish of a few natives of the same who desired to know more of the past connected with the district, and the request has been backed up by the members of the Dipton and District Field Club. In its compilation I have ransacked many sources and have endeavoured to bring into one place all that can be got hold of appertaining to the history of the parish. How far I have succeeded in entirety I leave the reader to decide. That this work may be instructive and interesting to all into whose hands it may fall is my desire. To all who have rendered any assistance I tender my grateful thanks.'

A PROLIFIC WRITER

James William Fawcett in his younger days was a prolific writer and scarcely a week went over but he wrote articles upon local history and natural history for the local press and the Newcastle press. He had an amazing store of knowledge and this he dispensed liberally. He was a much-travelled man and some of his travel lectures were fascinating indeed.

It was his proud boast that he had been in more than one place untrodden previously by any white man. As a member of the Newcastle Society of Antiquaries he was happy in the company of kindred souls of Tyneside men who, like himself, had made no mean contribution to the historical education of their county. By the members of this society he was regarded as an authority, and his knowledge was often sought. He knew the ancient City of Durham too, and spent many days searching in its old records. He knew the history of every old church in the district. He had delved among records and was familiar with all its past. He knew the birds, plants, insects, and all there was to know of his district's natural history.

He was a keen student of the geological formation of the county too. But perhaps the most interesting part of his life and one that he did not make public was his term in the Imperial Service Intelligence Department. His knowledge of several languages fitted him for this post. He was with Kitchener in the Sudan and became a firm friend of this great general; and in the last war sent him on more than one special mission. These missions were packed with interest and of them he could tell an amazing series of stories.

He lived to a good old age, and his passing, to the younger generation of today, may have been unnoticed. But he has left a heritage to our district and county and in N.W.Durham particularly we are immeasurably richer by his life amongst us and the knowledge he imparted during his lifetime.

COUNCILLOR BELLAM'S TRIBUTE

By the passing of Mr J.W.Fawcett North-West Durham has lost its chief historian who had outstanding literary abilities. Speaking in appreciative terms of Mr Fawcett, Councillor G.A.Bellam told our reporter that Mr Fawcett used his abilities in the acquisition of knowledge which he was at all times willing to place at the service of those who sought it.

Councillor Bellam said his personal knowledge of Mr Fawcett went back as far as 1902 after he had returned from his travels abroad to settle down at Satley. He was then engaged in activities associated with natural history and historical societies over a wide area. He was prominent in forming naturalist field clubs in Blackhill, Dipton and Burnopfield , was secretary of the Durham Historical Society and was also connected with the society for publishing parish registers. Author, too, he published the following books: 'Tales of Derwentdale' a bestseller of its time; 'History of Dipton', which will long be the standard book of reference; 'Life of the Late Bishop Westcott of Durham'; 'Historical Places in the Derwent Valley'; 'Birds of Durham'; 'History of Tow Law'; 'Life of Charles Attwood, Founder of Tow Law' and many other works.

FIRST VOLUME OF LANCHESTER

He was keenly interested in ancient parish registers of the district, and among those he transcribed were those of Satley, Muggleswick, and the first volume of Lanchester. These bear testimony to his wide knowledge and untiring industry and conscientious keenness for accuracy that characterised all his work.

Up to a few years ago, when ill-health overtook him, he was a regular contributor to our and other newspapers and contributed papers to the local field clubs. Councillor Bellam added that anyone who, in the future, attempts to write a standard history of North-West Durham will find that he will have to base his work chiefly on the materials collected and arranged by Mr Fawcett.

'It seems a pity,' observed Coun. Bellam, 'that all Mr Fawcett's learning and knowledge brought him no better material reward. A suitable epitaph would be "His thirst for knowledge did not abate and he followed it until the night."'

INTERPRETER TO ARABIC FORCES

When Mr Fawcett finished his career as an interpreter to the Arabic Forces in Egypt he lived a lonesome but nevertheless busy life in his stone-built cottage at Satley where he resided as a boy.

When he was 12 years of age he was rate-collector in Butsfield township. For that work he received 30s a year *out of which he had to pay his own postages. At the age of 13 he could speak 14 different languages. When he was 19 he qualified for the position of Spanish interpreter at Malta, for which there were 2,000 candidates from English universities.*

Mr Fawcett knew every part of the British Empire from Gibraltar to Hong Kong, and from England to Australia. Before he was 25 he could speak 33 foreign languages. For 17 years he was Lord Kitchener's sleeping companion.

He held 13 degrees of various universities of the world. In 1897 Mr Fawcett was a member of parliament for the Kennedy district of New South Wales, and a few years later was Chief Stipendiary Magistrate at Kennedy.

ATTENDED DURHAM MODEL SCHOOL

Mr Fawcett, or Major Fawcett as he was known by his friends, had but a scanty elementary education. He saved his coppers to buy books, and at an early age walked from Stanley to Dipton to take lessons in Hebrew and Latin.

When he was 14 he passed an examination for a higher education at the Model School, Durham. After leaving school he entered upon a career which was one of uninterrupted success and prolonged intellectual triumphs. No prize for which he was a candidate seemed to evade his grasp. Books he loved, and he possessed a large and wonderful collection of documents and historical works.

Unfortunately, Mr Fawcett, after living such a busy and useful life, had to eke out an existence as best he could as he had no pension from the Government. He claimed to have an intimate knowledge of every town and village in Durham County, and on one occasion he was visited by a professor from a university in California USA, who journeyed all the way to Satley for his pedigree. He was formerly a Durham man.

During the 17 years that he was an interpreter, Mr Fawcett visited the High Courts of Justice in Spain, Italy and Egypt, and when with Lord Kitchener he had the rank of Bimbashi, equivalent to that of a major, conferred upon him. He spoke highly of Lord Kitchener, who had been his friend and companion for many years.

A SURPRISE MEETING

During the time that he lived at Queensland, Australia, Mr Fawcett, who was a warden at St Peter's Church, entertained a visiting preacher to lunch. The preacher had returned to Australia after completing 25 years' service as a church missionary in India.

Some years later, when he returned home to Satley, Mr Fawcett met the Vicar of the church, and to his surprise discovered that he was the missionary he had met at Queensland. He was the Rev. Thomas Lewis John Warneford, whose grandson, Lieut. Rex Warneford, V.C., of Satley, brought down a German Zeppelin during the Great War.

Fifty-six years ago Mr Fawcett was with the first Britishers who got into Khartoum after the murder of General Gordon. In what was Gordon's flower garden, he found a little rose-bush, watered it and carefully tended it. It rewarded his goodness by producing white roses. Slips of the bush were sent to Satley, where his parents planted them in their garden. They are only common white garden roses, but they are descendants of the rose bushes planted by Gordon.

The churchyard at Satley is a peaceful, rural timeless scene. As the years passed, the sounds of war faded, Consett steelworks rose to a peak of production and then began its terrible decline….

Photo of masthead image by Val Scully

Fig. 47   Consett Guardian Office

RAY THOMPSON

In 2008, Ray Thompson decided it was time to honour Satley's forgotten hero. He knocked on the door of Fawcett's childhood home and told the owners about the remarkable man who had once lived in Satley Grange. Galvanised by Ray's enthusiasm and determination, the community formed the 'Satley J.W. Fawcett Local History Society' and set about raising interest and funds to erect a headstone.

Under the title 'Satley's Forgotten Son', Ray typed out a three-page summary of the life of his old friend, including personal reminiscences and extracts from the newspaper cuttings he had gathered. When it was published in the Lanchester Village Voice in September 2008, people in the wider area were astonished to learn about the great man who had lived and died in their midst about whom so few had heard, a man who 'though he may have died in obscurity, was one of the most outstanding personalities in his day in our northern district.'

For all his world-wide travels and experiences, his roots were deeply embedded in his beloved Satley. He was a prolific contributor to local and regional publications and published many learned papers. He also published the parish registers of Satley, Muggleswick and Lanchester, works requiring great diligence and dedication. Nowadays they are treasure-troves for genealogists. It is well to remember that his vast literary output and research was accomplished without the aid of the technological advantages we would now consider essential. No telephone, no electricity. After darkness fell his work had to be done by lamplight.

Today, this truly remarkable man lies in an unmarked grave in a forgotten corner of the churchyard in Satley, his village which he loved so well. How sadly ironic there is nothing to commemorate a man who achieved so much and in particular researched and published the burial records of his parish. 'A son of Satley, of whom even great cities would have been justly proud.'

Interest was stirred. Encouraged, the newly-formed local history society booked the village hall for 17 June 2009 and Ray set about preparing his slide show.

He contacted the newspapers and the Northern Echo sent out ace reporter Mike Amos to interview him. The feature Mike produced not only told the wide readership of the Echo about Fawcett, but also conveyed what a great character had become his champion. [76] On Thursday 4 June, under the heading 'Heroes and Villains', the Northern Echo carried the story:

JAMES Fawcett was 12 when appointed the local rate collector, could speak 14 languages when he was 13, 33 by his 25th birthday and for 17 years was aide-de-camp to Lord Kitchener. He lies in an unmarked grave.

Rex Warneford was the first man to shoot down a Zeppelin, was at once awarded the VC and the Legion d'Honneur and died in a flying accident ten days later. Tommy Raw was a cattle thief.

Their link is the small village of Satley, somewhere between Tow Law and Lanchester, in west Durham, and a talk and slide show to be given in the village hall on June 17.

It's Tommy Raw who's the problem.

Since he could hardly call his presentation "Three Local Heroes", Ray Thompson has settled for "Two-and-a-half".

"He was a hero to half the locals, but he was no Robin Hood," says Ray. "Tommy would steal from anyone."

Ray, 77, lives in Castleside, a few miles up the A68. A former electrician and union convenor at Consett Steel Works – "They called me Red Ray," he recalls, cheerfully – he's now a keen local historian.

"I bought myself a computer, then a laptop, then a scanner, then a projector, then I went on a course and got into power pointing," he says.

His 53-year-old Norton motorbike, immaculately maintained and enthusiastically ridden, is a bit of local history, too. Any proceeds from the village hall talk, he hopes, will at last furnish a headstone for James William Fawcett.

Ray Thompson has won the backing of the parish and church councils and of local residents and has made a temporary marker for the grave, next to Fawcett's father's. A chap at the first informal meeting immediately gave £100.

"I was appalled when I discovered that he didn't even have a headstone. Probably some of the newer families are keener to do something than the longer established ones: a prophet is not without honour except in his own country, and all that. It would be wonderful to remember him at last."

It was said of James Fawcett that he always arrived home late from his lectures, because he simply had so much to say. It's possible distinctly to know the feeling. On, swiftly, to Rex Warneford, born in Darjeeling in 1891.

Photo Courtesy of Ray Thompson

Fig. 48   Rex Warneford V.C.

"A real daredevil, distinctly middle-class, not much of a team player," suggests Ray Thompson. "His only problem with the First World War was that he thought it might be over before he got into it."

Warneford was the vicar of Satley's nephew. His parents divorced, he spent school holidays in the village. He joined the Royal Naval Air Service, on several occasions came perilously close to being busted, was flying from Brussels in June 1915 when ordered to look out for returning Zeppelins.

"London was becoming seriously worried about Zeppelins," says Ray. "We hadn't the guns or the aircraft to tackle them and there was a real fear of a poison gas attack."

Flying solo, Warneford was attacked by the Zeppelin's machine guns and returned fire with his revolver, his only armament. Finally able to fly above the Zeppelin as it prepared to land, he dropped his six bombs on the German dirigible which plummeted from 6,000 feet, killing its crew and two sisters in the nunnery onto which it fell.

Forced to crash land after his own plane was damaged in the explosion, Warneford carried out running repairs to the fuel pipe – some accounts say with his cigarette holder, others with piping from his flying jacket – swung the propellor, jumped into the cockpit as the plane was moving and escaped just as German troops burst from the woods.

"It was all like something from the Hotspur," says Ray, hardly surprisingly. "Britain's morale was lifted massively. We'd shown we could tackle the Zeppelins."

Warneford's funeral was attended by 50,000 onlookers and a firing party of 50. A photograph of him and his plane hangs in the vestry of St Cuthbert's church in Satley, his image was used on Ascension Island stamps.

Unlike James Fawcett, Rex Warneford died a hero.

SO what of Tommy Raw, hero and villain, the man whose name was used countless years after his death as a warning to Derwentside's children: "Tommy Raw will get you..." Excommunicated, he had been buried in an unmarked grave near Castleside, the year of his death marked with the single word "Anno" and not the customary "Anno Domini".

"My theory is that Tommy thought God had done nowt for him, so he was going to do nowt for God," says Ray.

Some time in the 19th Century, the headstone from Tommy's grave beneath an oak tree was moved and is now part of a barn wall near Satley. "We get people from all over coming to see it," says Angela Steel. "If they make a film about him, I hope it stars Mel Gibson."

In the 1920s, locals dug up his remains and photographed them on a tablecloth. That image is in the slide show, too – Satley Village Hall, 7.30pm, Wednesday, June 17, all welcome.

The event generated so much interest that on 9 July, the paper published a follow-up article under the headline, 'Talk Unearths a Long-lost Cousin.'

We wrote on June 4 about the remarkable James Fawcett (1862-1942) from Satley, near Tow Law. There is a happy post-script.

Fawcett, it may be recalled, was a prodigious youngster who could speak 14 languages at the age of 13, was appointed Spanish interpreter on Malta at the age of 18 and became (among much else) right-hand man to Lord Kitchener.

Ray Thompson from Castleside, a bit farther along the A68, is trying to raise funds at last to afford the forgotten

Fawcett a headstone in Satley graveyard. As the June 4 column noted, his talk and slide show in Satley village hall was meant to help the cause.

It overflowed, raised £200, attracted a "well-spoken" lady from Bedale, North Yorkshire, who'd read of it in the column but had no idea where Satley might be. "Bedale," echoes Ray, "ye gods."

Supposed in her 60s, the lady had been told as a child that she had a cousin who was Kitchener's interpreter. All her grandmother knew was that he was called Fawcett.

"She always cherished the hope that there had been a great man in the family and that one day she might find out more," says Ray. At the slide show, of course, she succeeded.

"She said she'd had a wonderful night, thoroughly enjoyed it and at the end gave me £20 to help get Mr Fawcett a headstone. To tell you the truth, that incident alone made all the efforts worthwhile." [77]

With a grant from the Durham Community Foundation, the money was raised and a local stonemason commissioned. On Sunday 10 June 2013, the headstone was unveiled. The invitations, made by the indefatigable and inventive Ray, wittily featured the famously arresting Lord Kitchener poster.

Fig. 49   Lord Kitchener Poster

Image in Public Domain

YOU are invited to the unveiling of a headstone for my old friend James William Fawcett of Satley, renowned scholar, naturalist, Antiquarian, Linguist, Author: A son of Satley of whom great cities would have been justly proud.' The ceremony will be held in the churchyard of St Cuthbert's Church, Satley, on Sunday 10th June at 2.30 pm. This unique event will appeal to all with an interest in our history. Everyone welcome to a friendly 'get-together' in the nearby Punch Bowl Inn afterwards. The Society is grateful for the generous support given by the County Durham Community Foundation for this project.

Fig. 50   Ray Thompson and Andrew Martell, Deputy Lord Lieutenant of County Durham and Trustee of the County Durham Community Foundation with the headstone

Ten years later, when David Marrs, a local historian from Dipton, suggested that J.W. Fawcett would be 'an interesting chap to research,' the Land of Oak & Iron publications group volunteers knew exactly where to start…

LEGACY

As another obituary had put it over seventy years ago:

> *There are quite a few classics from his pen, published histories, that are invaluable to the student of local history. His book upon the Derwent Valley is one. He wrote many other histories, and all have stood the test of time, and will continue to do so. He had a wonderfully keen insight, and loved to delve into the past, tracing records and old manuscripts. In his cottage at Satley he had round him many valuable old records and much valuable data. He was indeed a wonderful personality and is worthy of no mean tribute not only from this district but the whole county, for it is through the indefatigable industry and skill of such men as he that much of our history is known and kept alive.* [78]

J.W. Fawcett was an extraordinary man, of that there can be no doubt: linguist, explorer, civil servant, historian, naturalist, chronicler, archivist, journalist, writer, raconteur, teller of tales. In so many ways, he worked to explore, celebrate and preserve the history of the Land of Oak & Iron. We hope this book will ensure that his legacy is a lasting one, and we look forward to hearing from anyone who would like to contribute to our community's knowledge of this legend of a man.

NOTES

[1] *Proceedings of the Society of Antiquaries of Newcastle upon Tyne. Third Series. Volume X, pp. 274-6:* 'In 1851 the population was 318 persons (157 males and 161 females) in 55 houses. The geological formation is millstone grit, above which are several outcrops of coal, the borderline between the carboniferous and millstone grit passing through the township….drifts have been made to work this coal but…were soon closed…several ganister quarries and also a freestone quarry at Woodburn where stone slates, flagstones and kerbstones are worked. The soil and subsoil are clay, and the chief crops are wheat, barley, oats, potatoes and turnips. In 1856, there were 12 farms, subdivided into 30 by 1922….much woodland, considerably depleted in the Great War. Two stone cists have been opened, one in 1883 in a pasture field on the Satley Grange Farm, and the other containing human remains and an earthen vessel, in the corner of a cultivated field between East and West Butsfield in 1885.'

[2] Undated Article from *Consett Chronicle*, c.1927: 'My father's dear old friend – one of God's own gentlemen – lived at Satley Grange. William French lived at Steeley. I knew his family well. William ('Young Willie', we called him) and …(with the hare-shod lip), and Alice. Their old Residence, the old farmhouse, has been converted into a hemmel and a barn, and a new farmhouse erected. The tenants before them were the Greens – a well-known family of Wesleyan methodists. John Black lived at Fine House. He was just a labourer, but also carried on the illicit manufacture of whiskey. He had his stills in the Black Bank Plantation and in Robin's Fancy. He was often hunted by excisemen, who came from Burnopfield in these days. John Walton was the farmer at the Hythe.

'One Whitfield, an old rascal, lived at Robin's Fancy. He was a buzzom-maker and a drunken wastrel. He made his buzzoms in the upstairs rooms. One night he went home drunk and went upstairs to make buzzoms. He lit a candle and stuck it in a buzzom for a candlestick – with the result – you know what. It used to be a laughable farce in the Satley district and elsewhere, how old Nanny rushed upstairs when the place was burning, and tossed her set of best china out of the upstairs window to save it from being burnt. The place was a black-thatched building, and is still in ruins. I went to see the old place and found the walls still partly standing, the site of the old coalhouse, the well, and the garden. The fire-raiser then went to Byerley House, then a black-thatched building, burnt it down in the same manner – all within a twelvemonth. Then the people of the district rose up and cleared them out. They went to the Wokingham district, where they had at least a couple more fires.

'Jacob Hopper lived at one of the farms at East Butsfield and William Bulman at the other. The latter afterwards became a steward to the last squire of Woodland, who bought the estate after we had left the district, and later on emigrated to British Colombia. He left behind him, however, his eldest son, the only child of his first wife, and Jack ("Poor Jack") has led a wandering life about the farms, Consett Works and the workhouse. Jack was driven to this by the ill-usage of an abominable stepmother. I met him, one day, with an old sack on his back, tottering along the road to the Butsfields, to the farmhouse of some kindly farmer. We were lads together, and I felt heart-sorry for poor old Jack.

'Leonard (we always called him Lenny) Rippon lived in the ivy house. I was told that he lived to the age of 83. I remember him and his cuddy well. I don't know when the cuddy died, but if his life was like that of his master, he must have been a bonny old cuddy when he left this earth for cuddyland, for he was an old cuddy when I was a lad 70 years ago.

'Willy Langton and Hannah lived in the old black-thatched house. They would be the last tenants. The place is now a ruin I saw, partly roofless, and without windows or doors. Willie worked on the roads, and had a son, 'Young Willie' who served his time at Consett to be a joiner.

'Henry Nicholson lived down at Butsfield Burn. His wife's brother, Cuthbert Foster, lived with them. I have many memories of 'Cuddy' marching up and down the village street of Satley, half drunk, swinging his arms around like the spokes of a cart-wheel or the wands of a windmill, and giving a shriek or yell every now and then. They told me that Cuddy died in Lanchester Workhouse. He must have squandered over a thousand pounds before he went there. A nice ending to one of the last of an old local yeoman family.

'Up at West Butsfield lived John Willis in one of the farms. Robert Hall in another, and Jack Carrick in the other. I was told that John Willis was blind for many years before his death. The Primitive Methodist Chapel has seen many changes before it became a place of worship. Once it was a school, then a cottage inhabited by a family named Thompson; then successively hen-house, duck-house, goose-house and cow-byre. John Galley lived at Bute's Plantations, and the Nicholsons at Woodburn. One of their lads went away to be an engineer, and I was told he only died recently. I'd like to have seen him before he died. John and George Scott lived at Springwell, and Neddy Walker at Dean House. I once saw Neddy building a small stone bridge over a gutter in his land, and making one of his lads bend his back until he got the arch fixed over it. I little thought then that I'd do the same thing on the other side of the world, with one of my own lads as the mould. Thompsons lived at Low Hermitage. They had a family of lads and lasses. Robert Bulman lived at the Abbey, with Bessy, his housekeeper, and William Robinson at Byerley House. He was the second tenant in the new house after the old rascal Whitfield burnt the place down. Before going to Byerley House the Robinsons were our neighbours in Satley Village. George Whitfeld (no relation of the buzzom- maker) lived at Filed House (we called it 'Malley's Oppen' when I was a lad), and Tom Hardy at Philadelphia. Jack Howe lived at Lamb's Cross public house, where he carried on the business of a stone-mason, beer-brewer, and whiskey-stiller.

'The Garthwaites (Garfoots we called them) lived at West House or Wood's End. I was told that Aaron died at the age of 95. George Maddison lived at West Carr. He kept cows, and sold milk at Tow Law in its early days, making sufficient profit to enable him to build a row of cottages in the new town, which were long known as 'Milk and watter Raa,' significant of the manner of how the money was obtained to build them.

'George Ayre lived at West Shields. John Greenwell lived at Broomshields. The place had not got the handle-hall in those days. His three maiden sisters lived at Broomshields Cottage – now a farmhouse. They all lived to good old ages so I found out – John 84, Mary 88, Elizabeth 89, and Eleanor 96. John was the Squire and kept a number of men employed about the estate all the year round. They all had regular upstanding wage – 12s per week. I remember George Lawson, John Bell, William Pearson, and Matthew Peart among the number. My dear old father was an occasional worker there.

'William Nicholson lived at East Broomshields. His grandsons still have the place. John Hunter and Betty and Willie Towns and Betty lived at the two farms at Rare Deans. I remember Will Towns losing his arm at Inkerman crossing as just the other day, although it is over 60 years ago. He lived at Hall Hill in the new house which was built of bricks made and burnt in one of the fields on the farm. The brick-makers came from Lincolnshire and lodged in Satley while working. Anthony Shotton lived at Land House, Willie Gibbon and Betty at Patrick's Close Cottage (Partridge Close), and Tommy Neasham at Low Mill. He would be the last miller there, for now the dam is gone and the watermill in ruins. Tommy Buddle lived at Ragpathside (Rackwoodside we used to call it) and Willie Bland at Black House. George Burlison was blacksmith at Browney Bank and a right good man he was. He used to make all kinds of agricultural implements – hay-rakes, ploughs, harrows etc and he made them good. I saw one of the hay-rakes the other day which he made 60-odd years ago, and it was as good as new. Neddy Charlton, a Consett Iron Company's official, lived in the old farmhouse at Broadwood. There was no hall in those days.

'There are some of the men of the Satley district as I remember them 60 or 70 years ago. They are all gone now, and so are their families, and the place remembers them no more. I many a time wonder what would I have been had I stayed in England. I am now owner of one square mile of country in my house across the seas – all cut up into farms and paid for by the hard work of my dear old father and myself. Had I stopped in England I suppose I'd have been an ignorant old clodhopper, like so many of my contemporaries here, or a cross-bred between the public-house and the workhouse, as others are.

'Sixty-seven years ago my parents were readers of the Consett Guardian (from its first issue) and it's a pleasure for me to contribute these memories to its columns so many years after. May it have nothing but success is my only wish.'

[3] *Satley Registers*, p.150: 'William Fawcett was born at South Shields Farm, Cornsay Township, Satley Parish, on 28th November 1830; baptised at Satley Church in 1831, educated at Satley School, 1840-1845, under George Watson and Alexander MacDonald, was a farmer at South Shields, Satley, 1851-1860; at Wooley Close, in Brancepeth Parish, 1860-1867; and at the Grange, otherwise Satley Grange, 1867-1897; a private resident in Satley Village, 1897-1900; was a useful parishioner wherever he resided; Parish Constable for Brancepeth 1861-1866; Overseer for Brancepeth, Brandon and Byshottles 1863-1866; [first] People's Churchwarden of St Cuthbert's Church, Satley, 1870-1878; Waywarden for the Township of Butsfield 1876-1888, and Rate Collector for the same 1876-1888; [first] Chairman of the Satley Conservative Association 1886-1900; Freeholder of Satley 1890-1900; one of the Trustees for the Greenwell Charity belonging to Satley School 1891-1900; one of the Managers of Satley School 1891-1900; Lay Representative of the Parish, &c; took a prominent, but useful, part in every movement connected with Satley Parish. Died at Satley on Easter Tuesday, 17th April, 1900, aged 69. Buried in Satley Churchyard. Headstone there.'

[4] *Satley Registers*, p.150. 'Margaret Sarah Charlton was born 29 December, 1845, second daughter of James Charlton, farmer and cattle dealer, of Bavington Mount, in Stamfordham Parish, Northumberland… died at Cornsay, 24th June 1912, aged 66 years, by whom he had issue three sons and four daughters.'

[5] 'Two Hitherto Unrecorded Burial Cists in Satley Parish, County Durham.' *Proceedings of the Society of Antiquaries of Newcastle upon Tyne*, Fourth Series, vo.IX (May 1939 – January 1942) pp.225-6:

'Lying on the North-west side of the village of Satley is a small grass farm called Satley Grange, (formerly occasionally Steeley Grange). In the year 1899 it, with other lands, was sold, and the new owner separated from it some 33 acres, called 'The Allotments', and added them to a cottage called Byreley House in order to make a 'small-holding.' These allotments were originally part of Satley Fell, a portion of Lanchester Common, which was divided by Act of Parliament in 1773. They were allotted to Satley Grange farm and formed into five fields by enclosures of stone walls and thorn hedges, and brought under cultivation.

'In 1885 the then tenant, William Fawcett, who had been connected with the farm for forty years, decided to 'lay it away' as well. In one corner of this field there was, and had been since memory of man, a mound or heap of soil. By most persons it was called an old 'Whicken Heap,' or place where whickens' - couch grass, sods, weeds, etc. - had been carted to when ploughed lands were cleaned. He carted the heap away, and when he reached the level of the adjoining land found a large flagstone in what had been the middle of the heap. This was raised and it was found to cover a cavity some three feet by two and about two feet deep. The hollow was empty, except that in one corner lay an earthen pot. There were signs of the place having contained water at one time. The late Canon Greenwell, who was an old friend of the finder and a frequent visitor to his house, saw the cavity soon after the opening and declared it an ancient British burial.

'Three years later (in 1888) another similar burial cist was found in a pasture field between the hamlets of East and West Butsfield, on the north side of the lane between the two places. It contained the skeleton of an adult, lying on its right side, which fell to dust on exposure to the air. Canon Greenwell was present at the "find."

'Both graves lay north and south, and both contained a food vessel, which the Canon took possession of. We know of no record made of either of these finds made by the Canon, but we do know that he intended bringing his work on prehistoric remains up to date and had got many additions. He had two other records that we know of, but we cannot give any dates or particulars. One was found somewhere near the village of Esh and the other was on Hedley Common or Fell, between Tow Law and Hedley Hill.'

[6] *Keys To The Past* website, article 10339. [Accessed 6th April 2019]

[7] *Proceedings of the Society of Antiquaries of Newcastle-upon-Tyne.* First Series. 1921

[8] *Proceedings of the Society of Antiquaries of Newcastle-upon-Tyne.* First Series. Volume IV, pp. 255-6.

'For the last sixty years and more than that, the farmers who have resided on the farm called Steeley near the village of Satley have complained when ploughing a certain field that a narrow patch running in a slanting direction across it and only about three or four yards in width was always very bad to let the plough through on account of the large number of stones which lay at a depth of nine to twelve inches beneath the surface. Some of the farmers when ploughing this field had the misfortune to either break or damage the sock or coulter of their plough near this particular place...

'None of the tenants appear to have taken the trouble to investigate the strip and have the stone taken out until the present one had a portion of it cleared of the stones in the spring of 1889, and another portion in the spring of the present year, 1890. These stones were taken out of the ground, the larger ones broke in two, and the whole carted away to repair the walls of the adjoining fields. On the writer of this note becoming informed of what was going on, he paid several visits to the place and saw the operations. He saw at once that the long narrow stony strip was none other than a portion of an ancient British road and as perfect as it was in the time of its builders... the remains of this road are situate about a quarter of a mile to the north of the village of Satley and run a direction from south-east to north-west for about 300 yards. These are the only remains of a British road that I have been able to find in this neighbourhood and in what direction the road ran southwards I am unable to say as no similar examples have been brought to light in cultivated ground in that direction. The direction of the road northwards seems to me to be to meet the ancient British road which ran down the Derwent Valley on the south or right bank of the river, traces of which are visible between Muggleswick and Allensford and also near to Lintz Green The opening out of this long-hidden antiquity verifies the etymology of the name of the village of Satley near to which it lies. The prefix SAT- is derived from the British word sathe signifying a trampling or a treading; a place beaten down by the continued walking over of men or animals a well-worn track. If I read the old British language correctly; whilst the affix -LEY is from the termination of the same language signifying a woodland clearing, grassland, an open space in the forest. Putting the two syllables together we have Sathelle, since corrupted into Satley and signifying pastureland near the well-trodden road in the clearing by the main road.

'Mr Hedley thought the road in question could not be ancient British as the known roads of the Britons were not paved and are now merely hollow ways. The portion of the paved road ascending a bank near Muggleswick appear to be medieval.'

⁹ *Satley Registers,* p.vii

¹⁰ Fawcett, J.W. 'The Greenwells of Broomshields' in *The Monthly Chronicle of North Country Lore and Legend, 1991,* p.43.

¹¹ Durham County Record Office, E/W 50, p.10712

¹² Fawcett, J.W. 'Maltese Memories'. *Consett Guardian,* 4 April 1930

¹³ *Consett Guardian* April 1942: 'At twenty-five he could speak thirty-three foreign languages. He remained in the Government service for seventeen years and acted as interpreter in the High Courts of Justice in Spain, Italy and Egypt. During his Egyptian service he worked for Lord Kitchener personally for seven years, having the rank of bimbashi or major.'

¹⁴ Fawcett, J.W. 'The World's Great Linguists'. *Consett Guardian* 3 June 1927:

'It is not everybody who is successful at mastering languages. And one is inclined to think that there is a linguistic facility, something more than a powerful and retentive memory, which absorbs language-forms like a sponge absorbing water. And when those who realise keenly their linguistic failings, remember that they can only write and speak one language, and possess a very poor smattering of several others, they stand in awe of the man who is master of half-a-dozen. But what shall we think of the man who can speak fifty languages?

'Charles Lever once wrote with contempt about those people who learn languages, and classed them with those who played games – as if the gift for languages and ability for playing ping-pong went together. It is true, however, that men of action are apt to be impatient with those who possess the linguistic gift, because they have an idea that this gift is no indication of any real power of mind. But most of the world's great linguists have been something more than linguistic, as we shall see.

MEMORISING AT SIGHT

'Sir W. Robertson Nicoll, in an obituary notice on Dr Robert A. Neill, a great classical and Oriental scholar, who was for many years fellow and tutor of Pembroke College, Cambridge, described Neil's method of study as a student at Aberdeen. "His verbal memory was like nothing I have ever seen in this world. He was a born linguist. He would take Liddell and Scott's dictionary, and with his feet on the fender, read over a page, and then hand over the book to me. I would find that he could give practically the English word for every Greek word just by means of one reading.: So this Aberdeen student became a great classical scholar, his edition of Aristophanes represents a lifetime of study. Then, in addition, he was a keen student of Sanskrit and Oriental languages. Thus we see that the linguist starts with a peculiar endowment, which includes a keen memory.

'There have been several men who have gained an outstanding place as remarkable linguists: - Sir John Bowring, and English diplomat, Cardinal G,.C. Mezzofanti, and Italian ecclesiastic; H.C. von der Gabelentz, the German linguist and ethnologist. Bowring, who died in 1872, is known to many as author of the popular hymn, "In the Cross of Christ I Glory." He is credited with knowing two hundred languages, and is said to have spoken one hundred of these. However, it is likely that acquaintance with many of these would be slight. But he had a sound knowledge of forty languages – no mean performance. Sir John Bowring was a widely-read and a far-travelled man. He published books on Russian, Spanish, Polish, and Serbian poetry. He lived in Holland and Denmark for some time, and made a collection of Scandinavian poetry. In 1849 Bowring became Consul at Hong-King, and in 1855 negotiated a treaty between Britain and Siam.

'Cardinal G.C. Mezzofanti was born at Bologna in 1774, and became Professor of Arabic there at the age of 23. In 1833 he became keeper of the Vatican Library, and died in 1849. Unlike other great linguists, Mezzofanti's peculiar talent, remarks one authority, was more like that of "calculating boys," and not combined with any outstanding intellectual power. He spoke with fluency some 50 or 60 languages, besides having an acquaintance with others. A more able man was Von Gabelentz, the German linguist, who applied his knowledge of languages in working out philological principles. While still in his teens, young Von Gabelentz studied Arabic and Chinese, and he continued to study Chinese while at the Universities of Leipzig and Göttingen. In 1830 he entered the public service of the Duchy of Attenburg, and when he retired in 1868 after long service, it was to give his undivided attention to his learned researches. He is reputed to have learned 80 languages, 30 of which he spoke with fluency and elegance. And his great ability for linguistic study, he used for the advancement of the Science of Languages.

JUVENILE LINGUISTS

'Some people with the linguist faculty start very young. Robert Boyle, the eminent natural philosopher, could speak Latin and French in his earliest years, and was sent to Eton at eight years of age. John Stuart Mill could read Greek at five, for his father had taken the boy in hand, and was training him to be a philosopher, and at 14 he had acquired Latin and Greek, had grappled with Mathematics and had made the acquaintance of Logic and Political Economy. One might say there was no boyhood in the life of John Stuart Mill, for it was drilled out of him by his educational regimen.

'Then some men are never too old to learn languages. It is said of an eminent Scottish educational publisher that he commenced to master Dutch when over 80, in order to publish a grammar of that language.

'Mr Newberry, editor of "The Newberry Bible"; Dr Robert Young, who produced a very fine "Analytical Concordance of the Bible"; Dr John Brown, of Haddington, author of "The Self-Interpreting Bible"; Dr John Kitto, a voluminous writer, and many more, were largely self-taught men. Dr Young began life as a printer; Dr Brown acquired his knowledge of Latin, Greek and Hebrew whilst a shepherd; Dr Kitto, who was stone deaf, was a workhouse boy and served his apprenticeship to cobbling.

EXCAVATORS AND ARCHAEOLOGISTS

'Then men became linguists in order to aid them in travel, and in excavating the sites of ancient ruins. The celebrated Swiss traveller, J.L.Burckhardt, who died at the early age of 33, went out to the East in 1809, after studying at Cambridge. He disguised himself as a Musselman, studied Arabic and mastered the Koran, passing stringent tests so that he might pose as a native doctor of the Mohammedan law. He travelled up the Nile, went through Syria, and on to Mecca as a Mohammedan pilgrim. He then projected an expedition into Central Africa. But while waiting for a caravan to Fezzan, he as seized with fatal illness and died in 1817. He bequeathed eight hundred volumes of valuable oriental manuscripts to Cambridge.

'Another romantic story is the life and work of Heinrichs Schliemann, the German linguist and scholar who excavated the site of the ancient buried city of Troy. Schliemannn was the son of a Protestant pastor and was apprenticed to the village grocer, but he went off to sea. Finally he settled in Hamburg, where his mastery of languages gained him promotion in a business house. Besides his native German, Schliemann could speak Dutch. English, Spanish, French. Italian, Portuguese and Russian. Business took him to St Petersburg, and launching out on his own, he found himself a millionaire at 40. Then he settled down to his studies, mastered the classical languages, went to Paris and studied Archaeology. In 1868, he went out to the East and started excavations for the site of ancient Troy, and with the spade, Schliemann dug up a great chapter of buried history, which many believed to be pure myth. Thus the ancient stories of Homer were proved to have foundation in fact. Most of the next twenty years were spent in the Levant and in publishing his epoch-making books which roused controversies by their theories.

'Another great scholar and linguist was the late Lord Acton, who was considered the best-read man in Europe. He possessed a vast library, which he bequeathed to Mr John Morley, on his death in 1902. He has been described as an "historian of almost incomparable learning."

'Elihu Burritt was another linguist who deserves mention. He was known as the "learned blacksmith" and while working at the anvil mastered mathematics and several oriental and modern languages. Burritt was United States Consul in England from 1865 to 1870. Our list of great linguists might be considerably extended, but we have named the most representative. But, none can excel the record of Bowring, Mezzofanti and Von Gabelentz for linguistic attainments.'

[15]   Durham County Record Office, E/HB 2/869.

[16]   Letter from James F. Robinson of Vale of Derwent Naturalists' Field Club in *Newcastle Weekly Chronicle Supplement*. 14 Nov. 1891, p.5.

[17]   *Transactions of the Society of Antiquaries,* Series 3, Volume 8. Listed pp.66-68, 88-92)

[18]   *Satley Registers,* p. ii.

[19]   *Satley Registers,* p. iii.

[20]   *Dictionary of National Biograph*y, Volume 3, p.829.

[21]   19th Royal Hussars (Queen Alexandra's Own) on National Army Museum website.

[22]   Royle, Trevor, *The Kitchener Enigma,* The History Press. 2016, Chapter 9.

[23]   *The Parish Registers of St Cuthbert's Church, Satley: containing the Baptisms, Marriages and Burials from 1560 to 1812, Gravestone Inscriptions, Local Pedigrees &c. Transcribed, Annotated and Indexed by J.W.Fawcett, B.A., LL.B. 1914*

[24]   *Satley Registers,* p.iv.

[25]   *Satley Registers,* p.v, note 6.

[26]   Reverend Warneford (1834-1905) was vicar of Satley 1891-1904, and had a son, Reginald William Henry Warneford, (1860-1903). After various curacies in England, 1857-1866, he was chaplain to the Bengal Ecclesiastical Establishment, 1866-1891 for 25 years, but not as a missionary. There is no reference to any Australian connection but he had periods of leave in 1881 and 1889-1891 when he could have visited Australia. (David Butler.)

[27]   Sub-lieutenant Reginald Alexander John Warneford R.N. (1891-1915), brought down LZ37 over Belgium in 1915. 'His parents separated, his mother re-married, and Rex and his possessions were shipped by P&O steamer to live with his grandfather, Rev. Thomas Warneford, at Satley Rectory on the wild moors of County Durham.' From the website of King Edward VI School, Stratford-upon-Avon.

[28]   *Durham Advertiser,* April 1942.

[29]   *Newcastle Weekly Chronicle Supplement*, 14 February 1891, p.3.

[30]   Allen, David Elliston. *The Naturalist in Britain, A Social History.* Princeton Paperbacks. 1978.

[31]   Fawcett, J.W. *A History of the Parish of Dipton.* 1911, p. 68.

'The study of the sciences, all of which are parts of natural history, from the earliest periods, have by no means been confined to the sterner sex. Certain it is that the greater part of the facts discovered and arrived at in each separate science have been searched out by man, yet, though they stand predominant, much has been made known by woman.   Man, standing as he does at the head of all created nature, the crowning piece of organic life, endowed with varied mental qualities, and possessing the most ambition and perseverance, peers further into the deep unfathomable depths of science, and working with more unwearying energy, attains greater results than the opposite sex; yet in all these works of research, how often is he assisted and cheered in his labour by the feebler yet far-seeing help of a weaker though sometimes firmer mind?

'As we study the biographies of the greatest naturalists and scientists, those men who have toiled hard in the vast storehouses of nature, bringing forth and advancing doctrines and theories of the natural sciences, frequently do we find them receiving assistance from the weaker sex. Sometimes it happens these women are content to hide their important productions beneath the name of their husband, wishing only to render him their often very valuable assistance, and to share with him the praise, if any be accorded. At others, we find them striking out for themselves, and winning by their own persevering energies a name in the niche of fame.

'Up to almost recent years, woman, thinking it was out of her place, cared little to exert herself in sciences that by length of time belonged to the stronger sex, but a breach having been made, and the way laid open, numbers are beginning to climb the paths of science, vying not only with others of their own sex, but with those whose prerogative, if it may be so called, the field of erudition had so long been. Besides the thought of woman that it was out of her position to appear as one cultivated and learned, it had long been regretted that the cultivation of the mind in a woman was a mark of mental or moral obliquity, and anyone who did happen to leave the centre of the beaten track of the very common-place erudition of a common-place clique of society, was looked upon with a mixture of pity and dislike. Happily, in these days of advanced education, woman finds that the way to success is not barred so much as it was formerly, and though there are one or two obstacles in the way, she can raise herself by honest heroic endeavours to be one of the "upper ten thousand of erudites," and occupy a position well up in the scale of cultivation and learning. Having surmounted what was for a long time considered an impregnable barrier, we now have women occupying important positions, and almost all the professions can now boast of a female as one of its members.

'In this brief paper of mine, I wish to say something of woman as a student of nature. We are passionately fond of flowers, and this passion ought not to be restricted to one, for it should lead us on to be full of enthusiasm for all that Dame Nature so liberally spreads out for the delectation of her worshippers, and become ardent lovers of nature. This would increase our mental powers for nature throughout the extent and variety of her productions and processes as man's great teacher, and because she is man's great teacher, she is also woman's great teacher, for are not we one of another? Apart from the study being peculiarly healthy and ennobling, it leads to practical results of utility, and as nothing exists for nothing, it leads and tends more towards the effectual training of intellectual powers the deeper we go into it.

'And now let us see what woman has done and is doing in the great world of natural history. In it she chiefly excels as an authoress; and as the greater part of her writings are the outcome of experience, many of them have become works of much importance. Zoology and ornithology are not subjects which have taken up much of her attention. Chief amongst them are Mrs. Loudon, Mary Howitt, Miss Bond, and Maria Ellen Catlow, writers of no small repute. Maria Catlow also holds an important position as an entomologist and is not lacking in knowledge of other sciences; and Miss Ormerod, the consulting entomologist of the Royal Agricultural Society, is well-known for her researches in entomology.

'Botany, the science treating of our wild flowers, is the one which finds most students and writers.   Amongst the latter are Anne Pratt, "Haunts of the Wild Flowers;" Agnes Catlow, "Garden and Greenhouse Botany;" Lady Wilkinson, "Weeds and Wild Flowers;" Mary Roberts, "The Woodlands;" Anna Maria Libert, a cryptogamic botanist; and Mrs Gatty, "British Seaweeds."

'Besides the many who have given the result of their labours to the public at large, there are others who have rendered great help to the botanical world by their discoveries of various plants. These are found more frequently in our colonies, and especially Australia. In that great island continent a great help has been afforded towards enlarging the flora of Australia by such women as Amelia Dietrich, perhaps the greatest of female Australian botanists; Mrs. Ellis Rowan, Miss E. Testor, Mrs. Molloy, Mrs. Louisa Atkinson, Mrs. Forde,

Miss Scott, Mrs. Hodgkinson, Mrs. Calvert, Mrs. Glendinning, Mrs. Parker, Mrs. F. Spencer, Mrs. J.W.R. Stuart, Miss Bowkett, and several others.

'But we need not look so far away for female botanists of note, for in the county of Durham - amongst others - two deserve especial notice. One is Miss Deborah Wharton, of Old Park, Durham, whose hortus siccu, or collection of British plants made in the county of Durham, A.D.1760-1802, is now in the University Museum, Durham; the other is Mary Eleanor, Countess of Strathmore, of Streatlam and Gibside, who died in 1800, and who was wife of Lieutenant Stoney, afterwards the notorious "Stoney Bowes." Geology and its kindred sciences find female writers of no mean repute in such a one as Margaret Pleus, "Geology for the Million." Such then is, I think, sufficient proof that woman is not lacking in knowledge and power in the study of natural history.'

[33] Fawcett, J.W. A History of the Parish of Dipton (and the Township of Collierley) in the County and Diocese of Durham. 1911, p.70.

[34] *A History of the Parish of Dipton (and the Township of Collierley) in the County and Diocese of Durham.* 1911, p.85.

[35] *A History of the Parish of Dipton (and the Township of Collierley) in the County and Diocese of Durham.* 1911, p.85

[36] *Notes on the History, Geology and Botany of the Vale of Derwent, being papers read before the Vale of Derwent Naturalists' Field Club.* Wordsworth Press. 1891.Volume 1, p. 97.

[37] Michael Turner. 'Thomas Robson 1812-1884: The Forgotten Bird Man.' *Northumbrian Naturalist.* Volume 75. 2013, pp.42-45.

[38] *Newcastle Weekly Chronicle Supplement,* Saturday 24 January 1891

[39] *Newcastle Weekly Chronicle Supplement,* Saturday 17 January 1891.

[40] *Newcastle Weekly Chronicle Supplement,* Saturday 17 October 1891.

[41] *Newcastle Weekly Chronicle Supplement,* Saturday 14 November 1891.

[42] Letter published in *Australian Town & Country Journal,* 29 Jan 1898

[43] Brady, E.J. *The Land of the Sun.* Edward Arnold & Co. 1924, p. 274

[44] Lavallin Puxley, W. *Wanderings in the Queensland Bush.* Allen & Unwin. 1923. P.18

[45] Lavallin Puxley, W. *Wanderings in the Queensland Bush.* Allen & Unwin. 1923. P.23-4

[46] *The Queenslander,* 27 August 1892.

[47] /Native Art' in *The Queenslander,* 2 June 1894: 'Rude drawings found in caves, on smooth rocks, and on trees in various parts of Australia show that the aboriginal inhabitants were not altogether without appreciation of the beauties of art. Though the drawings are of the roughest they are sufficient to place the authors far above the animals with which it is the custom to compare them. Art, such as it is, is even yet practised in some parts of North Queensland. The specimen we give on this page is a facsimile of a set of drawings found in a cave on the Upper Herbert River, and a copy of which was sent us by Mr. J. W. Fawcett. The figures are scratched with a bone or hard stick, and charcoal and ochre have been rubbed into the marks thus made. What the hieroglyphic design in the lower corner signifies is a mystery, but the others are easily identified as representations of the aboriginal conception of the human form, of a kangaroo, an opossum, a boomerang and shield, and a native wooden sword; all objects with which the artist would be familiar. There is merit in these drawings when it is considered that they are the work of savages of so low a type as the aborigines of Australia unquestionably are.'

[48] *The Queenslander,* 24 March 1894. Brisbane Courier, 28 March 1894

[49] *Queensland Police Gazette* 1896, p.18.

[50] 'A Bunch of Queensland Grasses.' *The Queenslander,* 2 June 1894

[51] *Western Champion and General Advertiser for the Central Western Districts,* 4 June 1895

[52] *Queensland Police Gazette* 1985, p.228.

[53] *Queensland Police Gazette* 1894, P.250

54 The Brisbane Courier, 22 March 1898.

55 *Notes on the History, Geology and Botany of the Vale of Derwent, being papers read before the Vale of Derwent Naturalists' Field Club.* Wordsworth Press. 1891. (A list of the contents of these two volumes is available on the website.)

56 *Clarence and Richmond Examiner* 27 June and 4 July 1899.

57 *Sydney Morning Herald,* 9 February 1898.

58 Fawcett, J.W. *History of the Parish of Dipton.* 1911. Introduction.

59 *The Vasculum,* Vols 1-5, 1916-19, pp. 9-11.

'In the band of naturalists drawn together by the personality of the late John Hancock was one – himself no mean naturalist – who held his memory in special regard.   To this friend, Canon Tristram of Durham, occurred the happy idea of perpetuating one trait of Hancock's character, to wit, the encouragement of the beginner, the young student of nature, to whom a word of help means so much in directing and strengthening his hobby and widening his outlook.

'With this object in view, and with the hearty support of the Natural History Society of Northumberland, Durham and Newcastle-upon-Tyne, Canon Tristram set to work after Hancock's death, while his memory was yet green, and by his spirited and personal endeavour, collected from a few generous friends a modest sum for investment, the interest of which enabled him to found a competition, which, with loving remembrance, was linked with the name of his old friend as "The Hancock Prize."

'The competition, as originally constituted, took the form of an essay, describing the observations in any branch of natural history made during the course of a day's ramble in the country or on the coast.   The administration of the scheme was vested in the hands of the Council of the Natural History Society and the award was to take the form of a medal or prize of books, but later the winners were allowed the option of choosing instruments suitable for the pursuit of their subject.

'The competition was intended not for those who had enjoyed the advantage of special scientific study, but primarily and essentially for the benefit of those whose opportunity had been more restricted and who, working to some extent in the dark, needed the encouragement of a helping hand. Systematic knowledge was not desired but rather an intelligent observation of those things seen during a day's outing. Literary style was not the object in view, for to all it may not come easy to write with a flowing pen of those things seen, but every encouragement was given to him whose book knowledge was limited, to go out into the fields, the woods or the shore, to use his eyes and put down on paper, however simply, what he had seen, the worth of which would be duly weighed and considered.

'The condition attached was that the competitors should be residents of the counties of Northumberland and Durham.

'All cannot climb to these heights, nor can everyone gain the Prize, but many have done excellent and useful work, and in the doing have learnt something of the truth that: -

> "Earth's crammed with heaven;
> And every common bush afire with God;
> But only he who sees, takes off his shoes:
> The rest sit round and pick blackberries."

'The object aimed at by the late Canon Tristram and the Council has been attained with a measure of success, may be fairly claimed, and it must have been gratifying to him to see the result. Perhaps the best has been the discovery of unknown talent, of quite a large body of previously obscure naturalists – miners, quarrymen, and others – brought into touch with the leading naturalists of the district: and thus encouraged, helped, and their work drawn into the general stream of scientific record. Perhaps the most of this talent has now come to light, and it is to the juniors that one must look for future work. Hope is entertained by the Council that the Hancock Competition may become yet more widely-known and that each would-be competitor will take heart and strive his utmost to emulate the good work of former winners, will try again if not successful at the first attempt, and be encouraged by the thought that: 'the trying shall suffice, The aim, if reached or not, makes great the life!'

[60] *Satley Registers,* Editor's Introductory Note.

[61] *Satley Registers,* p.156.

62 *Hobart Mercury,* Tasmania, Tuesday 28 December 1909, p.5.

LORD KITCHENER.
ARRIVAL IN AUSTRALIAN WATERS.
SOME PERSONAL IMPRESSIONS

'The Dutch steamer *Van Outhoorn* arrived at Port Darwin last week from the Netherlands Indies ports, bringing Field-Marshal Lord Kitchener, with his A.D.C., Captain Fitzgerald. Colonel and Mrs. Foster were also passengers.

'Immediately the vessel anchored (says the *"Sydney Telegraph"* correspondent), a boat from *H.M.S. Encounter* came alongside, with Major-General Hoad and Colonel Kirkpatrick. Without waiting for the port health officer to grant pratique, these officers boarded the *Van Outhoorn* and welcomed the Field-Marshal to Australia. Afterwards Lord Kitchener was taken off to the *Encounter* in a boat from that cruiser, and a Field-Marshal's salute of 19 guns echoed round the cliffs of the harbour. Following this salute, Mr. Justice Herbert, with his secretary, Mr. Nicholas Holtze, put off to the *Encounter.* The Resident welcomed the great soldier on behalf of the State of South Australia.

'At 5.30 p.m. Lord Kitchener landed at the railway jetty, and was welcomed by Cr. Barnes, chairman of the district council, and Councillors Bell, Kelsey, Kirkland, and Witherden. He was also introduced to Mr. Somerville, the railway superintendent.

'Cr. Barnes, in welcoming the visitor said: "My Lord, on behalf of the residents of this territory, we beg to extend to you a very hearty welcome to Port Darwin."

'Lord Kitchener replied: "I thank you most warmly. I am very glad indeed to be in Port Darwin today."

'Three rousing British cheers cut the words short, and Mr. Justice Herbert then escorted the Field-Marshal to the train waiting on the jetty, and the party proceeded to the railway station, where vehicles were in waiting. A party, consisting of Lord Kitchener, Major General Hoad, Colonel Kirkpatrick, Staff-officer and Captain Fitzgerald, A.D.C., Captain Colomb, of *H.M.S. Encounter,* Mr. Justice Herbert, and Mr. Holtze, then drove to Point Emery, which is the eastern head of the entrance to the harbour; thence through the experimental gardens to Fannie Bay, and from these points were able to see and grasp the great natural advantages which the harbour possesses for defence. Returning to the Residency, the party was entertained at dinner by Mr. Justice Herbert.

'After dinner the Residency party, consisting of Mr. Justice Herbert and Mrs. and Miss Herbert, Lord Kitchener, Major-General Hoad, Colonel Kirkpatrick, Captains Fitzgerald and Colomb, and Mr. Holtze, attended a concert in the Town Hall given by the band of *H.M.S. Encounter.* This proved a most successful function. The residents were intensely delighted that Lord Kitchener honoured them with his presence. This was a greater pleasure because it was thought possible that no opportunity would be afforded for many to see the great soldier. Lord Kitchener entered thoroughly into the enjoyment of the evening, and appeared particularly to enjoy the comic songs, with pointed hits at the state of the army and navy. At the close of the concert Lord Kitchener and party boarded the Encounter. Interviewed by a press representative, Captain Fitzgerald, A.D.C., stated that Lord Kitchener arrived at Singapore after his visit to Japan in the steamer Assaye, and stayed there only one day, joining De Carpentiere at Singapore. They voyaged to Batavia, where they landed, and were the guests of the Commander-in-Chief of the Dutch forces in the East. After spending one day in Batavia, Lord Kitchener proceeded to Buitenzorg, where the Governor-General was residing, and there he was welcomed and entertained by the Governor-General. Leaving Buitenzorg, but still the guest of the Governor-General, he was taken by rail and motor to all the most famous beauty spots in Java, and finally, after six days in Java, joined the *Van Outhoorn* for Port Darwin on the 11th inst. The stay in Java was thoroughly enjoyed by Lord Kitchener, as was also the voyage through innumerable Dutch islands, but the lack of progress of colonisation seemed to the party a matter for much surprise.

'Arrived at Wake Island, the Van Outhoorn met with a most serious mishap, which threatened to upset all the Australian programme of the Field Marshal. The water is so deep at this port that no anchorage is possible, and accordingly steamers keep under way the whole of the time. The Van Outhoorn was steaming backwards and forwards waiting for her boats to return to the ship when, in broad daylight, she grounded hard and fast on the shore, and remained fast for twelve hours. So firmly did she ground that no hope was entertained of floating her off for ten days, and, accordingly, a boat was despatched on a long voyage to the nearest cable station to cable for *H.M.S. Encounter* or some other vessel to be sent to assist the *Van Outhoorn;* but, fortunately, the worst fears were not realised, for the vessel was floated after twelve hours, without much apparent damage.

'Captain Fitzgerald says that Lord Kitchener carefully studied the charts of this harbour, and has examined the natural features for defence, and that he is very much impressed indeed with the great natural advantages existing there for defence. It is understood that Lord Kitchener considers the harbour can be most easily and effectively fortified, and that in this respect it offers greater natural advantages than Singapore.

'Captain Fitzgerald stated that Lord Kitchener is looking forward to his Australian tour with most intense pleasure, and that he is greatly pleased and impressed with Port Darwin, his first port of call. Speaking for himself, Captain Fitzgerald said one could not but be impressed with the immense possibilities of this port when a railway was put through the continent. When reminded that the Commonwealth declined to take over the Territory, the captain said that, although this was probably a keen disappointment to the Territorians, they must not despond, for the geographical position of the port, with its great natural advantages, must inevitably make this a great centre in years to come.

LORD KITCHENER'S ITINERARY. (Melbourne, December 27)

'The Prime Minister has received from Lord Kitchener the following telegram setting out his proposed movements within the Commonwealth: - "We hope to reach Brisbane on Saturday, January 1. In Sydney I dine with the Lord Mayor on January 5, and with the Grand Lodge of Masons, N.S.W., on January 7. We leave Sydney on Monday, January 10, to unveil a memorial at Bathurst, and thence to join the Melbourne express, as may be arranged later. In Melbourne the Victorian Government reception will take place on January 17.

I propose the following programme after January 19:- Leave Adelaide by mail steamer Mooltan on January 20, and arrive at Fremantle on January 24; return from Fremantle by mail steamer *Osterley* on January 27, reaching Adelaide on Monday, January 31. Will stay in Adelaide till Thursday, February 3. Arrive in Melbourne, Friday, February 4, and leave for Tasmania by the steamer *Loongana* the same day, arriving in Launceston and Hobart on February 6. Will leave Hobart on February 7 and arrive at Ross camp on the same day. Will leave Tasmania on February 8, and arrive in Melbourne on February 9. Will leave Melbourne for New Zealand on Saturday, February 12."

[64] *Archaeologia Aeliana,* lists of members (Third Series, vol.XVII, 1920, p.xxviii)

[65] *Archaeologia Aeliana,* lists of members (Fourth Series, vol.VII, 1930, p.xvii)

[66] *Townsville Daily Bulletin*, Monday 28 September 1931, p.4.

[67] *New South Wales Government Gazette*, Friday 5 May 1893, p.252

[68] *Sydney Evening News*, Friday 20 February 1885.

[69] 'In *Archaeologia Aeliana, lists of members* (Third Series, vol.XVI, 1919, p.xxi) Odd Moments' column in *The Australian Worker*, Sydney, 25 January 1917.

[70] 26 January 1921 in *Proceedings of the Society of Antiquaries of Newcastle-upon-Tyne,* Third Series, vol.X (January 1921 – December 1922), pp.36-37.

[71] Deeds, etc., relating to Northumberland', read by Secretary 25 July 1917 in *Proceedings of the Society of Antiquaries of Newcastle-upon-Tyne,* Third Series, vol.VIII (January 1917 – December 1918), pp.66-68.

[72] John Gall, *Lanchester Local History Society Booklet Number 3.* 1992

[73] *History, Topography and Directory of Durham,* Whellan, London, 1894:

'Woodlands, in this township, affords a pleasing instance of the triumph of art and industry over the most difficult and discouraging obstacles to improvement. After a long discussion as to the wisdom of enclosing this portion of Lanchester common, the idea was abandoned, and a large tract, including over 1500 acres, was sold by the commission for about £8000, and another parcel of 300 acres, at a rent-charge of £30 per annum. This was principally bought by Thomas White, Esq., of Nottingham, who planted the smaller parcel, one-half with large trees, in addition to which he also planted many acres of fruit trees, under the shelter of another planting of over 200 acres. His spirited example was followed by others with success, and this once dreary and uninteresting tract of country now presents a most pleasing landscape, clothed with thick woods and plantations, and has become more thickly populated than would otherwise have been possible.

'Woodlands is the seat and property of W.B. van Haansbergen, Esq., J.P., and occupies a charming and elevated situation, three miles west of Lanchester, and two north of East Butsfield. The park is beautifully laid out, and the surrounding district, for a considerable extent, is thickly clothed with fir, forming a pleasing diversity in the somewhat wild and rugged landscape.'

[74] *The Proceedings of the Society of Antiquaries of Newcastle Upon Tyne,* Series 4, Volume X, Number 2. January 1943, p.103.

75 *The Consett Chronicle,* Thursday 2 April, 1942, p.5, d-e.

76 *Northern Echo*, Thursday 4 June 2009, p.14. 'John North' written by Mike Amos.

77 Havery, Gavin. 'Historian's grave gets headstone after seventy years.' *Northern Echo*, 2 July 2013.

78 *Durham Advertiser*, 3 April 1942, p.6, f-g.

APPENDIX A

Dendrological Notes from North-West Durham.

From Transactions of the English Arboricultural Society,
Volume II, 1895-6, p.17-30

The county of Durham, small though it be in size, possesses some fine woodland, with intersperses of varied scattered and venerable woods, remnants of former forests; all containing some large and noble specimens of the various species of our British forest trees, with variegations of thriving plantations, the homes, it is to be hoped, of sturdy giants of the future.

Durham in the early period of British history, then a portion of the country of the Brigantes, a wide and almost trackless district, was covered with thick forests and dense woods, of which the chief trees were the robust oak, the beautiful birch, and the graceful pine. Part of the district now forming this county, and which contained the largest woodlands, were the upper reaches of the rivers Tees, Wear, and a portion of Derwent, the two former of which were known up to even a late period as Teesdale and Weardale forests. These districts are now destitute of much of their former woodlands, and present only a bare appearance to what they were in the early days of Britain's history.

The Bishops of Durham, princes and autocrats in their own diocese, possessed several extensive stretches of woodlands, designated forests, in which deer were preserved for sport, and adjacent to these were the parks where the beasts of the chase were hunted. For all these forests, some of which were only called woods and parks, the Bishops appointed foresters and park-keepers, whose duty it was to look after, keep in order, and watch the several separate places. Amongst the forests and woods were those of Weardale, Teesdale, Birtley, Marwood, Gateshead, Benfieldside, &c., and the parks Aycliffe, Auckland, Beaurepaire, now Bearpark, Consett, Evenwood, Ferryhill, Marwood, Muggleswick, Raby, Rainton, Stanhope, Wolsingham, &c. Amongst the woods, that of Muggleswick is stated in 1602 to have been, at that date, 'the goodliest wood' in the county, and though since then many successions of trees have been planted and cut down, any person seeing some of the fine and stately 'denizens of the forest' now upon the steep banks of the

Hisehope and Horsleyhope burns, will not, I think, fail to form some idea of the 'goodliness' of the wood in former days.

First and foremost amongst our British forest trees are those venerable fathers of the forest, the OAKS. They, the monarchs of our woods and the pride of every patriotic Englishman, were held sacred by peoples and nations, whose height of ambition long since fell and decayed away, until now they are almost forgotten. Greeks, Romans, Gauls, Scandinavians, and Britons all regarded it as a tree of reverence, and the priests and teachers of the latter people esteemed all its productions as holy.

The county of Durham contains many fine oaks of great age and size, and the district which seems to be specially adapted to the growth of these trees is the Vale of Derwent. This valley has been famous for oaks for many centuries. More than six hundred and sixty-six years ago, when the towers of Durham Cathedral were in course of construction, we learn, from depositions taken in a suit between the Bishop of Durham (Richard de Marisco) and the Prior (Ralph Kermech) and Chapter, about 1227-1228, that one Walter de Andre, a knight, having been sworn and questioned concerning the rights of the Bishop in the forests, stated that, "He is certain that it is unlawful for the monks to take oakwood in the forest without the leave of the Bishop or his agents, but deadwood, ash and willow, and what is required for ploughs (ash), they can take, as the knights and other magnates do by forest right; as is also testified by all the other witnesses," and he adds that "he has seen the monks draw wood purchased in the wood of H-- de Bolbec (a relation of Walter de Bolbec, who founded the Abbey of Blanchland in 1175), which is beyond the Bishop's forest and the water of Derwent (stretching between Shotley and Minsteracres on a portion of Bolbec Barony and Common, the latter of which was divided in 1765), for making the towers of the Monastery of Durham, which wood for some time was collected his land at Conekesheved (this is a former name of Consett, but which was the land I cannot say, for this is the only mention I know of the Bolbecs having land in that locality), which as he believed they would not have done if they could lawfully and without licence have taken it in the forest in which is equally as good wood, and it is on this (the south) side the water, and much nearer for them."

Chopwell woods, formerly, perhaps, part of the original forests of Durham, were, until about the year 1850, famed for their sturdy old oaks; and we may judge that the timber was of a quality both strong and durable, when it is known that in the year 1649, Charles I, King of England, gave timber out of the crown woods at Chopwell towards the repair of the Tyne Bridge between Newcastle and Gateshead. Besides these evidences of the stately oak in the Derwent valley, we have other proofs of the former existence of extensive forests, and that on what are now bleak hillsides, in the form of the trunks of large oaks which are frequently found amongst the peat on the fells and moors of the west.

Though by far the greater part of the ancient oak forest has long been laid low by the axe of the spoiler, we have still a few straggling specimens of old grey gnarled oaks left, some of which are real "Kings of the Forest," both in age and size. One of the largest and oldest in the Derwent valley is found in close proximity to the Foxholes farmstead, between Alansford and Muggleswick. It measures seventeen feet in circumference at the base, and twelve feet beneath the lowest branches, and reaches a height of over thirty feet, the top being greatly broken. On its aged trunk it bears numerous proofs of having suffered from storm and tempest, and the greater number of its branches have been shattered and torn off by the effects of the weather.

Another old oak with furrowed trunk and shattered limbs, broken yet stately, and still bearing in the season leaves both green and thriving, is found in Gibside woods, where it is truly called the "King of the Wood," for it must be many centuries old, having a girth of sixteen feet.

Another, and maybe the oldest in the North of England, is found in this valley not far from Friarside Chapel. This noble old oak is thus described by my friend Mr J. F. Robinson, the President of the Vale of Derwent Naturalists' Field Club, in one of his papers read before the members of that society; "This oak is really a conglomeration of two trees, or trunks, from one root. The original tree had apparently attained its full growth before the second commenced to grow, as it is very much decayed, while the later growth is strong and vigorous. The original trunk is enclasped by the other so closely that the two form virtually one tree, seventeen feet in girth, one half of which is decayed and several hundred years old, while the other half is sound and very much younger."

Other fine sturdy and stately specimens, though not so large as the above, are found either singly or in small clumps above Alansford, near Shotley Bridge, Ebchester, Hamsterley, Chopwell, Lintzford, Gibside, Ravensworth, and Bradley, and other places in or bordering on the Derwent valley.

The Browney valley contains some fine old oaks, rivalling those of the Derwent in age and size. It was from a couple of woods in this valley, Beaurepaire (now Bearpark) and Backstanford, a mile and a half further down the river, that much of the timber for the cloisters of Durham Cathedral — which were commenced in 1368 and finished in 1498 at a total cost of £838, a considerably larger sum in the currency of the present day — was obtained. A venerable oak in this valley is that which overhangs the river just above the weir of the now dismantled Relly Paper Mills. This tree, which has been dead many years, is quite hollow, and consists of a trunk reaching eleven feet high and fourteen feet in circumference at the base, and has lost a portion of one side. There is little probability but that it is the remains of one of those which formed part of the forest existent here more than six centuries ago.

On the first of December, 1758, a very large oak, known as the " Great Oak, "was cut down in the woods of Langley, near Durham — in the Browney valley. It measured twenty-four feet ten inches in circumference at the base, was computed to contain about ten tons of timber, perfectly sound, and was supposed to be one thousand years old. The timber was sold by the Bishop of Salisbury, to one John Marks, timber merchant, of Downton, near Salisbury, for the sum of £40.

Numerous oaks are found in other parts of the valley, though not of so great dimensions. Some fine specimens exist in the woodland fringes of the river between where it receives the Panburn and the Smallhope, a few of them measuring twelve feet and more in circumference. Several other large trees have been found in the valley of the upper Browney and its tributaries, the Pan and Rippon burns.

Oak timber forms the chief wood of the roofs of most of our old churches, and it is not at all improbable that much of it in the local forests. An instance of its durability was afforded in the winter of 1884, when the old oak timber forming the bell loft of St. Michael's Church, Heighington, which was computed to have been there for four hundred and fifty years, was sold by public auction.

The BEECH (*Fagus sylvatica*) is a noble tree, attaining an immense size, and living to a considerable age. Attaining its full stature at fourscore, it always presents, when full leaved, a fine appearance, and as one of the most magnificent objects of nature, its appearance is much appreciated by artists. Many splendid specimens of beeches are to be found in the county of Durham, and the Vale of Derwent is almost as remarkable for its beeches as Buckinghamshire itself, which as some suppose gets its name from this tree.

Lofty and massive trees are found all the way up the valley from Swalwell to Alansford, Gibside, Lintzford, Hamsterley, and the woods about Shotley Bridge being the best localities.

The upper part of the Browney valley and its numerous tributaries equally vie with the Derwent in the magnificence of its beeches. In what is known as the Gill in the Browney valley between East Butsfield and Satley is a clump of beeches, thirty-three in number, presenting as fine specimens as any that may be found in the county. The largest measures ten feet in circumference at the base, and reaches to a height of about sixty feet. Several of the others are over eight feet in girth. A second clump, twelve in number, stand near the junction of the Panburn with the Browney, the whole of which measure on an average, eight feet in girth, and attain a height of some forty feet. Several large ones formerly grew on the Broomshields estate. They were planted prior to 1818, and many of them were cut down in the years 1884 and 1885. Some of them measured nine feet in girth at the base, and were over fifty feet in height. A few about the same size still (1891) remain. Several noble trees grow by the sides of the Lobley Hill turnpike at Browney Bank, nearly equidistant from Lanchester and Satley, the girth at their bases is large, but they begin to branch off almost immediately from the ground. An avenue of noble beeches is an imposing sight. Many of the old residences had one running from their fronts to the main road, remnants of which still remain. There is a beautiful avenue of beeches on either side of the road for a short distance, and then only on one side of what is known as the Ivesley and Waterhouses cross-road, leading from the Lanchester and Crook road, about midway between the two latter places. This avenue is the remnant of one which formerly skirted each side of the private road which led for a short distance eastwards along the hilltop, and then descended northwards to what is now the ruined Rowley Castle, the ancient seat of the Gillet family. Another beautiful beech avenue formerly led from Delves Lane, Consett, to the now also ruined Crook Hall, the former seat of the illustrious family of Bakers. Very few of these noble trees now remain, many of them having either been cut down or blown down by the heavy winds; the last one which fell was blown down in 1885. A row of these trees, but younger and of lesser dimensions, still stand on either side of what was the fishpond at the bottom of the old lawn, in front of the hall.

The ASH (*Fraxinus excelsior*) abounds all over England, and for strength, beauty, and long life, is a tree of the first rank. Loving such localities as border a stream, it grows to an immense size, and its sylvan beauty is only equalled by the Walnut. It is remarkable for being frequently found growing on the walls of old ruins, crags, and rocky heights— places where the hand of man could not have planted it; a fact owing to its having a winged seed, which is easily carried away by the wind into such odd out of the way places. Some fine specimens are found in this county. In the winter of 1887 and 1888, a remarkable tree of this species was cut down in the grounds of Bradley Hall, near Wylam. Its girth was over twenty feet, and it contained nearly six hundred cubic feet of timber. It covered nearly an acre of ground, and was cut down owing to its proximity to a building wherein prize cattle were housed, which it was feared it might damage, if blown down by the winter storm. A couple of men were employed two days in hewing it down and cutting it up. Other noble specimens, though not so large, are found in most of the woods of the Derwent valley. Two remarkable ones formerly grew within the roofless walls of Friarside Chapel. They were cut down about 1860. There are several trees in the Browney valley measuring more than forty feet high, and six and seven feet in girth at the base. One was cut down in 1888 in the fringes below Colepike Hall, which measured ten feet in girth, and was forty odd feet high.

The ELM (*Ulmus campestris*), one of the finest of our British forest trees, is tall and graceful, and attains a considerable height, with tier after tier of spreading branches. Some fine specimens are to be found in the valley of the Derwent in the neighbourhood of Shotley Bridge, and in the Wear valley in the grounds of Stanhope Castle, and near to the picturesque "Jack's Crag." Several of those near the latter place must be very old, for their trunks are hollow. A few of this species arc found in the Vale of Browney, but they are not large, neither do they present any remarkable features.

The BIRCH (*Betula alba*) is one of the prettiest of our forest trees, and possesses more elegance and grace than any other. It never attains dimensions like the Oak or Ash, yet it is by no means a small tree. That this tree formed part of the large forests of Durham, we have many evidences, for numerous remains of birches have been found in-situ on the high moorlands of the west. A few specimens, of what may be termed large dimensions, are found in the woodland fringes of the upper Vale of Browney. Two on the Hole House grounds, below Colepike Hall, measure six feet in circumference at the base, one attaining a height of over forty feet, the other fifty feet; and three further up the valley, in the neighbourhood of Browney Bridge, though only about thirty feet in height, average six feet in girth.

The ALDER (*Alnus glutinosa*), a great companion of the Birch, is one of the commonest of our native trees. Loving a marshy situation, it forms a picturesque part in the scenery of lakes and rivers. It seldom attains a larger growth than that of a large shrub, though occasional fairly-sized trees are met with. In the woodland fringes of the upper Browney, there are several measuring over three-and-a-half feet in girth, one or two exceeding five-and-a-half feet: but none of them attain a height of more than thirty feet.

The HOLLY (*Ilex Aquifolium*), the finest of our evergreens, thrives nowhere so well as in this, its native country. Slow-growing, but sure, it takes many years to attain a fair height. Though having a fine appearance at all times, it appears best when laden with its clusters of red coral-like berries. Though the berries, in general, are ripe only in the winter months, and especially about Christmas, I have known trees to have berries upon their branches all the year round. One tree in the Browney valley contained ripe berries the whole twelve months of the years 1883, 1884, and 1885, in abundance; however, during the winter of 1889 it bore very few, and only for two or three weeks; and in 1890 the berries were ripe by October 8th, but they were few in number, and had all disappeared by January 7th, 1891. On a sandy, gravelly bank, bordering one of the haughs in the woodland fringes of the upper Browney, are some fine and remarkable specimens. From one root in this wood grow no fewer than twelve trees, the largest measuring three feet in girth, and about twenty-five feet high, with a clean trunk; and from a second root, not far distant, spring nine trunks, all over eighteen inches in girth, the largest measuring three feet, and reaching a height of more than twenty feet.

A fine scenic tree is that commonly called The PLANE. This tree is only a false-leaved Plane, as its botanical name shows — *Acer pseudoplatanus* — the proper appellation being that of the Sycamore. In favourable situations it attains a large size, and when growing alone becomes a grand and noble shader, and one ever admired for its massive foliage. It is a tree commonly found in the neighbourhood of simple dwellings and villages. A few, unrivalled perhaps for form and beauty, are to be found in the neighbourhood of the village of Satley, many of them exceeding seven feet in circumference — one or two measuring nine feet and over. Other noble trees of this species are found in the grounds of Stanhope Castle, and in the rectory gardens in that town. Beneath the shade of three Sycamores in a field called Guy's Close, near Greenhead farm-house, more than a mile to the west of Stanhope, lie the remains of the first resident Quakers of Weardale, John Muschamp and his wife Ann. A row of these grand trees is to be found in Wolsingham churchyard, skirting the older portion of the burial ground. The largest measures eleven feet in circumference four feet from the ground; and as they were planted about 1734 by the Rev. William Watts, who was rector sixteen years - from 1721 to 1737 - they have attained a fairly good age, seeing that they may now be said to be about one hundred and sixty years old; and they are yet healthy and vigorous.

Various species of WILLOW are found, all of which are of elegant and picturesque outline; but the one which is best known, and which attains the greatest height in this county, is The White Willow (*Salix alba*). Growing by the margin of the rivers, streams, brooks, and water-courses, its graceful and slender form always presents a pleasing object to human view, harmonizing well with the wave and ripple of the water. Some fine specimens are to be found in the upper Browney valley, where their fringe-like foliage give them a fine lands apical appearance. A grand specimen of the White species was cut down on the Broomshields estate in the winter of 1882. It measured over seventy feet in length, was eight feet in girth at the base, four feet in circumference at a height of forty-one feet from the ground, and contained seventy cubic feet of useable timber, and several feet of waste.

Another specimen, of larger girth, was cut down in 1884, which contained upwards of seventy cubic feet, with much waste, the upper parts being greatly subdivided. A tall White Willow stood at the confluence of the Rippon Burn and River Browney at Browney Bridge, about a mile and a half north-east of Satley, which reached to a height of upwards of seventy feet. On several occasions it suffered severely from the strong winds which sweep down the valley; and in the heavy storm of August, 1889, the greater part of it was destroyed. Another, and perhaps the best in this district, stands near the centre of a grass-haugh further down the river. It measures eight-and-a-half feet in girth at the base, and attains a height of sixty feet or more. It begins to branch off almost from the root, and forms a fine object, giving a graceful air to the woodland fringe which surrounds it.

Other specimens, measuring over six feet in girth at the base, and tapering gradually to a height of more than forty feet, are found by the side of the stream above and below this specimen. Two specimens of this tree, which is best known in this county as the Huntingdon Willow, formerly grew in a yard at the back of a dwelling house in Front Street, Wolsingham. The introduction of the parent of these two trees, and how they came to grow there, has such a fine Joseph-of-Arimathea-and-the-Glastonbury-thorn flavour about it, that it is worthy of a public record. The Rev. Peter Ionn, a native of the village of Great Strickland in Westmorland, and who for thirty-eight years was curate of Wolsingham, and head-master of the Grammar School there, and perpetual curate of Eshe and Satley a short time, received his appointment at Wolsingham in the year 783. He was then a young man, being only twenty-one years of age; and soon after quitting his west country home for the picturesque valley of the Wear, he met his "fate," if so I may call it. Like the indomitable Caesar, "he came, he saw, he conquered." Yes, he finally won the affections of a handsome lady, the eldest daughter of a gentleman farmer of the old town. One evening during the courtship he visited the home of his affiance, taking with him a favourite walking stick. At the back of the house was then a small garden, and happening to enter it, he chanced to thrust his stick, a young willow sapling, into the soil, and there forgetfully (young men are very forgetful in their courting days) left it. It was some days after before he brought himself to recollect where he had left his wand; and when he did, he found on going to seek it, that, like Aaron's rod, it had budded leaves; and, generous man! he left it to grow, which it accordingly did. Two separate cuttings were afterwards made of it, and planted some distance apart. Mr. Ionn married in 1788, and this was done a short time previously. The two trees grew amain until between 1830 and 1840, several years after Mr. Ionn had joined the great majority, when they towered far above a malting house since removed, which stood near them. They were the admiration of all who either knew or saw them, their fine trunks and ribbon-like branches standing out grandly against the mottled roofs and blue sky. During some heavy gales soon after 1860, they were very much broken, and becoming unsound, were eventually cut down.

The WHITE HAWTHORN (*Crataegus oxyacantha*) grows well in this its native country, attaining in some districts a great size. Though we have no Hawthorns in the county of Durham, to carry our memories back to the time of the Tudors, with reminiscences of Richard III., whose crown was found in a fruited Hawthorn bush after the battle of Bosworth, in 1485; or of the unhappy Queen Mary of Scotland, who was executed in 1587, whose favourite was existent at Duddingthorn, near Edinburgh, as late as 1836: we have a few which have histories, and others which, from their great size, must be of no small age.

Two historic thorns deserve special mention. About halfway between Lintz Green House and the Pont Burn, on the Medomsley and Burnopfield road, in the Derwent valley, on the right-hand side going east, is a fir plantation, a portion of the Priestfield farm, in which up to about 1850 there stood the ruined remains of an old chapel. Against the western gable of this building grew a large thorn, some three feet - more or less - in girth. The remains of the chapel are now obliterated, and the thorn is cut down and was lying where it had fallen, the last time the writer visited the spot (March 12th, 1890). It bore marks of having grown against the wall; and as these marks were very plain, and there has been no wall for it to wear against during the last fifty years, and seeing that the Thorn when it becomes what may termed a tree, makes wood very slowly together with its great thickness, this Thorn, which may be called the "Chapel Thorn," must be, if not more than a century and a half old.

Another important Thorn is the "Wesley Thorn." In a field at the west end of High House Wesleyan Chapel, between Weardale St. John's and the Ireshope Burn, are two White Thorns. Under the taller of these the venerable John Wesley, the founder of Wesleyan Methodism, preached to an assembly in June, 1774. Though nearly destroyed in 1837, it still stands a monument of age and history.

There are a few of what may be termed large Thorns in the Browney valley. One measures five feet in girth, and is twenty feet in height. It is what is locally termed "scroggy," i.e., having numerous small branches full of angry prickles, and has been gradually dying for many years. From its gnarled trunk and great thickness, there is little doubt but that it is one of the, if not the, oldest in the district, and cannot be far short of two hundred years old. Near it is another with a girth of four feet and three-quarters, rising fifteen feet in height. Neither of them bear marks of the axe. A short distance further up the valley are two unique specimens; one is six feet ten inches in girth at the base, from which rise nine stems; the other has a circumference of five feet, and has twelve different stems growing from the root. Both, or rather all, are more than twenty feet high. There are several other fine specimens in this valley, and also in the vale of Knitsley, above the hamlet of that name. It is a picturesque sight, and one of fine effect, to see the gnarled rough trunk of an aged Hawthorn, in the month of May, supporting a crown of branches white with innumerable blossoms, which fill the air with a strange yet fragrant sweetness. Aye, 'tis a glorious sight !

There are some large Fir plantations in north-west Durham, chief of which are the scenic woods of Chopwell, planted after 1850 by the Commissioners of Woods and Forests, in the Derwent valley, one of the fairest portions of sylvan landscape in the North of England; woodlands chiefly in the valley of the Smallhope, an affluent of the Browney, planted at various dates between 1773 and 1811, by Thomas White, Esq., to whom the Society of Arts presented ten gold, and one silver medals, for so doing, some of the trees of which were cut down in the decade of 1830 and 1840, and other land planted after 1850, the planting being done by Jonathan Richardson, Esq., the whole of which presents a fine portion of woodland scenery; Bute's plantations, planted soon after 1850, near the head of the Browney; those on the Broomshields estate, near Satley, planted after 1840, one wood of which, 79 acres or more in extent, was ruthlessly cut down in the winter of 1889-90; the Black Banks, on the south side of the Wear below Wolsingham; and Shull, with its wide-spreading plantations in the Harthope, one of the affluents of the Wear.

Some of the finest LARCHES in the county are found in the valley of the Bedburn, a tributary of the Wear, near Hoppyland Hall, many exceeding a girth of ten feet three feet from the ground. One of the finest specimens of Larch that I have seen, formerly grew near the centre of a small grass-haugh by the margin of Pan Burn, not far from the footpath leading from Satley to Cornsay. This tree was a stately and magnificent one, and was greatly admired by persons travelling along the footpath near it. Its trunk was straight, tapering gradually to a point at a height of seventy feet. Its branches drooped gracefully even to the top), and their evenness gave the tree a very symmetrical appearance, somewhat resembling a cone. It is greatly to be regretted that this fine tree was ruthlessly hewn down in the winter of 1888-9. It measured over nine feet in girth at the base, seven feet at a height of five feet, four-and-a-half feet at a height of twenty-eight feet, and contained upwards of fifty cubic feet of timber. Some fine Larches were cut down about the same time in the grounds of Hole House farm, near Alansford. One, which was known as the "King of the Forest," contained over one hundred and twenty cubic feet of measurable timber, besides waste; whilst thirty others averaged seventy cubic feet. A beautiful avenue of Larches extends for some distance along the road from Roughside to Blanchland.

The SPRUCE occasionally exceeds five feet in girth at the base, and a height of over fifty feet.

The SCOTCH FIR — Pine it really is — is considered a native of Britain, and one of the proofs of this is the number of roots of this species found in a burnt state in many of the peat-mosses. At the southern catchwater of the Waskerly Reservoir a large number of stumps of this tree have been laid bare, showing that they must have formed part of a large forest in that neighbour-hood. Many of the trees, judging from the roots, have been of very great size, and from their charred appearance, appear to have been burnt off. This tree does not attain any great height in this district, the largest not reaching much more than forty feet in height, and less than four feet in girth.

Having already made my paper a long one, I shall, in conclusion, just briefly refer to the remaining, and rarer species in the locality. The LIME (*Tilia Europaea*) is a handsome tree, growing to a considerable size. A row of these lofty trees, numbering twenty-five — at one time there were twenty-six - grow on the south side of the main street of Stanhope, and the "Lime-tree Walk" is a delightful and much-frequented shady pathway. These trees, planted about 1740, are amongst the finest specimens of the North of England. Other noble Linden trees are found in the grounds of Stanhope Castle, on the Palace Green, Durham; and there is a fine avenue of old Limes in the Grounds of Blackwell Grange, near Darlington. In the grounds of Walworth Castle are (or were) two extra-ordinary Horse Chestnut trees, standing about thirteen yards apart, having branches of great size and weight touching and taking root in the soil in several places, like the famous Indian banyan tree. The branches of both trees meet, and cover an elliptical space of about one hundred and fifty yards in circumference.

There is a tine POPLAR tree in Stanhope rectory gardens, which was planted about 1830, and is now supposed to be one of the finest and most picturesque in the northern counties.

The YEW (*Taxus baccata*) seems to favour natural woods in rocky and mountainous districts, and there are a great number of these fine old native trees with gnarled stems, twisted branches, and sombre foliage, in the picturesque Castle Eden Dene, in the Derwent valley, near Friarside, and in a few localities in Teesdale and Weardale.

Some fine specimens of the CEDAR OF LEBANON (*Pinus cedrus*) are found in the grounds of Ravensworth Castle, and Blackwell Hall, where are also several CYPRESS trees (*Cupressus sempervirens*) and one of the TULIP tree (*Liriodendron tulipifera*).

On the Grounds of Bishop Oak, in Wolsingham Park, is a NORFOLK ISLAND PINE (*Araucaria eccyeses*) perhaps the finest in the North of England.

Photo: Terry Coult

Fig. 51 Remaining beech trees at the junction of the Pan Burn and the Browney

Figures 52, 53 and 54 (following pages)
from photographs taken in 1874 by G.C. Atkinson.
Atkinson's Remarkable Tree Survey.
Transactions of the Natural History Society of Northumbria
Volume 55, Part 2, February 1990.

Fig. 52   "The King Oak" at Gibside, 1874

OAK. "The King" A very grand tree, grows in the ravine, 100 yards E from the House. Girth, 15 feet 1 inch: height, 103 feet: bole 55 feet of clear stem, and then a few moderate branches. It is a noble tree, containing a great deal of capital timber. Several other fine oaks grow near it.

The tree stands on sloping ground, and the mean surface level is midway between the highest and lowest. This noble tree is computed to contain 500 cubic feet of timber: the bole is very magnificent, tapering very little for 55 feet: the spread is trifling.

From a framed description in the stewards office, dated Dec. 1800, the girth, at 7 feet from ground, was 13 feet 4 inches: in 1808 the girth at 7 feet was 13 feet 8 inches: now, in June 1874, the girth at 7 feet is 14 feet 9 inches. (*1 June 1874. G. C. Atkinson*)

Fig. 53   Group of Cedars of Lebanon at Ravensworth Castle. 1874

A noble group of old Cedars grows 270 yards N of Castle, of which four, in a line a few yards apart (E. and W.), are very large. The girth of themost E., at a height of 5 feet, is 12 feet 1 inch. That of the next on its W., at a heightof 5 feet, 12 feet 9 inches. That of the most W., 5 feet, 14 feet: spread of branches, not great: height of this last tree, 51 feet.

The boles of all are short, varying from (the W. one which is) four feet to seven feet; and then good in heavy branches: a good deal decayed. *(May 28, 1873, G. C. Atkinson)*

Fig. 54   Horse Chestnut at Walworth Castle 1874

Two magnificent trees of this kind grow about 60 yards from the Castle, on its E. side, about 60 yards apart N. and S.; the N. a female and the S. a male tree. Both trees, especially the S. one, shew a great tendency to bow their branches to the ground, and then strike root and rise again. The boles of both are about 9 feet, with a height of about 63 feet: the girth, however, of the S. tree is 15 feet, and its spread 105 feet, while that to the N. is only 13 feet 9 inches. They are noble trees, in full vigour, and well become their position near the quaint old Elizabethan castle. *(Oct. 22. 1874. G. C. Atkinson.)*

APPENDIX B

Publications in Australia

A list of all the articles and books that have so far
come to light.

An Australian Pioneer – Robert Towns. MacKay Mercury, Queensland. 28
October 1890

The Aborigine Association

In late 1892, Fawcett wrote letters to newspapers all over Australia announcing
the inception of the Australian Aborigine Association, of which he was
president. These were published in papers such as The Queenslander, The
Australian Town and Country Journal, The Melbourne Argus, The South
Australian Register, The West Australian and The Western Mail. Subsequently,
he had various short articles on Aborigines published in newspapers, starting
with *Aboriginal Numerals*, which appeared in The Queenslander on 27 August
1892.

The Naturalist in Northern Queensland

This regular column was written for The Queenslander and published on
the dates given below. It was also syndicated in The Brisbane Courier and
occasional extracts appeared in other newspapers.

I	*Introductory*	24 March 1894
II	*The Great Kangaroo*	21 April 1894
III	*The Red Kangaroo*	18 May 1894
IV	*The Opossum*	26 May 1894
V	*The Tree Kangaroo*	2 June 1894
VI	*The Duck-Billed Platypus*	9 June 1894
VII	*The Dugong*	16 June 1894
VIII	*The Australian Crocodile*	23 June 1894

IX	*Ornithological Jottings*	30 June 1894
X	*Ornithological Notes*	7 July 1894
XI	*Kingfisher Family*	14 July 1894
XII	*Australian Shrikes*	21 July 1894
XIII	*Robins & Wrens*	28 July 1894
XIV	*The Thrushes*	15 September 1894
XV	*The Green Oriole*	22 September 1894
XVI	*The Blood Bird*	29 September 1894
XVII	*Parrots*	6 October 1894
XVIII	*Pigeons and Doves*	13 October 1894
XIX	*The Emu*	20 October 1894
XX	*Waders*	27 October 1894
XXI	*Natatores*	3 November 1894
XXII	*Snakes in general*	24 November 1894
XXIII	*The Deaf or Death Adder*	1 December 1894
XXIV	*The Brown Snakes*	5 December 1894
XXV	*Lizards*	15 December 1894
XXVI	*Entomological Notes*	5 January 1895
XXVII	*Botanical*	12 January 1895
XXVIII	*Flowering Time*	19 January 1895
XXIX	*Botanical*	26 January 1895

2 February 1895, *The Queenslander* published two new columns by their resident naturalist: In *The Birds of Queensland,* he covered the *White-bellied Sea Eagle,* the *White-Breasted Eagle,* the *White-Headed Osprey,* the *Whistling Eagle,* the *Brown Hawk,* and the *Nankeen Kestrel;* in *The Forest Trees of Queensland* he only managed to cover the *Bunya Bunya* and the *Red Cedar* before his journalism career went into a hiatus when he was imprisoned that June.

Books and miscellaneous articles published after his release

A Narrative of the Terrible Cyclone and Flood in Townsville, North Queensland, January 25th, 26th, 27th, 28th, 1896 compiled by J.W. Fawcett from personal observations, Townsville Daily Bulletin and Townsville Evening Star; with illustrated supplement from Blocks supplied by Northern Miner Newspaper Company was published by R.H. Thomas, bookseller and stationer, Townsville. 1896.

Songs and Recitations of the Australian Bush was published by D.W. Hastings & Co., Townsville in 1897.

Life and Labours of the Right Rev. William Grant Broughton, D.D., The First and Only Bishop of Australia was published by Sidney Hobart of Brisbane. 1897

The History of Wesleyanism in Tasmania. Launceston Examiner, Tasmania, 12 July 1897

The Last Resting Place of Governor Philip. Australian Town and Country Journal, 29 January 1898

Giant Trees – a letter written in response to an article about Forestry in the last issue of The Agricultural Journal was published in the Warwick Examiner and Times, 16 July 1898

Panicum in the Bundaberg District – a letter written in response to an article in the May Edition of the Queensland Agricultural Journal about Summer Crops was published in The Bundaberg Mail and Burnett Advertiser, 3 August 1898

A Brief Life of the Rev. John Cross, Forty Years a Chaplain in the Colony of New South Wales. Sidney Hobart, Brisbane.1898

A Brief Life of the Venerable William Cowper, D.D., Archdeacon of Cumberland in the Diocese of Sydney, and Forty-nine Years Minister of St. Phillip's Church, Church Hill, Sydney. Sidney Hobart. 1898

Sermons by the Rev. John Cross, Chaplain of Port Macquarie, 1828-58. Sidney Hobart. 1898

The Uses of Forests: A Plea for Forest Conservancy was published in two parts in the Clarence and Richmond Examiner on 27 June 1899 and 4 July 1899.

The Old Garden 'In Odd Moments' column in The Australian Worker, Sydney, 25 January 1917.

APPENDIX C

Publications in England

What follows is a simplified list of Fawcett's known publications: it has been distilled from a detailed chronological inventory researched and compiled by David Butler, to whom I am greatly indebted. For the use of researchers, scholars and those with more than a passing interest in the works of J.W. Fawcett, David's original list can be downloaded from the Land of Oak & Iron Local History Portal.

The Birds of Durham (1890)

The Naturalist, A Monthly Illustrated Journal of Natural History for the North of England included numerous reports by Fawcett between 1890 and 1909

Tow Law- Its Foundation and Early History (1890)

The Durham Magazine and County Historical Record. Comprehending Antiquity, Biography, Dialect, Folklore, Genealogy, History, Legend, Natural History, Song, Superstition, Topography, Trade.

Introductory Address
The Bishops of the See of Lindisfarne
The Durham Book
The Parish Registers of the County of Durham
Regal Progresses through the County of Durham
The Bishops of the See of Lindisfarne
The Parish Registers of the County of Durham
The City of Durham and her Topographers
The Heraldic Visitations of the County of Durham
The Monumental Inscriptions of Durham Cathedral
The Name "Durham" and its varied Etymologies
The Parish Registers of the County of Durham
The Heraldic Visitations of the County of Durham

The Monumental Inscriptions of Durham Cathedral
Durham Private Journals
Genealogical Collections
An Armorial of Durham

Dendrological Notes from North West Durham.
English Arboricultural Society. 1890

Notes on the History, Geology and Ornithology of the Vale of Derwent,
being the Papers read before the Vale of Derwent Naturalists' Field Club.
Wordsworth Press. 1891. Including 3 papers by J.W.F.

 Notes on the Birds of the Derwent Valley
 Women as Students of Nature
 Lanchester: Descriptive and Historical

Historic Places in the Derwent Valley. 1901

Brooke Foss Dunelm: a memorial. 1901

Tales of Derwentdale. 1902

Annals of the City of Durham

Blanchland Church. Descriptive and Historical with List of Incumbents. 1904

Durham Churches, Descriptive & Historical, with Lists of Incumbents. 1904

The Capercailzie. Weardale Naturalists' Field Club Transactions, vol.1, pt.2
(1904),

An Eminent Durham naturalist – Thomas John Bold. Notes on the History,
Geology, and Entomology of the Vale of Derwent, being Papers read before
the Vale of Derwent Naturalists' Field Club, vol.5 (1905)

The Parish Registers of Muggleswick in the County and Diocese of Durham,
containing Baptisms, Marriages, and Burials, from 1784 to 1812. 1906

A brief history of the township of Chopwell, read at Chopwell 11 May 1907.
Transactions of the Vale of Derwent Naturalists' Field Club, New Series,
vol. I, pt. 1 (1908)

*Memorials of Early Primitive Methodism in the County of Durham,
1820-1829.* 1908

*The Parish Registers of All Saints Church, Lanchester, in the County and
Diocese of Durham. Volume 1, containing Baptisms, Marriages, and Burials
from
3rd November, 1560, to 30th March, 1603.*
Transcribed, Annotated, and Indexed by J.W. Fawcett. 1909

*The Church of St. John the Baptist, Newcastle on Tyne;
Descriptive and Historical*

*A History of the Parish of Dipton (and Township of Collierley) in the County
and Diocese of Durham.* 1911

*The Parish Registers of St. Cuthbert's Church, Satley, in the County and
Diocese of Durham, containing Baptisms, Marriages, and Burials from 1560 to
1812, Gravestones, Inscriptions, Local Pedigrees.* 1914

Society of Antiquaries of Newcastle-upon-Tyne: papers, notes and letters
included in the Proceedings of the Society and in their journal, *Archaeologia
Aeliana*. This is a simplified list: for more details, please see Appendix D.

On the Remains of an Ancient Road near Satley. 1890.

Notes on the Chantry Chapel and Cantarists of Alnwick Castle,
1362-1548. 1917.

Deeds, etc., relating to Northumberland. 1918.

Early Northumbrian deeds. 1918

The Rev. Robert Patten: Cleric, Rebel, Historian. 1918

A Sixteenth-Century Newcastle Clergy List. 1918

A Calendar of Fourteenth Century Newcastle Burgesses. 1918

Ladykirk on Tweed. 1919

The Rev. Thomas Randall, B.D., and some of his MSS. 1919

The Addison Family. 1919

The Election of a Morpeth Grammar Schoolmaster. 1919

Inscriptions in Northumbrian Churches and Churchyards. 1919

Notes on Northern events in 1648 and in 1659-60. 1919

More about the Rev. Robert Patten. 1919

Chantries in Northumberland

Early Schools, &c. in Northumberland. 1920

Fowberry, Northumberland. 1922

Sheepmarking on the Fells. 1921

Alexander Davison, Swarland House.

The minor historians and topographers of the County of Durham.

Hunstanworth: Its geography and history. 1922

Local Notes from the Testementa Karleolensia. 1922

The Parish of Hunstanworth. 1922

Butsfield township, by Satley, Co. Durham. 1922

The Rev. Thomas Hobbes Scott. 1922

The Incumbents of Hunstanworth, Co. Durham. 1922

Some Local Authors. 1922

The Manor of Consett. 1922

The clergy of the County of Durham in 1534. 1923

Old Benwell Tower Chapel and its graveyard. 1923

Woodhorn, Northumberland [calendar of deeds] 1923

Lanchester Collegiate church and its deans. 1923

The Collegiate church of Chester-le-Street, Co. Durham, and its deans. 1923

The Collegiate church of Darlington, Co. Durham, and its vicars and deans. 1923

Cells and hermitages in Co. Durham. 1923

The office of coroner with reference to those of the County Palatine of Durham, and especially of Chester Ward. 1923

The Lords Lieutenant of the County of Durham. 1923

Sir John Duck, the butcher baronet of Durham. 1923

Prebendaries of the collegiate church of Lanchester. 1924

The Township of Knitsley, Co. Durham; Its Geography and History. 1924

Some forgotten or ruined churches or chapels in the County of Durham. 1924

The manor of Satley. 1924

James Craggs, Postmaster General of Great Britain, 1715-21. 1925

The minor historians and topographers of the County of Durham. 1925

The manor of Crook Hall, by Leadgate, County Durham. 1925

The compilation of parish clergy lists, with special reference to the Diocese of Durham. 1926

The manor of Pontop, County Durham. 1926

Archdeacon Thorpe's Visitation of Northumberland in 1792-3. 1926

Witton Gilbert Bridge. 1930.

Roman Antefix [tiles] 1938.

An Un-printed Satley Charter, c.1190. 1939

Two hitherto unrecorded burial cists in Satley Parish, Co. Durham. 1942

Interments at Winnowshill Friends' Burial Ground. 1942

Rowley Baptist Chapel, Co. Durham, and its graveyard. 1940

The place name Satley, and some coin finds there. 1941

Some Durham Bonds, read 24 May 1942, following the death of JWF.

Calendar of Deeds, Documents, &c. relating to Haddricks Mill by Gosforth, Northumberland,

APPENDIX D

Fawcett's Contributions to the Society of Antiquaries of Newcastle upon Tyne

'On the remains of an Ancient Road near Satley.' 1890. *Proceedings of the Society of Antiquaries of Newcastle upon Tyne.* First Series. Volume IV, page 255-6.

'Notes on the Chantry Chapel and Cantarists of Alnwick Castle, 1362-1548', read by the Secretary 30 May 1917. *Proceedings of the Society of Antiquaries of Newcastle-upon-Tyne,* Third Series, vol. VIII (January 1917 – December 1918), pp.50-53

'Deeds, etc., relating to Northumberland', read by Secretary 25 July 1917. *Proceedings of the Society of Antiquaries of Newcastle-upon-Tyne,* Third Series, vol. VIII (January 1917 – December 1918), pp.66-68

'Deeds, etc., relating to Northumberland, etc.', sent 31 October 1917. *Proceedings of the Society of Antiquaries of Newcastle-upon-Tyne,* Third Series, vol. VIII (January 1917 – December 1918), pp.88-92

'Early Northumbrian deeds', read by Secretary 29 May 1918. *Proceedings of the Society of Antiquaries of Newcastle-upon-Tyne,* Third Series, vol. VIII (January 1917 – December 1918), pp.154-157

'The Rev. Robert Patten: Cleric, Rebel, Historian', read by Secretary 31 July 1918. *Proceedings of the Society of Antiquaries of Newcastle-upon-Tyne,* Third Series, vol. VIII (January 1917–December 1918), pp.169-171

'A Sixteenth-Century Newcastle Clergy List', read by Secretary 28 August 1918. *Proceedings of the Society of Antiquaries of Newcastle-upon-Tyne,* Third Series, vol. VIII (January 1917–December 1918), pp.188-190, 194-196

'A Calendar of Fourteenth Century Newcastle Burgesses', note read 25 September 1918. *Proceedings of the Society of Antiquaries of Newcastle-upon-Tyne,* Third Series, vol. VIII (January 1917 – December 1918), pp.193-194

'Ladykirk on Tweed [and extracts relating to Upsetlington]', taken as read 29
January 1919. *Proceedings of the Society of Antiquaries of Newcastle-upon-
Tyne,* Third Series, vol. IX (January 1919 – December 1920), pp.9-10

'The Rev. Thomas Randall, B.D., and some of his MSS', read 26 March 1919.
Proceedings of the Society of Antiquaries of Newcastle-upon-Tyne,
Third Series, vol. IX (January 1919 – December 1920), pp.24-26

'The Addison Family', note sent in 26 February 1919. *Proceedings of the
Society of Antiquaries of Newcastle-upon-Tyne,* Third Series, vol.IX
(January 1919 – December 1920), p.28

'The Election of a Morpeth Grammar Schoolmaster, note sent in 26
February 1919. *Proceedings of the Society of Antiquaries of Newcastle-upon-
Tyne,* Third Series, vol. IX (January 1919 – December 1920), p.28

'Inscriptions in Northumbrian Churches and Churchyards', communication
read 26 March 1919. *Proceedings of the Society of Antiquaries of Newcastle-
upon-Tyne,* Third Series, vol. IX (January 1919 – December 1920), pp.30-31

'Notes on Northern events in 1648 and in 1659-60', read 30 April 1919.
Proceedings of the Society of Antiquaries of Newcastle-upon-Tyne,
Third Series, vol. IX (January 1919 – December 1920), pp.46-48

'More about the Rev. Robert Patten', read 30 April 1919. *Proceedings of the
Society of Antiquaries of Newcastle-upon-Tyne,* Third Series, vol. IX
(January 1919 – December 1920), pp.48-49

'More about the Rev. Robert Patten', read 28 May 1919. *Proceedings of the
Society of Antiquaries of Newcastle-upon-Tyne,* Third Series, vol. IX
(January 1919 – December 1920), pp.54-56

'Chantries in Northumberland', taken as read 27 August 1919. *Proceedings
of the Society of Antiquaries of Newcastle-upon-Tyne,* Third Series, vol. IX
(January 1919 – December 1920), pp.86-90

'Early Schools, &c. in Northumberland', sent in and taken as read 27 October
1920. *Proceedings of the Society of Antiquaries of Newcastle-upon-Tyne,*
Third Series, vol. IX (January 1919 – December 1920), pp.264-266

'Fowberry, Northumberland' [abstracts of deeds] *Proceedings of the Society of Antiquaries of Newcastle-upon-Tyne,* Third Series, vol. X (January 1921 – December 1922), pp.21-25, 48-51, 74-77, 87-90, 114-117, 148-150,188-190, 221-222

'Sheepmarking on the Fells', read 26 January 1921. *Proceedings of the Society of Antiquaries of Newcastle-upon-Tyne,* Third Series, vol. X (January 1921 – December 1922), pp.36-37

'Alexander Davison, Swarland House', note sent. *Proceedings of the Society of Antiquaries of Newcastle-upon-Tyne,* Third Series, vol. X (January 1921 – December 1922), pp.65-66

'The minor historians and topographers of the County of Durham', taken as read. *Proceedings of the Society of Antiquaries of Newcastle-upon-Tyne,* Third Series, vol. X (January 1921 – December 1922), pp.169-175

'Hunstanworth: Its geography and history', taken as read. *Proceedings of the Society of Antiquaries of Newcastle-upon-Tyne,* Third Series, vol. X (January 1921 – December 1922), pp.201-206

'Local Notes from the Testementa Karleolensia', taken as read. *Proceedings of the Society of Antiquaries of Newcastle-upon-Tyne,* Third Series, vol. X (January 1921 – December 1922), pp.218-219

'The Parish of Hunstanworth', taken as read. *Proceedings of the Society of Antiquaries of Newcastle-upon-Tyne,* Third Series, vol.X (January 1921 – December 1922), pp.230-237

'Butsfield township, by Satley, Co. Durham', taken as read. *Proceedings of the Society of Antiquaries of Newcastle-upon-Tyne,* Third Series, vol. X (January 1921 – December 1922), pp.274-281

'The Rev. Thomas Hobbes Scott', taken as read. *Proceedings of the Society of Antiquaries of Newcastle-upon-Tyne,* Third Series, vol. X (January 1921 – December 1922), pp.295-299

'The Incumbents of Hunstanworth, Co. Durham'. *Proceedings of the Society of Antiquaries of Newcastle-upon-Tyne,* Third Series, vol. X (January 1921 – December 1922), p.316

Some Local Authors', taken as read. *Proceedings of the Society of Antiquaries of Newcastle-upon-Tyne*, Third Series, vol. X (January 1921 – December 1922), pp.317-319

'The Manor of Consett', taken as read. *Proceedings of the Society of Antiquaries of Newcastle-upon-Tyne*, Third Series, vol. X (January 1921 – December 1922), pp.345-348

'The clergy of the County of Durham in 1534', sent 31 January 1923. *Proceedings of the Society of Antiquaries of Newcastle-upon-Tyne*, Fourth Series, vol. I (January 1923 – December 1924), p.18

'Old Benwell Tower Chapel and its graveyard', taken as read 25 April 1923. *Proceedings of the Society of Antiquaries of Newcastle-upon-Tyne*, Fourth Series, vol. I (January 1923 – December 1924), pp.53-56

'Woodhorn, Northumberland [calendar of deeds]', communicated 25 April 1923. *Proceedings of the Society of Antiquaries of Newcastle-upon-Tyne*, Fourth Series, vol. I (January 1923 – December 1924), pp.56-57

'Lanchester Collegiate church and its deans', communication taken as read 30 May 1923. *Proceedings of the Society of Antiquaries of Newcastle-upon-Tyne*, Fourth Series, vol. I (January 1923 – December 1924), pp.75-78

'The Collegiate church of Chester-le-Street, Co. Durham, and its deans', taken as read 25 July 1923. *Proceedings of the Society of Antiquaries of Newcastle-upon-Tyne*, Fourth Series, vol. I (January 1923 – December 1924), pp.117-120

'The Collegiate church of Darlington, Co. Durham, and its vicars and deans', taken as read 29 August 1923. *Proceedings of the Society of Antiquaries of Newcastle-upon-Tyne*, Fourth Series, vol. I (January 1923 – December 1924), pp.124-126

'Cells and hermitages in Co. Durham', communicated 26 September 1923. *Proceedings of the Society of Antiquaries of Newcastle-upon-Tyne*, Fourth Series, vol. I (January 1923 – December 1924), pp.136-140

'The office of coroner with reference to those of the County Palatine of Durham, and especially of Chester Ward', portions read, 31 October 1923. *Proceedings of the Society of Antiquaries of Newcastle-upon-Tyne,* Fourth Series, vol. I (January 1923 – December 1924) pp.146-150

'The Lords Lieutenant of the County of Durham', parts read 31 October 1923. *Proceedings of the Society of Antiquaries of Newcastle-upon-Tyne,* Fourth Series, vol. I (January 1923 – December 1924), pp.151-152

'Sir John Duck, the butcher baronet of Durham', read 28 November 1923. *Proceedings of the Society of Antiquaries of Newcastle-upon-Tyne,* Fourth Series, vol. I (January 1923 – December 1924), pp.169-173

'Prebendaries of the collegiate church of Lanchester', read 27 February 1924. *Proceedings of the Society of Antiquaries of Newcastle-upon-Tyne,* Fourth Series, vol. I (January 1923 – December 1924), pp.201-202. Read by the Secretary

'The Township of Knitsley, Co. Durham; Its Geography and History', read 24 May 1924 in *Archaeologia Aeliana* (Society of Antiquaries of Newcastle upon Tyne), Fourth Series, vol. I (1925), pp.35-41

'Some forgotten or ruined churches or chapels in the County of Durham', taken as read 30 July 1924. *Proceedings of the Society of Antiquaries of Newcastle-upon-Tyne,* Fourth Series, vol. I (January 1923 – December 1924), pp.269-272

'The manor of Satley', taken as read 24 September 1924. *Proceedings of the Society of Antiquaries of Newcastle-upon-Tyne*, Fourth Series, vol. I (January 1923 – December 1924), pp.299-302

'James Craggs, Postmaster General of Great Britain, 1715-21', taken as read 25 February 1925. *Proceedings of the Society of Antiquaries of Newcastle-upon-Tyne,* Fourth Series, vol. II (January 1925 – December 1926), p.21.

'The minor historians and topographers of the County of Durham', read 26 August 1925. *Proceedings of the Society of Antiquaries of Newcastle-upon-Tyne,* Fourth Series, vol. II (January 1925 – December 1926), pp.82-85

'The manor of Crook Hall, by Leadgate, County Durham', read 25 November 1925. *Proceedings of the Society of Antiquaries of Newcastle-upon-Tyne*, Fourth Series, vol. II (January 1925 – December 1926), pp.113-116 Read by chairman

'The compilation of parish clergy lists, with special reference to the Diocese of Durham', read 24 February 1926. *Proceedings of the Society of Antiquaries of Newcastle-upon-Tyne*, Fourth Series, vol. II (January 1925 – December 1926), pp.146-151

'The manor of Pontop, County Durham', placed before the Society on 24 February 1926. *Proceedings of the Society of Antiquaries of Newcastle-upon-Tyne*, Fourth Series, vol. II (January 1925 – December 1926), pp.155-158

'Archdeacon Thorpe's Visitation of Northumberland in 1792-3', read 28 April 1926. *Proceedings of the Society of Antiquaries of Newcastle-upon-Tyne*, Fourth Series, vol. II (January 1925 – December 1926), pp.162-166. Read by the Secretary

'Witton Gilbert Bridge.' *Proceedings of the Society of Antiquaries of Newcastle-upon-Tyne*, Fourth Series, vol. IV (January 1929 – December 1930), p.97.   Note to the Society.

'Roman Antefix [tiles]' *Proceedings of the Society of Antiquaries of Newcastle-upon-Tyne*, Fourth Series, vol. VIII (January 1937 – December 1938), p.31. Letter to the Society.

'An Unprinted Satley Charter, c.1190', read 26 April 1939. *Proceedings of the Society of Antiquaries of Newcastle-upon-Tyne*, Fourth Series, vol. IX (May 1939 - January 1942), pp.68-70   Read by H.L. Honeyman.

'Two hitherto unrecorded burial cists in Satley Parish, Co. Durham.' *Proceedings of the Society of Antiquaries of Newcastle-upon-Tyne*, Fourth Series, vol. IX (May 1939 – January 1942), pp.225-226

'Interments at Winnowshill Friends' Burial Ground.' *Proceedings of the Society of Antiquaries of Newcastle-upon-Tyne*, Fourth Series, vol. IX (May 1939 – January 1942), pp.226-228

'Rowley Baptist Chapel, Co. Durham, and its graveyard', read 25 September 1940. *Proceedings of the Society of Antiquaries of Newcastle-upon-Tyne*, Fourth Series, vol. IX (May 1939 – January 1942), pp.230-232. Read by H.L. Honeyman

'The place name Satley, and some coin finds there', read 27 August 1941. *Proceedings of the Society of Antiquaries of Newcastle-upon-Tyne*, Fourth Series, vol. IX (May 1939 – January 1942), pp.272-273

'Some Durham Bonds (From the MSS Collection of J. W. Fawcett)', read 24 May 1942. *Proceedings of the Society of Antiquaries of Newcastle-upon-Tyne*, Fourth Series, vol. X (July 1942 - December 1946), pp.95-97 Read by the Secretary following the death of J.W.F.

Calendar of Deeds, Documents, &c. relating to Haddricks Mill by Gosforth, Northumberland, by J. W. Fawcett, n.d. Manuscript notes of documents, 1537-1847, in the library of the Society of Antiquaries.

APPENDIX E

Notes on the Birds of the Derwent Valley
by J. W. Fawcett, The Grange, Satley, Darlington

IN compiling the following contributions towards the ornithology of the Derwent Valley, allow me to say a few words by way of introduction. The greater portion of the information given to me for the above purpose is that by Mr. Thomas Grundy, who for many years was a gamekeeper for gentlemen in the Valley of the River Derwent. Mr. Grundy was born at Ravensworth in 1815, where his father was gamekeeper to Sir Thomas Henry Liddell, sixth Baron of Ravensworth, in the County of Durham, in whose service and that of his son, he acted as such for sixty years.

In 1836, when twenty-one years of age, Mr. Grundy went into the service of Mr. Walker of Bradley Hall, west of Crawcrook, adjoining the River Tyne, as gamekeeper, and after residing there for eleven years returned to Ravensworth, in 1847, where he acted in the same capacity for seven years, until 1854.

Mr. Grundy, who is now advanced in years in his boyhood was, like many other of the children of that period, unable to obtain that great benefit to mankind, which is now so common, i.e., education - thanks to the various Education Acts; hence he was unable to commit to paper any of the important items of ornithology which he came across. Knowing that Mr. Grundy wished some one to write these notes down, and so preserve them, The Writer, for that reason, and the great importance of which he considers such to be, undertook to do so, feeling that, by so doing, he is rendering an important benefit to the ornithological world.

The knowledge which Mr. Grundy has of the birds of the lower portion of the Derwent Valley is unrivalled, and from what short notes he has given to me - thanks to his wonderful and retentive memory - I must say he has been a close and keen observer of the birds, and quite different from many of the gamekeepers in the county.

In the following list the writer has, for various reasons, kept Mr. Grundy's notes intact, and whatever additions have been made to them will be found at the completion of his (Mr. Grundy's) list.

1. *Turdus viscivorous.* Missel Thrush. A common resident in well-wooded districts. It feeds chiefly on berries, and at Christmas time yew berries form its particularly favourite food, and on them it gets very fat. Its note is about the first that is heard in the year, about February, or even in January.

2. *T. musicus.* Song Thrush. A common resident.

3. *T. iliacus.* Red wing. A regular visitor. Two or three eggs of this bird were obtained on the Bradley Hall Estate, about 1836, by Mr. Thomas Robson, at that time clerk for Crawley, Millington, and Co., Swalwell. They were lying on the grass, and had probably been dropped by the birds while feeding.

4. *T. pilaris.* Fieldfare. A regular visitor:

5. *T. merula.* Blackbird. A common resident.

6. *T. torquatus.* Ring Ouzel. A resident. I found a nest of this bird on the summit of Pontop Pike, about 1840, containing five eggs.

7. *Saxicola amanthe.* Wheatear. A regular summer visitor.

8. *Pratincola rubetra.* Whinchat. A regular summer visitor.

9. *P. rubicola.* Stonechat. A rare resident in the lower regions of the Derwent Valley. A pair nested near Burnopfield in 1887.

10. *Ruticula plœnicurus.* Redstart. A regular summer visitor.

11. *Erithacus ruticula.* Redbreast. A common resident.

12. *Sylvia cinerea.* Whitethroat. A regular summer visitor.

13. *S. curruca.* Lesser Whitethroat. The nest and eggs of this bird are very hard to find. In 1889 a pair nested in Burnopfield Gill, and another on the Bradley Estate between 1836 and 1847. Both nests were placed in bramble-bushes, and contained more substance (nesting material) and were deeper and firmer than the nests of S. cinerea. These are the only two nests I have found - T. Grundy.

14. *S. atricapilla.* Blackcap Warbler. Not a very common summer visitor. The male has a black and the female a brown head, and the nest is generally found among nettles.

15. *S. hortensis.* Garden Warbler. A very common summer visitor; its habits and nest are similar to those of the Blackcap Warbler.

16. *Regulus cristatus.* Gold-crested Wren. A resident. It used to be very common, but it is not so now. It is found in the warmer localities in the valley, especially where it is quiet. It breeds in spruce firs.

17. *Phylloscopus rufus.* Chiffchaff. Not such a common visitor as it used to be. It nests in very rough bramble covers.

18. *P. trochilus.* Willow Wren. A common summer visitor.

19. *P. sibilatrix.* Wood Wren. A very common summer visitor to the Derwent Valley. Burnopfield Gill is a favourite resort for it during the breeding season.

20. *Acrocephalus streperus.* Reed Warbler. A common resident on the marshes at Bradley and Ravensworth.

21. *A. turdoides.* Great Reed Warbler. Found nesting in the water-dykes (fences by the waterside, often very thick and bushy. - J.W.F.) near Swalwell. One nest was taken in a water-dyke between Blaydon and Scotswood Bridge, which was built between three reeds, and fully a yard in height.

22. *A. phragmitis.* Sedge Warbler. A common summer visitor.

23. *Locustella nœvia.* Grasshopper Warbler. A common summer visitor. Found two nests in 1888. They are generally found in young plantations on the side of a dry ditch. When the parent bird is disturbed from the nest, she will run along the ground in the grass for a great distance before she rises.

24. *Accentor modularis.* Hedge Sparrow. A common resident.

25. * *Cinclus aquaticus.* Dipper. A resident. Breeds in Milkwell Burn Woods.

26. *Acredula rosea.* British Long·tailed Titmouse. A common resident. The broods of the year always keep together during the winter months, and with the two old birds I have frequently seen fourteen or fifteen together. During the breeding season I have found as many as fifteen eggs in one nest, and have reason to believe that two females often lay in one nest, for I once found three old birds in a nest containing eggs; built in a blackthorn, on the Bradley Estate. (Certainly this is a very curious case, and may probably account for the numerous progeny of the long tailed Titmouse. It also leads us to believe that some of our birds are polygamous. I remember once finding three old House Sparrows in one nest. - J.W.F.)

27. *Parus major.* Great Titmouse. A common resident.

28. *P. Britannicus.* British Cole Titmouse. A common resident.

---

* This bird has bred in Ravensworth Woods. - T. Peacock.

29. *P. palustris.* Marsh Titmouse. A pretty common resident. This is a very plain bird, with an ash-colorued head.

30. *P. cœruleus.* Blue Titmouse. A common resident.

31. *Troglodytes parvulus.* Wren. A common resident.

32. *Motacilla lugubris.* Pied Wagtail. A common resident.

33. *M. melanope.* Grey Wagtail. A common resident.

34. *M. rayii.* Yellow Wagtail. A regular summer visitor; breeds.

35. *Anthus pratensis.* Meadow Pipit. A common resident.

36. *A. trivialis.* Tree Pipit. A common summer visitor. Its nest is built similar to that of the Meadow Pipit, but always in the middle of a wood.

37. *Ampelis garrulus.* Waxwing. It is a visitor only in severe winters, when it feeds on hips and holly-berries. I shot three on the Bradley Estate between 1836 and 1847 - Several (seven or nine) were shot at Norwood on the River Team, Ravensworth Estate, where they were feeding on holly-berries, between 1847-1854·

38. *Muscicapa grisola.* Spotted Flycatcher. A common summer visitor; breeds.

39. *M. atricapilla.* Pied Flycatcher. I have never found this bird nesting in Durham, but I saw one on the Gibside Estate early in the spring of 1886.

40. *Hirundo rustica.* Swallow. A common summer visitor; breeds.

41. *Chelidon urbica.* Martin. A common summer visitor; breeds.

42. *Cotile riparia.* Sand Martin. A common summer visitor; breeds in the bank of the railway cutting at Victoria Garesfield and at Rowland's Gill, and at the Scarbank near Winlaton Mill, and at Derwent Cote.

43. *Certhia familiaris.* Tree Creeper. A common resident; found nesting between the bark and trunk of trees, and between the jambs of old wooden buildings.

44. *Carduelis eligans.* Goldfinch. I saw one of these birds at Axwell, about Christmas 1885, feeding on horse knobs.

45. *Chrysomitris spinus.* Siskin. A common winter visinor. I have seen it feedimg on the flowers of the larch firs in February and March, at Bradley; and during the winter on the flowers of the alder.

46. *Ligurius chloris.* Greenfinch. A common resident.

47. *Cocothraustes vulgaris.* Hawfinch. I never saw this bird until recent years, about 1884. One was taken on the east boundary of the Gibside Estate in 1886.

48. *Passer domesticus.* House Sparrow. A commen resident.

49. *P. montanus.* Tree Sparrow. A resident. There is very little difference in the plumage of the male and female. They are not so common as the House Sparrow.

50. *Fringilla cœlebs.* Chaffinch. A common resident.

51. *F. montifringilla.* Brambling. A very rare winter visitor on the lower part the Derwent Valley.

52. *Linota cannabina.* Linnet. A common resident.

53. *L. linaria.* Mealy Redpoll. A common resident.

54. *L. rufescens.* Lesser Redpoll. A common winter visitor; feeding on the stubble fields.

55. *L. flavirostris.* Twite. Only seen in the lower part of the Derwent Valley in winter.

56. *Pyrrhula Europœa.* Bullfinch. A common resident.

57. *Loxia curvirostra.* Crossbill. A resident only in certain seasons. When it does appear it comes in plenty and breeds in larch firs, feeding on the fir cones. Eighteen were shot at the "Hollins," near Whittonstall, in winter time, for Mr. J. Hancock of the Newcastle Museum, in 1855. In the spring of the following year (1856) on March 1st, I found a nest containing three eggs in a spruce fir at Coalburns, near the Spen. On July 14th of the same year I found a nest containing four eggs in a spruce fir in the High Marley Hill plamtation.

58. *Emberiza miliaria.* Corn Bunting. A common resident

59. *E. citrinella.* Yellow Bunting. A common resident.

60. *E. schœniclus.* Reed Bunting. A common resident on the marshes at Byer Moor, Swalwell, and other places where the waters are still.

61. *Plectrophanes nivalis.* Snow Bunting. A frequent winter visitor.

62. *Sturnus vulgaris.* Starling. A common resident. I can remember the Starling breeding at Ravensworth for the last 60 years (since 1829). A nest was found in 1838 at Hesleyside.

63. *Garrulus glandarius.* Jay. A common resident in well-wooded districts; Gibside Woods being a favourite resort.

64. *Pica rustica.* Magpie. A common resident.

65. *Corvus monedula.* Jackdaw. A common resident; breeding in the Causey Arch and at Gibside.

66. *C. corone.* Carrion Crow. A common resident.

67. *C. Cornix.* Hooded Crow. A common winter visitor.

68. *C.frugilegus.* Rook. A common resident.

69. *Alauda arvensis.* Skylark. A common resident.

70. *Cypselus apus.* Swift. A common summer visitor.

71. *Caprimulgus Europarus.* Night Jar. A common summer visitor. I found a nest of this bird in Priest Close Wood, on Tyneside, on the Bradley Estate, and another in Beda Hills Plantation, between the Spen and Victoria Garesfield. Both nests were on the ground; but I cannot give any date of the finds.

72. *Dendrocopus Major.* Great Spotted Woodpecker. I have frequently seen them on the Gibside Estate, and they have nested in those woods, but I cannot give any date.

73. *D. Minor.* Lesser Spotted Woodpecker. I shot one on the Bradley Estate (can give no date), and have frequently seen them on the Gibside Estate.

74. *Lynx torquilla.* Wryneck. When a boy (about 1825 and after, it was very common about Ravensworth, and I have taken eggs out of old willow trees; each nest generally contained six eggs. I think that this little bird is now extinct, for it is years since I saw one of them in Durham.

75. *Alcedo inspida.* Kingfisher. It is common on the Stockley Burn, Stanley Burn, and Whittledean Burn, all on the Bradley estate; but I have never seen it on the Derwent, (See 120.)

76. *Cuculus canorus.* Cuckoo. A common summer visitor. I have found its eggs in the Meadow Pipit's nest frequently; once in a Robin's nest on the Bradley Estate, which was placed about a foot under a bank in a place where it was almost impossible for the bird to get. How it placed the eggs in the nest I cannot say, but I saw the bird leave the spot, and on looking in the nest found its egg. I once found a young Cuckoo in the nest of a Hedge Sparrow.

77. *Strix flammea.* Barn Owl. A common resident.

78. *Asio otus.* Long-Eared Owl. A common resident. It breeds in old

nests, generally those of a Crow or a Magpie, in dark fir plantations.

79. *A. accipitrinus.*   Short-Eared Owl.   Not very common.

80. *Syrnium aluco.*   Tawny Owl.   A common resident. I have found the eggs of this bird in old nests of Crows, holes in trees, and in walls, and in rabbit holes.

81. *Circus cyaneus.*   Hen Harrier.   A resident. A pair of these birds were shot and their eggs taken on Black Burn Fell Ravensworth Estate, some time before 1836.

82. *C. cineraceus.*   Montagu's Harrier.   This bird is not very common. Its eggs have been taken on Healey Fell, on the banks of the Derwent, Northumberland.

83. *Buteo vulgaris.*   Buzzard.   My father caught two of these birds in a rabbit trap at Ravensworth, but I cannot give any date.

84. *Aquila chrysaëtus.*   Golden Eagle.   One of these birds stayed all one winter and spring at Ravensworth, and I used to have to feed him on rabbits, generally a couple at a time, and sheep's liver. I am quite sure that this was a Golden Eagle, for at the same time the then Earl of Ravensworth had a living specimen shut up in a cage.

85. *Accipiter nisus.*   Sparrow Hawk.   A common resident. They hardly ever lay more than four eggs, but I once found a nest on the Bradley Estate which contained six eggs.

86. *Falco œsalan.*   Merlin.   I have found the nest of this bird, with eggs, on the moors south of Blanchland, fifty years ago (1839). The eggs are similar to those of the Kestrel in colour, but a little less in size.

87. *F. Tinnunculus.*   Kestrel.   A common resident. It breeds in Chopwell Woods, near Milkwell Burn, Spen Woods, Bradley, Ravensworth, and Gibside Woods.

88. *Ardea cineria.*   Heron.   This bird is commonly seen flying up the Derwent.   ·

89. *Anas. boschas.*   Mallard.   A common resident; breeding on Ravensworth ponds.

90. *Querquedula crecca.*   Teal.   A common resident; breeding on Ravensworth ponds.

91. *Mareca penelope.*   Wigeon.   A common resident; breeding on Ravensworth ponds.

92. *Columba palumbus.*   Ring Dove.   A common resident in all wooded districts.

93. *C. œnas.* Stock Dove. I found a nest of this bird with eggs in a hole in the wall in 1884; and another in a hollow tree in 1886.,

94. *Tetrao tetrix.* Black Grouse. Common on Blanchland Moors.

95. *Lagopus scoticus.* Red Grouse. A common resident.

96. *Phasianus colchicus.* Pheasant. A common resident.

97. *Perdix cinerea.* Partridge. A common resident.

98. *Coturnix communis.* Quail. A nest of this bird containing twelve eggs was taken at Crawcrook in 1886. Several eggs have been taken at various periods near Winlaton.

99. *Crex pratensis.* Corn Crake. A common summer visitor.

100. *Rallus aquaticus.* Water Rail. A common resident on the lower parts of the river Derwent, and on the Ponds at Gibside.

101. *Gallinula chloropus.* Moorhen. A common resident.

102. *Fulica atra.* Coot. A common resident; breeds on the ponds at Axwell and Ravensworth.

103. *Ægialitis hiaticula.* Ringed Plover. I have seen it very often on the Derwent Valley, but cannot say whether it breeds or not

104. *Vanellus vulgaris.* Lapwing. A common resident.

105. *Scolopax rusticola.* Woodcock. A resident; breeding in Chopwell Woods: It is thirty years (1859) since the eggs of this bird were first found in this district (Lower Derwent)

106. *Gallinago cœlistis.* Common Snipe. A common resident.

107. *G. gallinula.* Jack Snipe. A common winter visitor.

108. *Totanus hypoleucas.* Common piper. A common resident; breeding on the Derwent. In 1887 I found a nest on the channel bed of the Derwent, amongst the rough stones near Rowland's Gill.

109. *Numenius arquata.* Curlew. A common resident; breeding near Shotley Bridge.

The following additions to the Birds of the Derwent Valley are from notes gathered by the writer of Mr. Grundy's list, from personal knowledge; with the assistance of a few motes from Mr. J. F. Robinson and Mr. T. Peacock, the President and late Secretary of the Vale of Derwent Naturalists' Field Club, respectively.

110. *Acrocephalus streperus.*   Reed Warbler.   A nest with eggs was found near Ravensworth, June 8th, 1885.

111. *A. turdoides.*   Great Reed Warbler.   A Specimen (male) was shot near Swalwell Station, May 28th, 1847, by the late Mr. T. Robson.

112. *A. phragmitis.*   Sedge Warbler.   Common on Derwent side (lower portion). - T. Peacock.

113. *Cinclus aquaticus.*   Dipper.   Breeds at Ravensworth. - T. Peacock.

114. *Ampelis garrulus.*   Waxwing.   One shot at Lockhaugh. - J. F. Robinson.

115. *Muscicapa atricapilla.*   Pied Flycatcher.   One caught at Axwell Park, June, 1801.- Bewick.   It has been found nesting on the Derwent near Shotley Bridge, and Winlaton; and also nested at Ravensworth in 1885.

116. *Coccothraustis vulgaris.*   Hawfinch.   A nest containing two eggs, was found in an oak tree, fifty feet from the ground, at Axwell Park, May 29th, 1884.   One nest was taken at Axwell Park in 1884, and two in the same park in 1885.

117. *Pastor roseus.*   Rose-coloured pastor.   One was shot out of a flock of starlings in 186o, by T. Wilson, Esq., near Shotley Hall

118. *Corvus Monedula.*   Jackdaw.   A few nest in Causey, or Tanfield Arch. - T. Peacock.

119. *Alcedo arborea.*   Wood Lark.   Two were shot near Swalwell, March, 1844, by T. Robson.

120. *A!cedo inspidis.*   Kingfisher.   It has nested on the Derwent. near Gibside, Winlaton Mill, and Axwell:

121. *Buteo vulgaris.*   Buzzard.   In an account of George Bowes, Esq., of Gibside, debtor to Richard Harding, Esq., (formerly one of the owners of a part of the Gibside estate, Hollinside,) dated 1749, and now in the possession of Mr. J. F. Robinson; - for destroying certain birds occurs the following item: 'To shooting 5 Buzzards at ------. but unfortunately it is not finished, so we gain no idea of what was paid for shooting a Buzzard 40 years ago.

122. *Accipter nisus.*   Sparrow Hawk.   A pair nested in Tanfield Arch, 1887. - T. Peacock.

123. *Ardella minuta.*   Little Bittern.   One shot near Blaydon, May 12th, 1812.

124. Cygnus olor. Mute Swan. A pair, belonging to Major Joicey, bred in a pond at Tanfield Lea, but did not succeed in rearing their young. - T. Peacock.

125. Columba œnas. Stock Dove. Two pair nested in Axwell Park, March, 1885. It has bred in Causey Arch, or in holes in the banks near to it, every year since 1884 to 1889. - T. Peacock.

126. C. livia. Rock Dove. Found breeding near Shotley Bridge, 1867, by Mr. S. Yuille, keeper, Shotley Hall.

127. Porzana bailloni. Baillon's Crake. One was shot on the Derwent near Swalwell, July 22nd, 1874.

128. Gallinula chloropus. Moorhen. Breeds on Ravensworth ponds. - T. Peacock.

129. Scolopax rusticula. Woodcock. Has nested on the banks of the Derwent near Shotley Bridge.

130. Totanus fuscus. Spotted Redshank. One was shot near Blanchland, August, 1842, by Mr. Goundry.

If any reader could add occurrences of birds in the Derwent Valley not mentioned above, or could add any further knowledge of their range in that district, the writer will feel greatly obliged if they will kindly do so. In order to make the list as complete as possible, it is extremely important that all collectors of bird notes should co-operate and add to each others knowledge

ACKNOWLEDGEMENTS

Thanks to the Land of Oak & Iron project, the industrial and social history of the Derwent Valley area is being rediscovered and celebrated afresh. After the success of our first publication, *Men of Iron,* the suggestion that *Tales of Derwentdale* would be the ideal follow-up was an inspired one.

This book brings to life not only the traditional myths and legends of our area, but also the history of our natural environment. Fawcett lived from 1867 to 1942. In the intervening years, the heavy industry which once dominated our valley has vanished and nature's astonishing ability to recover is all around us; as is evidence of human resilience, the importance of community and a shared sense of history.

Thank-you to David Marrs, Karen Daglish and Kath Marshall-Ivens of Land of Oak & Iron, without whom this book would not exist.

Our profoundest thanks to David Butler, Archivist of Durham County Record Office and local historian, whose knowledge, interest, expertise, dedication and unfailing support has been the mainstay of this whole research project. Thank-you so much, David.

Two other people provided invaluable help at several points in the research: Terry Coult, retired Durham County Ecologist, and Trevor Royle, biographer of Lord Kitchener. Our lasting gratitude to you both.

The Bewick Society and the Natural History Society of Northumbria have helped in so many ways, but our particular thanks go to June Holmes, Peter Quinn and Michael Turner. Thanks also to Howard Cleeve, volunteer for The Newcastle Society of Antiquaries, which is also based in the Hancock Museum Library.

At the Literary and & Philosophical Society of Newcastle upon Tyne, we were assisted by Les Jessup, Richard Sharp and Paul Gailiunas, to whom I offer my gratitude.

THE LIFE AND WORKS OF JAMES WILLIAM FAWCETT

On the other side of the world, the librarians and archivists we contacted in Australia and Malta were invariably helpful. Our particular thanks go to:

Anne Watkins, Diocesan Archivist, Anglican Diocese of North Queensland

Janice Cooper of the Professional Historians Association of Queensland

Marisa Giorgi of Queensland Museum

Nick Shailer of Townsville Museum, Queensland

Rhett Lindsay of the State Archives and Records Authority of New South Wales

Robyn Maconachie and Debra Close of City Libraries, Townsville

Saadia Thomson Dwyer and Cynthia Cochrane of Queensland State Archives

Stephanie Schembri of the National Archives of Malta

Townsville Family History Association

Ray Thompson is a star. The initiative he started in Satley in 2009 involved John and Rosemary Gall, Tony Blenkinsopp and Chrissie Clark, all of whom welcomed this renewed interest in J. W. Fawcett. They have provided invaluable information, trusted us with rare books and sustained us with marvelous flapjack. Thank-you all and we hope you are thrilled with the result.

Val Scully and Geoff Marshall
Land of Oak & Iron

James William Fawcett

of Satley

1867 - 1942

Land of Oak & Iron

2019

Hosted by
Groundwork
NE & Cumbria